TAKEN TO THE GRAVE

A BOW STREET DUCHESS MYSTERY

BOOK SEVEN

CARA DEVLIN

First Cup Press

Any references to historical events, real people, or real places are used fictitiously. Names and characters are products of the author's imagination.

ISBN paperback: 979-8987612538

CHAPTER ONE

May 1821

The steady ticking of the long-case clock was the only sound inside the study at 19 Bedford Street. Hugh Marsden sat at his desk, wishing to be anywhere but where he presently was.

Two women in the chairs opposite his stared at him, each of them shifting anxiously. Their visit had been unexpected, and now he wished he'd given some excuse to turn them away. However, as one of the ladies was Lady Rebecca Poston, the beloved wife of Bow Street Chief Magistrate Sir Gabriel Poston, he had not. Hugh's curiosity as to why the magistrate's wife had come calling at such a late afternoon hour had influenced him to welcome her and her companion into his study.

Not exactly a Trojan Horse situation, but close enough.

He drummed his fingers upon the desk and sighed. "I'm not sure I can be of any assistance, Lady Rebecca."

She was several years younger than her husband, but just

as formidable. The way she glared down the slope of her nose at Hugh now, reminded him of when he'd been a young rapscallion and his own mother had managed to give him a proper dressing down with only a heavy, piercing look.

He sat forward, unwilling to fold as he might have back then. "You must understand—I respect Sir Gabriel too much to go behind his back in anything."

"My niece is missing, Lord Neatham," she replied.

"And yet Sir Gabriel does not believe that to be the case," he replied. "Not only that, but you've admitted he did not want you coming here to ask me to investigate."

A request she had roundly ignored.

Lady Rebecca's sister, Mrs. Caroline Silas, beat her scalloped hand fan rapidly to cool her face. She was not as self-possessed as her sister, and when she spoke, it was with a tremulous warble.

"My lord, please." The gusts from her fan tossed the ringlets framing her face. "My daughter is in trouble. Mr. Silas and Sir Gabriel believe she has merely eloped, but I *know* she has not."

Hugh clenched his back teeth. *Hell.*

"Why do they believe she has eloped?" he asked.

The sisters exchanged a look. Lady Rebecca urged Mrs. Silas on with nod.

"There is a man," she said. "Bethany is a bit wild, and she has not kept the finest company, I will admit to that. But to elope with no word, no note, leaving me to worry... No, she would not do such a thing."

Hugh kept his expression neutral, even though he wanted to groan and throw back his head in frustration. No doting mother would ever wish to believe their daughter, raised to be a perfect society lady, would fall in love with an unsuitable man, let alone run off to Gretna Green with him.

"Does Mr. Silas know you are here, requesting that I investigate?" He presumed he did not, just as Sir Gabriel did not, and when Mrs. Silas shook her head, he stood from his chair.

He needed to move. To think. Hugh didn't want to offend Lady Rebecca, but even more so, he didn't need to anger his last connection to his former life at Bow Street. After he'd been foisted from his role as principal officer and given instead the mantle of Viscount Neatham, Sir Gabriel had continued to involve him in several cases. However, after a handful of months last autumn, when Hugh had become somewhat of a distracted wastrel, Sir Gabriel had ceased approaching him. It had been all Hugh's own doing.

When the Dowager Duchess of Fournier, Audrey Sinclair, had gone to the Continent to spend the bulk of her required mourning period traveling, her letters to Hugh, and his to her, had been intercepted and collected by another private inquiry agent—one who had been hired to follow Audrey. In waylaying their correspondence, the inquiry agent had caused them both a great deal of confusion and hurt, each of them worrying that the other had fallen out of love. Hugh had not handled it well, and Sir Gabriel had not overlooked his shoddy performance.

However, after the events in January, in which he'd been beckoned to the port of Dover to help lift Audrey from suspicion of murder, everything had settled again. He was no longer in any doubt of her love for him, and he'd made sure that she was confident in his. For the last few months in

London, he'd taken every opportunity—few though they'd been—to get her alone and remind her of it.

He came to a stop in front of a window that overlooked Bedford Street. It wasn't a street devoted to fine residences befitting a lord, but to a mix of businesses and middle-class homes. As such, the arrival of the ladies seated at his desk would have gone unnoticed by fashionable society.

"My husband would be quite cross if he knew we'd come to see you," Mrs. Silas admitted. "He would prefer to keep Bethany's absence hushed up."

"Only because Caro's husband is convinced that she has run off with this cad, this Mr. Comstock," Lady Rebecca put in. "And he cares more for a pristine reputation in Parliament than he does for his own daughter."

"Now, sister, that isn't true." But Mrs. Silas winced and added more softly, "Not entirely."

Hugh had met John Silas once. He was with the House of Commons, and Hugh, the House of Lords. Still, he knew the man was a serious, well-respected member of the Tories. To have rumors swirling about that his daughter had ruined herself would be detrimental to his standing, and Silas did not have a title to fall back onto.

"Tell me about this Mr. Comstock," Hugh said, giving in to his curiosity.

Mrs. Silas beat her fan faster. "He is the most disgraceful of blackguards."

"What leads you to say that?" Hugh would take her opinion with a liberal grain of salt, if only because not very long ago, he, too, had been branded as a blackguard.

His half-brother, Bartholomew, had perpetuated a lie that had brought Hugh and his half-sister, Eloisa, to utter ruination. For years, the beau monde in London had believed Hugh had sullied his own half-sister, and his brother had happily allowed that lie to stand firm. Barty had wanted to cover up the truth—that his other brother, Thomas, was the degenerate abuser, not Hugh. The scandal had come out just over a year ago, and even with Barty's disgrace and disappearance from society, the Neatham title still suffered a black mark that would not easily scrub out. Hugh was loath to sully another man's reputation without proof.

However, Mrs. Silas's lips gaped in offense at his question. "I am *led* to say that because the man took my Bethany one week ago and never returned her!"

The choice of wording set him ill at ease. As if Bethany were an object, and Mr. Comstock had broken into the Silas household and stolen her.

Lady Rebecca patted her sister's arm, then more calmly said, "He is a mystery to us, Lord Neatham. Bethany made his acquaintance at Vauxhall while she was with her friend, Miss Gwendolyn Bertram, but we know very little else of him."

"He claimed to be the son of a squire," Mrs. Silas said. "The late Vernon Comstock. He seemed like a dandy to Mr. Silas and me, one of the young men about Town looking to catch a wife."

Hugh nodded, but also knew there were plenty of young men looking not for a wife but only to sow their wild oats. He paced back toward his desk. "The day she disappeared, did Mr. Comstock collect your daughter from your home, or did they meet elsewhere?"

Mrs. Silas deepened the sneer on her already pinched lips.

"He and his sister escorted Bethany on another outing, to Vauxhall."

At the second mention of the pleasure gardens across the river, Hugh glanced at the clock. In less than an hour, he would be leaving for Vauxhall himself. He was to meet Audrey there. Her mourning period had recently ended, and they'd agreed it would be a good place to make their first public appearance together. The rumors of their understanding had proliferated throughout the ton over the last few months, and Hugh was more than ready for rumor to become fact.

"Vauxhall seems a natural place for a young couple to go," he said, but Mrs. Silas scoffed.

"All kinds mix there."

"More importantly, Lord Neatham," Lady Rebecca said with an exasperated look at her sister, "my husband has since learned that the late Vernon Comstock had *one* child. A son, Mr. Travis Comstock. So, you see, he does not have a sister. We do not know who the young lady truly was. Nor if Bethany ever arrived at the pleasure gardens. If she planned to elope, she would have packed for the travel, and yet all her belongings are still in her room. She did not take so much as a handkerchief."

That bit of information struck a discordant note within him, rousing a strain of concern for the girl.

"I presume you've spoken to Bethany's friend, this Miss Bertram, to see if she knows anything of her whereabouts?"

"I could not," Mrs. Silas said, her voice pitched high into a near whine. "Mr. Silas forbade me to so much as breathe a word about her being missing. Instead, he wishes to wait until she returns as *Mrs.* Comstock and then smooth over the whole scandal, pretending that we knew of the discreet wedding all along."

To not post wedding banns and to marry quickly, with special license, usually indicated the need for a hasty wedding. The lady being in the family way, for instance. It was not the fashionable thing to do, but it happened, and so long as no scandal or uproar surrounded the events, it should not affect the Silas' reputations.

"And have you tried to call upon Mr. Comstock?"

It would be the first, most rational thing to do. However, Mrs. Silas gasped as if horrified. "Call on him ourselves? Of course not! Mr. Silas made inquiries and learned he leases bachelor's rooms at the Chesterfield on Portman Square. But he refuses to go."

Mr. Silas likely had too much pride and couldn't stomach chasing after the man who may have ruined his daughter. Hugh returned to his chair and folded his hands on the desk. He could understand the ladies' concern, and yet he could also see where the pair of lovers may have simply eloped. Who knew, this Travis Comstock may have purchased Bethany new things for their journey, rendering packing—and potentially tipping off her parents prematurely—unnecessary.

Still, the twinge of doubt would not be silenced, not even when he imagined Sir Gabriel's intimidating scowl.

"Very well, I will pay Mr. Comstock's rooms a visit and will see if I can learn anything more about him."

Lady Rebecca and Mrs. Silas both seemed to deflate with relief. He held up a hand. "That's not to say I am taking on this investigation. I am only going to look into Mr. Comstock's whereabouts for now."

"And if you find anything of concern, what then?" Mrs. Silas asked.

He knew what he would have to do, whether he wanted to or not. "If that is the case, I will speak to Sir Gabriel."

Lady Rebecca grinned in recognizable victory. "Thank you, my lord."

He bristled and wondered how long it would be until being addressed as "my lord" didn't feel like a cat's tongue licking his skin.

Lady Rebecca and her sister were moving toward the study door when Basil appeared in the threshold. To look at him, one might think he was butler of the house, dressed as he was in a fine black swallowtail coat, white waistcoat, tall stock, and cravat. However, he was far too concerned with Hugh's outward appearance to be anything other than a fastidious and snobby valet. The running of the new Viscount Neatham's household was not nearly as important to Basil as the supervising of the viscount's wardrobe.

However, Basil's patience over Hugh continuing to reside in his pre-peer status home, had frayed. After a full year of being viscount, Hugh knew it was time to change residence.

"It is five o'clock," Basil announced after the two women had exited. Mr. Whitlock, Hugh's butler, would see them out.

"I am aware," Hugh said, with another look at the clock. He'd been checking it all day, eager for the evening, and to see Audrey again.

Basil eyed him as he approached the study door and sniffed. "You will be changing, I hope."

Hugh edged past him, into the foyer of the small townhome. "Would you allow me to exit this house if I did not?"

"Heavens, no," he replied lightly, following as Hugh ascended the stairs.

"What is wrong with what I am wearing?" he asked, already shrugging out of his coat. "May I remind you that *you* were the one who dressed me this morning."

"But so much has changed since then, my lord."

Hugh rolled his eyes. Basil had been with him several years, though his decision to employ a valet had not been made entirely out of practicality. Hugh's father, the late viscount, had left him a generous living, one a gentleman could thrive upon. After his father's death, he'd wanted to strike out on his own and prove that he did not need or depend upon the viscount's money. However, when Hugh was tossed out of the ton for allegedly ruining Eloisa, and then when he permanently maimed Barty in a duel, he'd immediately leased a nice home and hired a small staff. He'd wanted to maintain a fragment of his respectable upbringing. Even more so, he'd wanted to prove that he *was* a gentleman and not the degenerate society believed him to be.

"What the devil has changed so much in the last nine hours?"

Basil rode Hugh's heels into the bedchamber and went straight to the bedside table. He picked up a small white silk box. Hugh groaned. He should have anticipated it being found and opened by his snoop of a valet.

"*This* is what has changed, my lord." He opened the box and held it out for Hugh to see.

"I know what it is, Basil, thank you. But why would it change what I am wearing tonight?"

Hugh took the box from his valet and replaced the cover.

The ring inside was a small sapphire, bedded down in a pillow of silk.

"It is only that if you plan to ask a certain question of a certain widow..." The valet trailed off, waving his hands in the air as if he couldn't decide on his next words. Hugh tossed his jacket onto the bed.

"I am not proposing marriage to Audrey at Vauxhall."

Basil released a breath and nearly doubled over. "Oh, thank goodness, that would have been a disaster." He snapped up the coat and disappeared into the dressing room. "In that case, I'll just fresh you up a bit."

Hugh stared after him. "How would that be a disaster?"

"A proposal at *Vauxhall*?" Basil returned with a new evening coat and a marked look of disgust. "Why not take her to a dance hall or a tavern down by the docks?"

Hugh glowered as he put on his coat. "How I ask her to marry me is none of your concern."

Basil crinkled his forehead but said nothing as he brushed the shoulders and lapels of the midnight blue coat. Now that her mourning was finished, she would be free to marry again. The past year had seemed everlasting, and he'd longed for this moment. But how he would propose, what words he would say, and where he would say them, were nothing he had given much thought to. He'd promised Audrey a respectable and romantic proposal. Unsurprisingly, Vauxhall did not meet those standards.

Once finished, Basil stepped back to observe him. "And a walking stick, my lord?"

He took up a black cane with a silver top that Hugh had not seen resting against a chair.

"Have I developed a limp that I am not aware of?"

"It is au courant. I took the liberty of ordering one from Bealman's," Basil said as he displayed how the walking stick was to be held and used. After he'd struck three increasingly amusing poses, Hugh held up his hands.

"You may keep it." He took up his hat and gloves from where Basil had lain them on the bed and opened the bedchamber door.

"Sir!" he bellowed. The boy would not be very far. Probably in the kitchen, sneaking food from the larder.

Sir was waiting for him in the foyer, a crumb of some pastry still attached to his bottom lip. He now stood nearly as tall as Hugh, after having had another growth spurt, and his voice had changed over entirely. It was rather disconcerting to hear not a squeaky street urchin whenever he spoke, but a growing young man.

"We're leaving," Hugh said as Whitlock opened the door for them. "You're at the traces."

CHAPTER TWO

Audrey entered the western gates to the pleasure gardens, and her stomach twisted into a tight knot. The time had come. Her first public outing with Hugh was about to commence, and only one week since the official end of her mourning period.

That day had dawned just like any other, and yet she'd risen from bed feeling lighter, freer than she had in twelve, long months. The buoyant sensation had carried her through the week, toward the planned evening out. Earlier that week, Hugh had dashed a note to her, asking her to meet him at Vauxhall for dinner and entertainment. People of all classes mixed there, and they were sure to be seen together by ton, gentry, and middle class alike. The whispers about their involvement had already started to take root, but walking arm-in-arm around the exhibits and dining in one of the supper boxes would make their attachment formally known.

The gossip sheets would be ablaze with the information. Already, the columns had revisited time and again the fact that the new Viscount Neatham, one of the most eligible bachelors in London, had not attended a single soiree or ball during the Season. And when Lady Veronica Kettleridge, the most stunning debutante of the last season, married an earl in early April, reminders about Lord Neatham passing her over the previous summer had resurfaced.

He had, quite deliberately, not put himself into any situation that would give the matchmaking mothers of the ton any opportunity to foist their daughters onto him. In fact, he had only just attended his first dinner party a fortnight ago, at Lady Shoreham's. The countess had encouraged Audrey to attend as a way to inch back into society, and she had accepted. Though separated by several seats at dinner, her brief conversation with Hugh in Lady Shoreham's drawing room had captured the attention of the other guests. A gossip sheet printed the following day remarked that perhaps the viscount *was* in the market for a wife after all, but that he already had one in mind for himself and was waiting patiently for the proper time to arrive.

It felt a little like a game, or a show, to be here tonight, on parade for all eyes to see, but there was a purpose behind it: If she was seen on the arm of the viscount, with any hope, no other suitors would come calling at Violet House. Already that week, she'd received several bouquets of hot house flowers from gentlemen and had needed to reject three invitations to stroll or ride through Hyde Park. The men were all perfectly amiable, all titled, and acquaintances of the late duke. But to give them any hope at all would have been unkind. Besides, not one of them wanted to court her because of any real affection. She was a wealthy widow, and her estate was the main attraction. Not that she faulted any of the men for their ambitions; it was simply how the beau monde operated.

After tonight, the only man who would press his suit would be the one she had, not so very long ago, believed she would never be able to have.

"I am so happy to see you out of those dreary silvers and grays," Cassie sighed as they ambled through the pavilion that fronted the orchestra box. As it was fine May weather, the orchestra was playing in the open air, rather than under the rotunda. The soft strains of the piano and woodwind instruments carried on the gentle breeze.

Audrey had cast off her widow's black while on the Continent but had returned to the more formal threads of half-mourning when she returned to London after the Dover debacle. She'd never been much for pinks or yellows or many of the other bright, girlish colors, but she'd been excited to visit Madame Gascoigne in March to order several gowns in shades of blue, green, and red. Her maid, Greer, had selected a promenade dress of teal silk for today, topped by a spencer of ginger gold. Much to the modiste's disappointment, Audrey did not care for the ruffles and flounces that were in fashion, but she'd consented to some cording and embroidery. She was also far too sensible to wear any of the elaborate bonnets or hats with high plumage that she saw bobbing and fluttering about in the spring breeze at the gardens.

"I do feel more like myself now," Audrey replied to her sister-in-law. Then winced. She was not the same woman she'd been since the last time she had gone out in London in fashionable dress. The year had changed her in several ways.

Mostly, she'd struggled to come to terms with the secret she'd been entrusted with. The one she had been burdened with ever since news of her husband, Philip, the Duke of Fournier, arrived, announcing that he'd drowned at sea off the coast of Marseilles. He had not drowned, however, and Audrey had been forced to uphold the charade. Instead, he had followed through with his plan to disappear into the Continent with the man he loved, Mr. Frederick Walker.

"Well, you look lovely, and I meant what I said earlier. As soon as we see Hugh, I will be perfectly content to walk with Ruth," Cassie said, glancing over her shoulder to where her maid followed at a distance.

"I think you are even more eager for me to be on Hugh's arm than I am," Audrey laughed. "Are you so tired of my company?"

Cassie balked. "You know that isn't true!"

"I am only jesting," Audrey replied, laughing again. It felt so good to smile, to feel light and playful. This last year, she and Cassie had grown closer than they'd been before Philip's "death", even if she'd been keeping such a large secret from her.

She'd grown accustomed to the persistent feeling of guilt over Philip's brothers and sister all believing him to be dead. It had been a hard truth to accept that to tell them now, to reveal he'd allowed them to mourn his death so that he could have the chance to live the life he wanted, with the person he wanted, would only more deeply injure them.

For so long, she'd taken on the weight of Philip's choice, one she had been unsuccessful in persuading him to abandon. She'd held all the guilt on her own shoulders, and it had been a great effort to cast it off. In truth, she was still working toward it, and wondering if she would ever truly succeed.

For now, however, she chose to think about the current

moment, for that was the only thing over which she had any control.

"Truthfully," she began, taking Cassie's arm into hers and lowering her voice, "I am a little nervous."

"That he will propose here, at Vauxhall?" Cassie said quickly. "I am worried too. It would be a wretched place to ask you to marry him."

Audrey slowed, taken aback by Cassie's presumption. The immediate spate of apprehension surprised her. Hugh had promised her an official proposal and a romantic one, too, but suddenly her half boots seemed to fill with rocks, slowing her. A public proposal would be too showy, too... performative. Not like Hugh at all.

"He won't. Not here, not tonight."

"Goodness, I hope not," Cassie said. But then gave a quizzing look. "What is it that are you nervous about then?"

Audrey wasn't sure how to describe the persistent, restless friction that had lingered just underneath her skin all week.

They passed another pair of women, strolling arm-in-arm. They canted their heads and smiled at Audrey and Cassie, saying a polite hello. This would be the way of their promenade this evening, and she'd best get used to it.

"It doesn't matter," she said once they'd strolled on.

"It does," Cassie insisted. "And I think I know what it is."

Audrey raised a brow, intrigued to hear her guess.

"You knew what it was to be married to Philip. You don't know what it will be like being married to Hugh. That's bound to leave you anxious."

She was probably correct. Audrey couldn't help but shiver every time she pictured becoming Hugh's *wife*. So much would change. All for the better, to be sure, but she still felt a fluttery sensation of unease, of worry that something would go wrong. That something would continue to stand in their way. Keep them apart.

She could make no sense of it, and neither could she have explained it to Cassie without sounding somewhat hysterical. So, she kept her lips sealed and continued toward the Grand Walk, where Hugh had said he would be waiting for her.

"I'm sure you're right," Audrey said, hoping to put the topic to rest.

"But I hope he does not wait too long," Cassie sighed. She squeezed Audrey's arm again. "You must be eager for...*companionship*."

She said this with a sly arch of her brow, and Audrey gaped. "Cassie!" she hissed but couldn't maintain her chastising expression when her sister-in-law dissolved into giggles. Audrey joined in as they entered the flat, neat gravel walk alongside the Chinese temple and arcades that housed the supper boxes.

Her next steps seemed to levitate as she caught sight of the gentleman waiting near the arcades, in the shade of one column. Out of the dozens of men walking and standing, Hugh Marsden could not but help stand out. Or perhaps, he simply drew Audrey's eyes in a magnetic way other men could not. He hadn't yet seen her, giving her the chance to observe him first.

He wore a dark blue coat over a deep sable waistcoat, buff trousers, and polished hessians. Even as a principal officer, he'd worn gentlemen's clothing, and though he had submitted to his valet's entreaties to add accessories that marked him as a peer—gloves, for instance—just because he now held the title of viscount did not mean he had changed his nature. He was still, at his center, a Bow Street officer. If he could have continued with his post and been viscount, he would not have thought twice about it. Unfortunately, peers did not *work*.

Hugh stood with his hands clasped behind his back, his attention on the two others standing with him—Lord Grant Thornton and Sir. But, as if feeling the press of her eyes, Hugh cocked his head. Then turned and saw her. The corner of his mouth tucked up into a mischievous grin as he came forward to meet her. His rich brown eyes surveyed Audrey in a way that increased her pulse as he approached. In that moment, all the restless, barbed irritation causing a friction under her skin vanished. It seemed Hugh's presence had been the only thing she required to dispel her muddled and chaotic thoughts.

"Oh, good gracious, what is *he* doing here?" Cassie muttered as Lord Thornton came toward them as well.

The fourth and final son of the Marquess of Lindstrom was Hugh's closest friend, and as such, Audrey and Cassie had come to be in his presence quite a bit. After last summer at Greenbriar, when he'd proclaimed Audrey's bullet wound to be non-fatal, Cassie had embarrassed herself by embracing him. Since then, she had progressed from pointedly avoiding the physician to openly expressing her derision for him. To be fair, Thornton had not tried very hard to change her opinion. If anything, he seemed to enjoy goading her along in her antipathy for him.

However, Audrey suspected that the pair of them were only using their mutual loathing as a shield against much different feelings.

"Be polite," Audrey scolded her just before Hugh reached them. He touched the brim of his hat, and she had to hold herself back from doing as Cassie had with Thornton, and throwing herself in his arms.

"Your Grace." Hugh's bright tone was as playful as his steady stare. "I had no idea you would be here."

She tamped down a grin, though not successfully enough. "What a fortunate coincidence."

From where he stood behind Hugh, Sir groaned.

"Here, here," Thornton concurred with a roll of his own eyes.

Hugh and Audrey ignored them. He held out his arm, and she settled her hand there. With a nod of greeting toward Cassie, Hugh went on, "Lady Cassandra, I must apologize, I came here entirely alone and have absolutely no one to stroll with you."

"Very funny," Thornton muttered. "Lady Cassandra." He held out his arm to her, though he looked anything but pleased to do so.

She treated the offer in kind. "No need, I have my maid." Ruth hurried forward to walk alongside Cassie, and then, to deepen the slight just a little further, Cassie turned to Sir. "Is this your first time at Vauxhall?"

Had the boy been wearing Neatham livery, as before, she would not have inquired, as he would appear to be a servant. However, after returning from Dover, Sir had made some changes. He'd cast off his servant's clothing and wore a version of what Hugh wore, but in darker colors and without a neckcloth. Instead, a tall collar sufficed. He appeared like any boy from Eton or Harrow.

"It is," he answered, his voice now a steadier tenor than it had been earlier in the year. "Bit overdone, if you ask me."

He was as tall as Cassie as he fell into step beside her, leaving Thornton to walk behind them. Audrey faced forward, catching Hugh's amused glance.

"Hello," he whispered into her ear. The small hairs on the back of her neck and arms prickled.

"You cannot say such things to me here, in public," she replied, just as softly.

"I said hello." She leveled him with a look. He winked at her. "Would you rather we speak of the weather?"

"Gracious no," she laughed as they slowly ambled toward the wooded area of the pleasure gardens. "Do not ever speak to me of the weather, or I'll be forced to turn you away."

"Thank you for the warning. I will endeavor to always be interesting." His arm purposefully brushed more closely against hers. "And while we are speaking of interesting things, I have just come from a meeting that might intrigue you."

She listened, rapt, as Hugh told her about Lady Rebecca Poston's visit to his home, and her sister's missing daughter. As he laid out what both the ladies had said, and why Mr. Silas and Sir Gabriel believed her disappearance to be due to an elopement to the Scottish border, Audrey shook her head.

"I am more inclined to treat it as a mysterious disappearance. Mrs. Silas is correct to worry. If this Mr. Comstock lied to Bethany regarding his false sister, he may have also tricked her into accompanying him here, to Vauxhall."

Hugh's frown mirrored the one she felt on her own lips. "I agree, he isn't to be trusted. Thornton has just informed me that Comstock had his membership at the Seven Sins rescinded. The rumor is that it was due to unprincipled behavior at the card tables."

Thornton seemed to be one of Hugh's primary resources when it came to gossip and information.

"Does he know everything about everyone in London?" she asked.

"He could probably write his own gossip column."

Audrey laughed and hooked her arm a little tighter around his. She felt a stirring low in her stomach being so close to him and wished they could be alone, just for one moment, so she could kiss him. It had been weeks since they'd last had the opportunity. Hugh had paid a call on Michael at Violet House, to where he and Genie had finally moved in March. It was the London seat for the Duke of Fournier, and it was only proper that Michael would now reside there. Audrey had remained, of course, but had needed to give up her usual room to Genie, as the attached bedchamber would now belong to Michael. It had been rather awkward, but there was no bitterness over any of it. Audrey's new bedchamber was perfectly adequate, and Genie had kindly refused to take over the smaller study at the back of the home that Audrey so adored.

It was into that study Hugh had slipped the day of his visit to Michael, to discuss some bill being presented in Parliament. He'd crossed the room, to where Audrey sat on the sofa, reading, and pulled her to her feet without saying a single word. The kiss had been hot and impassioned, but it had lasted only a few moments before he'd then needed to dash away again. Her blood had been high the rest of the day. Now, she longed to rest her head against his shoulder as they walked toward the Cascade, one of the pleasure gardens' most popular exhibits.

"Sir Gabriel doesn't want me to investigate," Hugh said.

"Why would he not want to search for his niece?"

Hugh didn't answer, but his expression remained pinched.

"But you will still search for her?" Audrey pressed. He wasn't a man to allow others to dictate his decisions, not even Sir Gabriel Poston.

"I am going to Mr. Comstock's rooms on Portman Square first thing tomorrow. But I believe we will learn more pertinent information from Bethany's friend."

Audrey straightened, her pulse skipping for a new reason. He'd said *we*. "Are you asking for my assistance?"

"Are you not my partner?" he asked with a sly, sideways glance.

Once again, the ground parted from the soles of her feet. "I am dangerously close to kissing you right here, in front of everyone."

"That would hasten the gossip along nicely."

"What can I do?" she asked.

"Your lips on mine should suffice."

She nudged him. "About Bethany."

He cut her a roguish grin. "Mrs. Silas mentioned a Miss Gwendolyn Bertram of Fitzroy Square. She doesn't want a scandal to break about her daughter's disappearance, but I think we must risk it to discover whatever we can."

A bubble of excitement expanded within her chest. The last handful of months had been deliriously dull. After the tumultuous week in Dover, Audrey had been grateful for the reprieve, however she couldn't deny the heady enthusiasm she now felt at being useful in an investigation. She'd told Hugh that she wanted to be his partner in everything, and he had not disputed it. In fact, he'd agreed that they worked well together—and he'd readily acknowledged that her curious ability to hold objects and see what were essentially memories was beneficial to any inquiry at hand.

As Audrey started to plan her outing to Fitzroy Square, to call on Miss Gwendolyn Bertram, she and Hugh neared the wooded area of the gardens that held the Cascade, an artificial waterfall, designed in such a way to trick the eye into seeing flowing water. The enormous structure was a three-dimensional staged contraption, centered by sheets of painted tin, which were moved by men, hidden from view from the spectators. With the additional help of gas lighting and sound effects, the shaped tin sheets appeared to be a falls, flowing into a body of water. Audrey had seen it a few times before, though the scene was changed from time to time to keep from becoming too dull.

Because of the need for gas lamps to reflect off the tin, the Cascade only operated at night, and only for twenty minutes. During the daylight hours, the entire structure was hidden from curious eyes behind a large screen, painted with the image of the Cascade. However, as they came upon it now, a thick crowd had gathered in the viewing area.

"What is it they are looking at?" Audrey wondered aloud as she noticed the men and women milling about, craning their necks as if to see something. It was far too early in the evening for the exhibit to open.

Hugh started for the large screen, keeping Audrey on his arm. Behind them, Cassie, Ruth, Sir, and Thornton followed.

"Is someone injured?" Thornton asked. The concerned expressions on those gathered and the low hum of discord indicated some emergency. When Hugh cleared a path to the front of the crowd, they were met with two men standing guard, one each at the edges of the screen. Their faces were pale, their mouths taut with matching frowns.

"What is happening here?" Hugh asked the closest one. Both wore dark red frock jackets, buttoned to the neck. Neither wore a hat, marking them as workers here rather than visitors.

"There's been an accident on the Cascade, milord," the man replied.

Thornton stepped forward. "I am a physician. Can I be of any help?"

The worker blinked. "Apologies, doctor, but there's naught you can do. The man's dead."

Audrey tensed. "That is awful. Was it a fall?" The last time she'd seen the Cascade it had been a mill scene, with a waterwheel turning and a bridge spanning the flowing water. The structure towered at least thirty feet high.

The worker hesitated, glancing over at his cohort on the other side of the screen. They'd been posted there, no doubt, to keep curious onlookers away.

"I'm afraid not, milady," he answered.

Hugh lowered his arm, and Audrey released him. "Has anyone sent for the police?"

"We've sent for the manager, milord. I imagine he'll want to call a constable." He lowered his voice to add, "It don't look to be a natural death."

Cassie let out a small gasp. "You mean he's been murdered?"

Audrey's stomach cinched tight as she and Hugh exchanged a well-worn look. Her penchant for coming upon dead bodies was a regular source of banter between them, and the way he squinted at her now showed his exasperation.

"I am Viscount Neatham, a former principal officer at Bow Street," he told the worker, who straightened a bit. "I will have a look, if you don't object."

The man hesitated, as if he did want to object, but under Hugh's practiced stare, he crumbled. "This way, milord."

He led Hugh behind the edge of the screen. Thornton followed, and Audrey stepped forward, too. But a small, gloved hand grasped her arm. "Where are you going?" Cassie hissed.

"Stay here with Sir and Ruth," Audrey said, knowing she had but a moment before the worker returned to his post and tried to block her from entering.

She peeled her arm free from Cassie's clutching grip and slipped behind the screen. The staging for the Cascade loomed before her, and in the shade from the screen and the surrounding trees, it appeared as it truly was—a hulking mechanism—rather than a magical vision.

"I'm sorry, milady," the worker said as he was returning to his post. "It isn't decent."

Having no intention of turning around, she gave him an indulgent grin. "Thank you for your concern, but I won't swoon. There is, however, a young lady out there who looks about to."

She said a silent apology to Cassie for the small lie, but when the young man hurried past her to check on the fainting lady, she pressed forward, toward the collection of men near the base of the Cascade. Hugh saw her approach and arched a brow. But he said nothing as another Vauxhall employee crouched to pull back the red coat he'd shed to use as a cover for the body.

The first thing Audrey saw was the blood. A gaping wound on the side of the man's head made no sense until she realized it was where an ear should have been. It was now gone. Removed? Her stomach churned, but she refused to cower. Bruises riddled the side of the man's face that was visible, and another red gash looked to have been drawn across his neck. The man's throat had been cut.

"Bloody hell," Hugh cursed as he crouched next to the body. "*No, no, no,*" he continued to mutter. He whisked off his hat and ran his fingers through his hair.

Audrey stepped closer to him, her skin prickling with concern. "Do you know this man?"

"Yes." His voice was barely a rasp. "This is Harlan Givens."

The name was not familiar to her. Just then, someone appeared at her shoulder. Sir stared down at the man, his eyes like saucers. All color leeched from his face.

"Father?" Sir whispered.

Hugh quickly covered the man with the coat again and straightened his legs. "Sir—"

But the boy staggered away and ran. He darted fast, into the trees.

"Thornton," Hugh said, and with the single word, his friend hurried off after the boy.

Audrey's skin flashed over with gooseflesh as she stared at the covered form. "This man is Sir's *father*?"

Hugh swore under his breath. "Yes. And he's most certainly been murdered."

CHAPTER THREE

Even after just one year away from Bow Street, the cold, cavernous gap separating Hugh from Bow Street Officers Tyne and Stevens when they arrived at the Cascade was unmistakable. He stood apart from the two men as they spoke to the four workers that had been with the body when Hugh and Audrey had entered behind the obscuring screen. Daylight had faded, and numerous lamps had been lit to illuminate the base of the Cascade. As word spread throughout the pleasure gardens of the body's discovery, the crowds on the other side of the screen had more than doubled. The cumulative voices had risen to a near cacophony as Hugh and Audrey had waited, choosing to stay with the body of Harlan Givens.

Shortly after Sir had run off, and Thornton had given chase, Audrey asked Cassie and her maid to set out to search the grounds as well. She'd then whispered in Hugh's ear a suggestion that he distract the workers. He'd known her intention, and even though a rock still sat in the pit of his stomach as he thought of what Sir had just seen, he'd gotten to work.

After drawing the four Vauxhall workers into a line for a discussion of the particulars regarding how and when the body had been found, making sure to angle them away from the body itself, Audrey had crouched beside Givens. As Hugh collected information, such as who had found the body (a lamplighter in charge of checking the gas jets for the evening's performance), when it had been found (just minutes before six o'clock), and whether any of them knew who Harlan Givens was or if they had seen him before at the pleasure gardens (a uniform *no* from all), she had hunched near the dead man's form. The distraction only lasted a minute or two. One of the workers threw a glance over his shoulder and spotted her.

"What's that in your hand, milady?" he'd asked.

When Audrey straightened up, she held a silver object in her ungloved hand. "This was sticking out of his pocket," she'd said. "Perhaps he'd been drinking and then fell from the bridge?" She'd pointed to the bridge high above, spanning the scene's waterfall.

Hugh suspected how much it pained her to sound so obtuse, but there were no other viable excuses for being found holding Harlan Givens's flask.

The worker took it from her hand and placed it onto the ground, next to the body. Hugh noted the lack of blood pooled around it. A sliced throat would have made more of a mess, but there wasn't much of anything near the body. He inferred that he'd been killed elsewhere and brought here, then.

"I doubt he fell. He's lost his ear, you see. That's the third one this month."

And *that* was that staggering revelation Hugh was now discussing with the manager of Vauxhall, Mr. Frederick Gye.

"Yes, yes, I told these fellows from Bow Street all about the other two bodies," he said with marked impatience as he and Hugh stood near the screen's edging. Gye kept peeking out at the milling crowd. Hugh couldn't be sure if it was with concern or excitement. The man's expression seemed to skip between the two.

"There have been two other murders at Vauxhall and no newspaper has printed even a single report of them. How is that possible?" Hugh asked.

The manager raised his hands and patted the air in a gesture for him to lower his voice. Irritated, Hugh grumbled, "The hyenas on the other side of this screen are not able to hear me."

"Mr. Gye," Audrey cut in, perhaps sensing Hugh's failing patience. "Newspaper reporters are ravenous for stories such as this. How is it that Bow Street has kept it quiet?"

"I have...connections there." He looked and sounded as though he'd like to keep it at that.

"And you asked them to stay quiet about the murders," Hugh said, "because it would be bad for business?"

Mr. Gye grinned and spread his arms. "Yes, exactly, Lord Neatham. Perfectly understandable, isn't it, to want to maintain calm and a sense of order?"

By the excitement on the other side of the screen, Hugh could understand the man's motives. One dead body may heighten the public's interest, but three in one month would give people pause.

"You can say goodbye to that arrangement, Mr. Gye. There is no chance that this is not going to be on every broadsheet in London by morning," Hugh said. "So, what has happened differently this time?"

Mr. Gye sighed, his disappointment plain. "This time, the body was not found before the gardens opened to visitors, as the other two were."

Hugh peered at the base of the Cascade where Givens's body had been. Shortly after Bow Street arrived, it was carted away. They had taken it through the trees, avoiding the more populated Grand Walk, but had surely been observed at some point before exiting the grounds. Hopefully not by Sir. It was a wretched thing to have seen, and not something he was ever likely to forget.

"Who were the other two victims?" Hugh asked.

The manager might have total control of the wildly successful amusement parkland, but he was not half as skilled at controlling his facial expressions. He wore his every thought on his face and in the hold of his posture. Right now, he arched an eyebrow and over a few protracted moments, seemed to consider naming the two other victims. It was more than apparent from his cagey expression that he knew them. However, his ultimate decision was to feign ignorance.

"I have no idea, and nor do I wish to. I leave all the unsavory details to Officer Tyne."

In the months after Hugh's departure from the magistrate's office, Tyne had risen in rank and had become a principal officer. He was now the lead on these hushed up murders. Tyne stood with the workers, speaking to them as they started to go about the business of readying the Cascade for its nightly performance. Mr. Gye had refused to shut down the exhibit. It would go on, as planned. Tyne glimpsed at Hugh, his expression wooden. The officer likely did not appreciate his presence.

"If those victims were found in the morning," Audrey started to say, oblivious to the tension exchanged between Hugh and Tyne, "does that mean they were killed here, at the gardens, overnight?"

Mr. Gye narrowed his gaze on Audrey, and again, his thoughts were obvious. To Audrey as well, it seemed, for she hardened her expression and braced for his reply.

"This is hardly a pleasant topic for a lady. Your Grace, allow my assistant to show you to the pavilion. A glass of wine, perhaps, to calm the nerves?" Mr. Gye cut off Audrey, who'd started to reply with an objection, by shouting, "Hammond!"

A tall man with unfashionably long black curls, streaked with silver at the temples immediately came around the corner of the screen. He stood at attention, though his shoulders and back still seemed to droop. His gloved hands were clasped behind him. "You called, Mr. Gye?"

His voice was soft in comparison to the manager's, who barked for the man to lead the dowager duchess to the supper boxes and to bring her a glass of wine.

"I only offer the finest selection," he said as an aside to Audrey. "From my own establishment, the London Wine Company. A recent acquisition."

Vauxhall was a fairly recent acquisition too, if Hugh recalled correctly. The Tyers-Barrett family had owned the pleasure gardens since its inception in the previous century, but the most recent generation had decided to lease it to Mr. Gye. He was a businessman through and through, eager to buy up establishments and profit from them. Hugh saw that as plainly as he did the man's thoughts and feelings. There was no artifice with him at all, and for that, Hugh was grateful. Or perhaps, Office Tyne should be grateful. This wasn't Hugh's investigation. His interest lay solely in the fact that the most recent body belonged to that of Sir's father.

"No, thank you, Mr. Gye," Audrey replied. "I will remain here with Lord Neatham. Now, about my question—"

"You need not concern yourself with such ghastly goings on, Your Grace. You can trust in Hammond to lead you safely to the pavilion. He's been steward here for many years, as were his father and grandfather before him, to the Tyers-Barretts."

The steward standing by kept his expression impassive, but his eyes betrayed him. They glittered with resentment as Mr. Gye spoke, and Hugh wondered if the new manager of Vauxhall had inspired some discontent among the workers here. Perhaps they had preferred to be overseen by the Tyers-Barretts.

"I do not doubt it," Audrey replied tightly, likely maddened by the coddling. "However, I insist upon staying. Now, how would the victims have gained access to the gardens overnight? Is there no security?"

The mention of security gave Hugh something to latch onto. Harlan Givens had been security at the Seven Sins. Might he have been working here as well? The others hadn't known him, but perhaps that was simply due to working different shifts.

"The grounds are patrolled throughout the night by private security. Hammond oversees all that," Mr. Gye answered swiftly, as though vexed to have to do so.

Hugh peered at the steward. "And was Mr. Givens, the victim here, on your staff?"

The steward frowned. "He wasn't. What would lead you to ask that?"

"Do not question the viscount, Hammond. You may go." Mr. Gye waved his hand, motioning for his steward to leave. Hammond did, but not before sending his employer another black glare.

Mr. Gye sighed. "The gardens are not enclosed by any walls or fencing, so I suppose one could trespass if one dared to."

"Were the other bodies found in this same state?" Hugh asked.

Mr. Gye blinked. "You mean, here? At the Cascade? No, they were out in the open, easy to find."

"I meant physically. Were they all killed in the same manner, with their throats cut, their ears taken?" he clarified, but before Mr. Gye could answer, Officers Tyne and Stevens approached. Stevens looked to Tyne to take the lead.

"We need to speak to Mr. Gye now," Officer Tyne said, his tone mockingly submissive. "Of course, only if you're done with your own questions, my lord."

Hugh grinned. "That's good of you, Tyne. I am finished. For now."

Stevens's own demeanor was less frosty than his superi-

or's. "Officer Mars—I mean, my lord, the men over there told us that guttersnipe of yours called the dead man '*father*'."

Hugh nodded. "That's correct."

Tyne scoffed. "What's it you call the boy again? Mister?"

"Sir," Hugh replied, unamused. The boy had not won himself many friends at Bow Street over the few years he'd gone there, time and again, smelling of refuse and ordering about the constables. He suspected Tyne took some pleasure in belittling Sir, if only to irritate Hugh.

"Where is he now?" Tyne asked.

"I'm not sure." Hugh paused, wondering at the question. "He saw his father's body and ran off."

"Why would he run?" Tyne pressed.

Hugh stared down the officer, who was unmistakably aiming to cast Sir in some guilty light. The utter fool.

"It was a shock, naturally," Audrey answered when Hugh's jaw remained locked tight. "He was upset."

"Poor lad," Stevens said. "Had to be a horrible thing to see."

Tyne sent him a flat look of annoyance before saying, "We won't keep you or the dowager duchess. Everything's under control here." Tyne then added, "My lord."

The tacked-on address smacked of sarcasm. That Hugh had ascended into a viscountcy surely gave the men at Bow Street something to disparage him over. At least Tyne had not called Audrey "your duchess" as he'd been inclined to do after their first investigation into the murder of an opera singer. Hugh had been teased relentlessly about the titled lady taking an interest in him, especially after she'd summoned him to Fournier Downs to solve another murder a few months later.

"Good to see you, Stevens," Hugh said, purposefully snubbing Tyne as he held out his arm to Audrey. She flexed her fingers around his forearm as they left the privacy of the large screen.

"Gracious, Officer Tyne was chilly. I had no idea he disliked you so deeply." She spoke softly as they cut through the spectators, ignoring looks of interest, and refusing to stop to answer questions of what lay behind the screen.

"I imagine he disliked me even before I became viscount." His title would have only bolstered the man's feelings. Hugh partly understood; those with peerage titles were often nothing but trouble to Bow Street officers. In the beginning, he'd felt much the same about Audrey and her family. Now, however, he counted them as friends.

"I suspect he is envious."

Audrey's shrewd suggestion was most likely correct. When wealth, power, and influence were unavailable commodities, those who possessed them could easily appear as the enemy.

"As he should be," Hugh replied, and at her stunned look, grinned. "He does not have you to tell him all the secrets Harlan Givens's flask gave up to you."

She rarely simpered as he'd come to notice many other ladies of the ton, young and old, doing. But the crafty expression inching across her lips right then was natural mischief, rather than practiced. She lowered her voice, brought herself closer on his arm, and told him what she'd seen.

"I was anxious at first, as all I could see was darkness. It makes sense, of course, because a flask would have been kept in his pocket most of the time."

Hugh nodded, understanding that the visions she was

given were often limited to what environment the object was in. The object would only hold so much energy too. Once depleted, the visions would cease.

"I had to push further back, so unfortunately when I did see something, it was quite grainy."

"What was it?" Anything at all, even something obscure, may assist them.

Audrey waited to speak until they'd passed a man and woman, strolling toward them on the walk. The man canted his head in a polite greeting, and the lady fawned with a bright, "Your Grace. My lord."

"Lord and Lady Stanwick," Audrey whispered once they'd passed. "She is good friends with Lady Dutton."

"Ah." Hugh recognized the name. He had, on several occasions, been invited to the dowager viscountess's gatherings over the Season, but as with all the others, he'd found excuses not to attend. He vastly preferred not mingling with members of the ton, and he suspected Audrey felt the same. He dreamed of whisking her away to his estate in Surrey and becoming contented recluses together.

"A street corner," Audrey said. Then, at his puzzled glance, explained, "My vision. I saw a street corner. A lamppost shed some light on two men, a fine carriage behind them. It had a cross, painted white, stamped on the door. But it was inverted."

"The cross was upside down?" She nodded. "Were the men with Givens?"

"Yes, but they were not friends. They were angry, accusing him of telling someone something that he shouldn't have." Before, Audrey had described how voices and sounds in her visions came to her in muffled form, like she'd dunked her head under the surface of bathwater.

"Anything else?"

She shook her head. "It went dark after that. But they did mention a boss, or 'guv' as they said. That Mr. Givens had crossed him."

And he'd wound up here, at Vauxhall, dead.

"The two men you saw," Hugh said. "They are most likely the men who killed Givens. How well did you see them?"

Audrey slowed her gait, and as he had several times before, Hugh wished that he could clear from her mind the wretched things she had seen. Her determination to put her ability to good use, to provide information that would otherwise be unattainable, never failed to impress him. But it was a burden for her, whether she admitted it or not.

"I saw one of them more clearly than the other. Dark hair, unfashionably long. Common clothes. Big, broad shouldered. Larger than Mr. Givens. The other man was slimmer, with a beard."

She'd come to a stop near the supper boxes, the gas jets lighting the area into a kaleidoscope of color. The orchestra was playing, though the tempo of the music had become less sedate and melodic. Vauxhall came to life after the sun set, and yet Audrey's pinched brow and distant eyes set her apart from all of it. Hugh touched her cheek, drawing her attention back to him. He did not drop his hand very quickly, and he noted two ladies in a supper box leaning in to whisper to each other.

"Did you know they were watching?" Audrey asked, having seen them too. Caressing her cheek while standing in the middle of the Grand Walk had certainly been an intimate gesture.

"I don't care who is watching. I just can't seem to keep my hands off you," he replied, winning a bashful grin and blush.

Their evening had not gone according to plan, but at least there would be talk the next day about something other than just a body being found at the pleasure gardens. They continued walking toward the gate.

"The men from my vision could also be involved in the other two murders Mr. Gye spoke of," she said.

"Possibly, but first we should know who the other two victims were and if they have any connection to Givens," Hugh said. "I'll call on Sir Gabriel tomorrow."

"After you visit Portman Square?"

For a moment, Hugh didn't take her meaning. But then with a burst of clarity, recalled the missing Miss Bethany Silas. Finding her was unquestionably important, though his interest in that inquiry paled in comparison to the murder of Sir's father and the other two recent murders at the pleasure gardens. Had he still been at Bow Street, he would have taken lead on the latter, and given the former to Tyne and Stevens.

Ahead, near the gate, the bright lights illuminated Thornton, Cassie, and Ruth, none of them conversing. Thornton was sipping a glass of what appeared to be Vaux-hall's famous and heady arrack punch, while Cassie stood stiffly. When she saw Audrey, she rushed toward her.

"No success finding Sir," she said, her distress high. "We walked everywhere too. All the way to the Hermit's Walk, even."

"You should not have gone there alone," Thornton

grumbled, the glass to his lips.

The secluded part of the gardens was in the farthest corner of the property and was known for its many scandalous rendezvous.

"Yes, because all the rogues in London have conspired to linger in the bushes there for the chance to jump out and ravish unsuspecting ladies."

Audrey gaped. "*Cassie*!"

Hugh held up his hand to stop his friend from saying anything more—Thornton had lowered his glass of arrack punch and parted his lips to do just that.

"We need to find Sir. Have you checked our rig in the coach field?" The boy might have been waiting for them there.

Thornton dropped his irritation with Cassie and focused on the larger problem. That was something about him Hugh always appreciated; his ability to change tack swiftly and give the new matter his entire concentration.

"I've been. He's not there," Thornton said.

"You should go to Bedford Street. He could be there by now," Audrey suggested, pressing her hand to Hugh's arm before releasing him and stepping aside. He hoped she was correct.

"I'm not interested in supper any longer," Cassie said.

"I don't think any of us are," Hugh agreed. He took Audrey's hand and lifted her knuckles to his lips. "I'm sorry the evening turned out as it did."

He was sorry for more than just the lost evening, though. Disappointment flooded his gut when he thought of what Mr. Gye had indicated—that Bow Street officials had agreed to keep the murders at Vauxhall from the public. Sir Gabriel

Poston had not wanted to investigate the disappearance of his own niece, and now Hugh questioned if the chief magistrate was the "connection" Mr. Gye had spoken of.

"As am I," Audrey replied. "I will send word about my meeting with Miss Bertram."

She took Cassie's arm and started for the exit, leaving Hugh and Thornton to stand there and watch them go.

"I would say I'm sorry the evening concluded early," his friend said after draining the dregs of his glass. "But had I known Audrey would bring Lady Freeze, I would have made other plans."

Hugh clapped him on the shoulder. "I'm sure Cassie feels the same way."

Thornton gave a passing waiter his empty glass. "What the devil was Givens doing here? I thought he was working security at the Seven Sins."

The gaming hell in Temple catered to the upper crust, or at least to anyone who could afford the exorbitant membership fees, be they male or female. The proprietor, Mr. Lars Vance, did not much care, so long as his members were flush.

It had taken Thornton's connections there to arrange a job for Givens, an offering that had been made to look as if Hugh had held no part in it. The arrangement hadn't been an act of charity for Givens, but rather for Sir's mother and younger sisters. Not that the position had cured the man of his many shortcomings. In early February, quite some time after securing the job at the Seven Sins, Givens had shown up at 19 Bedford Street one late afternoon. Mrs. Peets had complained loudly about a visitor at the back door, drawing the attention of Whitlock and Basil. Givens had been half-pissed, and he'd refused to leave until the master of the house spoke to him. Sir had been out, thankfully, and not wanting him to return to find his father present, Hugh had gone to the kitchen's back door.

"You'll no longer give Davy his allowance," Givens had said, slurring his words. "He's just a lad and as his father, that blunt should come to me. I'll see fit what's to be done with it."

Had Mrs. Peets not been looking on in shocked awe at the exchange, Hugh might have clocked the bastard in the jaw. Instead, he'd regulated his temper and replied evenly, "I won't be handing you a single farthing, and neither will Sir. If I ever learn you've touched his earnings, you will find yourself in a cell at Newgate. Do I make myself clear?"

He'd then slammed the door on the man's face. That was the last he'd seen of Harlan Givens. Until tonight.

"I am not convinced he was killed at the Cascade," Hugh said, thinking back to the insignificant amount of blood pooled underneath the body.

"You think his body was brought there?" Thornton asked as they now started for the gate. They'd given Audrey and Cassie a decent enough start for the coach field. To be seen leaving together might have inspired too much gossip for one evening. More importantly, it could inspire corresponding gossip involving Thornton and Cassie.

"I don't know, really, and I suppose it isn't my job to," Hugh answered. Though, he couldn't deny the bit of envy he felt for the work Tyne and Stevens had before them. "Let's go back to Bedford Street. It's far step across the river to take on foot, but he's resourceful."

"He'll be fine," Thornton assured him.

Hugh hoped his friend was right.

CHAPTER
FOUR

"This illustration looks nothing at all like me." Audrey crumpled the small pamphlet Greer had brought her just before they'd set out for Fitzroy Square. The ink on the newest scandal sheet in town, *All the Chatter*, had barely dried before it was left in print shop windows, coffee houses, and tea shops, and delivered to the homes of those who subscribed. A cartoon depicting Audrey and Hugh strolling together at Vauxhall would not have upset her. Letting London society know that they were courting had been the aim, after all.

However, the cartoon also included an unsavory background scene—sprawled on the walk behind the smitten and oblivious couple was the prone figure of a dead body. The caption read: *The dowager has cast off her black...but should Lord N beware the Bad Luck Duchess?*

"Bad Luck Duchess?" She tossed the crumpled paper onto the cushion next to her. "Who writes this rubbish?"

"Someone who was at Vauxhall last evening," Greer

suggested. "Or perhaps an informant. I imagine all the rags in town have someone in society that they pay for gossip."

She was correct, of course, as no Fleet Street reporter would ever have personal access to such things as balls and society events. They depended heavily upon informants. Those who loved gossip. She thought of Lady Dutton's friend, Lady Stanwick, and grimaced. The pairing of her and Hugh's first public outing alongside the discovery of a dead body was grossly unfortunate. But perhaps the cartoonist had been correct in calling her the Bad Luck Duchess.

She certainly seemed to have an abundance of it.

"As if I am not already treated as a pariah," she sighed. But then felt guilty. She should not be thinking of herself or her tenuous reputation. It was not nearly as important as the situations at hand.

The morning newspapers Michael subscribed to had been delivered before breakfast, and as expected, all of them had lurid headlines about the body found at Vauxhall. However, one newspaper, *The Morning Post*, had an even more shocking headline inked onto the front page: *The Secret Vauxhall Murders. Three Bodies in One Month!*

Mr. Gye's efforts to keep the previous murders from becoming public knowledge had been thwarted—and yet, only one publication had printed the story. As she and Greer had just been discussing, it seemed an informant had gone to *The Morning Post*. The evening editions would all run similar articles, spreading the truth throughout London before nightfall. Three murders would certainly cause a stir, though it was the murder of Sir's father that had plagued Audrey throughout the night.

Worry for the boy had kept her restless and unable to sleep soundly, and she wondered if Hugh had managed to locate him. He had shared some of Sir's past with her, including the fact that his father had treated him appallingly. However, as any son would, Sir had continued to hope for his father to remake himself and become a better man. Her heart broke for him. Harlan Givens may have been a dreadful parent, but he'd still been Sir's. Hugh had tried to protect the boy by taking him in, giving him an education, and a real chance at a future. She'd never brought it up with Hugh, but a part of her suspected he felt fatherly toward Sir. It made her love him even more.

The missing Miss Bethany Silas had also kept her awake most of the night, pacing her room at Violet House. The young woman needed to be her only focus right then, especially since Audrey was currently waiting in her carriage for her footman, Travers, to present her card at Miss Gwendolyn Bertram's home. She'd tried to formulate a credible excuse to visit Miss Bertram without giving away the truth about Bethany's disappearance. But no matter which path she started down she always ran up against a wall. There was no way around it—she would have to be frank, and hopefully neither Miss Bertram nor her mother were prone to hysterics or overreaction.

"Let us hope Mrs. Bertram has not yet seen the latest issue of *All the Chatter*," Greer said as they spied Travers returning to the carriage. "Otherwise, she will never let you in."

Audrey shot her maid a withering look but enjoyed the bit of drollness. Ever since Greer and Carrigan had become romantically attached, she had seemed to have a lighter step and a much lighter tongue as well. It was also possible that, after confessing that she knew about Philip, her maid felt a sense of relief. Audrey knew the weight that accumulated when guarding a secret; sharing with another person did relieve some of the burden. When they'd been in Dover in January, and Audrey had started to connect the murder of a private inquiry agent to a mysterious and anonymous note, which had threatened to reveal the truth about Philip, Greer had admitted that she'd known all along. Instead of judging her, Greer had wanted only to help protect the story. Help protect Audrey.

Travers opened the carriage door. "The lady is in, Your Grace."

She exhaled, relieved Mrs. Bertram would not turn her away.

"It seems she has *not* seen the latest copy," Greer murmured as Travers handed Audrey down.

"I will return shortly," she told her maid with an arched brow of teasing censure.

A maid allowed Audrey into the foyer of the modest but fine home. The Bertrams were upper middle class, with Mr. Bertram owning several merchant warehouses. While Sir had not delivered information on the Bertram family, Audrey had applied to an unexpectedly helpful resource: Genie, the new Duchess of Fournier. At breakfast, Audrey had avoided accompanying Genie to her modiste by saying that she would be taking tea with a new acquaintance, Mrs. Bertram.

"How did you meet Belinda?" Genie had asked, astonished.

Audrey had stumbled through a fib, and Genie had explained that her late father had business dealings with Mr. Bertram, and that she and Mrs. Bertram had gotten along well.

Now, as she entered the drawing room, Audrey at least knew to mention the Duchess of Fournier if things became awkward. However, the warm greeting she received put her instantly at ease.

"Your Grace, what a pleasure it is to receive you," a middle-aged woman, whom she took to be Belinda Bertram, said. She stood near a collection of chairs and sofas, and near her were two others—a young woman of about eighteen or nineteen, and a younger girl, of about eleven or twelve. Each significantly resembled Mrs. Bertram, who introduced her daughters as Gwendolyn and Flora. They each smiled, though Audrey thought Gwendolyn's was a bit more reluctant than her younger sister's.

Mrs. Bertram invited her to sit and announced that tea was on its way. After that, a silence descended. Audrey, normally somewhat awkward in social situations, pushed on a grin.

"Do forgive my unannounced call," she said to which Mrs. Bertram eagerly told her that she was not to apologize on any account.

"But to what do we owe the honor?" she tacked on, asking what her entire household must have been wondering.

She'd already decided to speak plainly, and so, she did.

"Concern for a friend's daughter." As expected, Mrs. Bertram's brow pleated in concern and confusion. "I am told Miss Bertram is good friends with Miss Bethany Silas."

Immediately, Gwendolyn's eyes went stony. Her lips thinned, and her chin hitched.

"She is indeed," Mrs. Bertram answered with a quick, curious look at her daughter. "What concern do you have about Miss Silas?"

Gwendolyn cast her attention to the carpet, while the younger Flora sat riveted, her eyes wide.

"I am afraid she has not been seen in a week." Audrey bit her tongue after that, knowing to allow the natural responses to occur—and to observe them closely for anything she might have missed had she continued speaking.

Mrs. Bertram's gasp of dismay, and her hand pressing to her chest, appeared genuine. But it was Gwendolyn's delayed reaction—pausing to inhale deeply before attempting to match her mother's distress—that Audrey paid closer attention to.

"A week? How awful! But where has she gone?" Flustered, Mrs. Bertram half-rose from her seat on the sofa before changing her mind and sitting again.

"I have offered my assistance to Mrs. Silas to help discover that," Audrey went on, manipulating the truth somewhat to avoid mentioning Hugh. "As you can imagine, she is quite distressed."

"Undoubtedly," she agreed. "Gwendolyn, dear, have you any idea what this is about?"

"Why should I know anything?"

"You are her closest friend, I've been told," Audrey said. "And there is some speculation that Miss Silas may have made an unwise decision regarding a certain young man..." She allowed her prompt to draw out. As expected, Mrs. Bertram's cheeks went florid.

She waved her hand toward her youngest daughter. "Flora, take your leave now. Immediately."

The girl jumped up and did as her mother ordered, closing the door to the drawing room behind her.

"Gwendolyn?" Mrs. Bertram gave an imploring look at her remaining daughter.

The young woman hesitated, her own color rising. She looked as if she'd have liked to flee the room just as her sister had.

"I demand you speak now if you know anything about this...this scandalous thing," Mrs. Bertram said, her horror increasing.

Gwendolyn jumped from her seat. "I...I didn't think she would go through with it."

Audrey stood as well. "Go through with what, the elopement?"

The young woman's dark hazel eyes went slightly blank as she looked at Audrey, but then she blinked and nodded. "Yes. That's right. The elopement."

Mrs. Bertram covered her face with her hands. "Oh! This is terrible. Simply terrible! Who is the young man, Gwendolyn? You must say everything you know. Poor Mrs. Silas!"

Something about Gwendolyn's blank stare a moment ago bothered Audrey. It was almost as if she'd been thinking of something else, but then grasped onto the offered explanation. Audrey fumed at herself. She should not have led the girl on with an answer but instead allowed her to find it for herself.

"I believe his name is Mr. Comstock. Mister Travis Comstock," she said, wrapping her arms around her middle, as if she had a stomachache.

"The wretched man. Who is he? Who are his people?" Mrs. Bertram stormed as she shot up from the sofa and began to pace. "Oh, Mr. and Mrs. Silas must be devastated. And their reputations! Shredded into tatters!" She lamented some more as she paced in a frothy panic. A maid entered with tea service, but Mrs. Bertram clucked at her to set it down and be gone.

"Mother, please—"

"How could you have known about this and said nothing?" Mrs. Bertram shouted.

"She begged me not to say anything!"

"What is their plan?" Audrey intercepted before the girl's mother could tirade against her some more.

Gwendolyn stared blankly at her again. "Their plan?"

"For after," she clarified. But still, the young woman appeared confused, and Audrey had to explain further. "After their elopement."

"Oh. Oh! Yes. Well, I'm not sure..." Gwendolyn laced her fingers together and began to fidget.

"I see," Audrey murmured. "Miss Bertram is there any chance that she has not eloped with Mr. Comstock?"

Based on her distracted reactions so far, she was beginning to think Gwendolyn did know something about her friend's disappearance, but that it might not have anything to do with a scandalous wedding.

Mrs. Bertram halted her pacing and stared at Audrey. "Where else could Bethany be?" The woman then paled and swayed on her feet before catching herself on the back of the sofa. "You don't mean to suggest...that they...they are living together in sin?"

That wasn't at all what Audrey was suggesting, though

this time, she kept her lips sealed and allowed Gwendolyn the chance to respond for herself. The rattled fluttering of her eyes as they skipped from her mother to Audrey, then to the floor, said multitudes even before she spoke.

"I really do not know anything further." Her voice was weak and soft. "Bethany had something planned but she didn't share every detail."

"You should have talked sense into her, Gwendolyn." Mrs. Bertram fanned herself as she staggered to sit again upon the sofa. "Oh, Your Grace, what disappointment in us you must feel. I do apologize for my daughter's silence. Please convey to Mrs. Silas my deepest concern and regret." She closed her eyes and fanned herself some more.

Audrey tried to meet Gwendolyn's gaze, but the young woman focused all her attention on her mother, who appeared ready to faint. No doubt she was avoiding having to look at Audrey.

It was time to leave, and with nothing new to go on. No facts. Only more speculation—speculation that Gwendolyn was lying. Audrey thanked them for their help and took her leave, neither Bertram ladies paying her much mind as she did.

With sinking spirits, she exited onto the front step, the maid closing the door firmly behind her. She hadn't gone three more paces toward the waiting carriage, Travers already opening the door for her, when the door to the Bertram's home opened again.

"Your Grace," a young voice called, and out onto the front step rushed Flora, her arm raised. In her hand was a single pink kid glove. "You forgot your glove, Your Grace."

Audrey turned. "My glove, you say?"

Not only was it pink—a color Audrey almost never wore—it was also much too small. In fact, it appeared to be sized for Flora herself. When the young girl's hazel eyes sparkled with a bit of mischief, Audrey caught on. She checked the door, which Flora had closed behind her.

"You were listening at the drawing room door, weren't you?" Audrey guessed.

"Yes," she said softly with a slight grimace of remorse. "But for a good reason. I want to tell you the truth."

Intrigued, Audrey gave the young girl her full attention. "Which is?"

"Bethie didn't elope with that man."

She stepped closer to Flora, peering at the door again. It wouldn't be long until her absence went noticed. "How do you know this?"

The girl rolled her eyes. "My sister thinks just because I am young, I don't have ears. But I do, and I heard Bethie talking about a sanctuary."

Sanctuary? The word put Audrey in mind of a church or some other safe haven.

"Bethie told Gwen not to worry, that she wanted to go to the sanctuary. That she was ready for it."

"Ready for what?" Audrey asked. But the girl only flipped up her hands and shrugged.

"I don't know, she just said 'it'. Gwen tried to tell her not to go, but Bethie doesn't ever listen to anyone."

So, Gwendolyn did know more than she was saying. If not for the presence of her mother and the harsh scolding she would receive, she might have eventually revealed more.

The front door to the home opened, and a startled maid peered out. "Miss Flora!"

Audrey winked at the girl. "Thank you, you've been most helpful, but it's not my glove. I do hope you find its owner."

Flora gave a small curtsey and winked in return before she turned and hurried back inside.

CHAPTER FIVE

Unlike the pampered individuals of London's upper crust, the working class did not sleep in most days until noon. They were setting off to their jobs or businesses when the sun touched the spires of the city and chased away night shadows. Costermongers set up their carts, shops lifted their awnings and opened their doors, newsboys hawked morning editions on corners, and in the case of Lucy Givens and countless other women living in the East End like her, so began a new day of monotony and struggle as she tried to care for her children.

Sir's mother was likely no more than thirty years of age and yet the few times Hugh had met her, she'd appeared at least a decade older. Her thin frame gave her a hollowed-out appearance, and there were usually yellowing bruises or fresh purple ones peeking out from under her shawl or cuffs.

Hugh stood on a short close, off Fenschurch Street, preparing to meet with Lucy Givens. Tyne and Stevens would have either paid her a visit last night or sent a constable to escort her to Bow Street. If they had not alerted her to her husband's death, then Hugh was hopeful Sir had.

He hadn't been at Bedford Street when Hugh and Thornton arrived there the evening before, and Basil had not seen him either. The valet had looked stricken upon hearing the news of Givens's murder and Sir's misfortune of seeing the body, and though at midnight, he'd said he was going to bed, Hugh had heard Basil shuffling about well into the early morning hours. Hugh remained in his study, lamps lit, an ear peeled for any sound near the kitchen, where Sir always let himself in. Of course, Hugh had imposed some rules for Sir to adhere to while living under his roof, and when he'd stopped being his 'assistant' and increased his tutoring sessions with Mr. Fines, the rules had become even stricter.

Sir was not to stay out past nine o'clock at night; if Hugh was not present, he was to leave word with Basil or Whitlock or Mrs. Peets about from where he could be fetched; he was not to associate with anyone connected to the Whitechapel gangs he'd once been connected to; and he was not to spend a single farthing of his weekly allowance on gambling or illicit substances.

All night, Hugh had clung to the theory that Sir must have gone to his mother. And when dawn crested over the city, he had dressed and hailed a hack to Fenschurch Street. It was moderately better than where Sir had grown up in Whitechapel. Though Hugh had offered to pay the monthly fee, Sir insisted it would be his own allowance that would keep the place. The smart lad paid the landlord directly, rather than giving the money to his mother, who would, undoubtedly, have lost it to her husband if he ever got whiff of it. Men like the unfortunate Harlan Givens could scent a coin as powerfully as a bloodhound could scent its quarry.

Hugh ascended the common stairwell to the third floor and brought his fist down upon the door. The wailing of a child and the chattering of other children came through the walls clearly, even before Mrs. Givens opened it to see who'd come calling. Her expression wasn't any more drawn or dejected than usual, and for a moment Hugh worried she did not yet know the news. That he would be the one required to give it. But then a weak smile touched her starched lips.

"You've heard about Harlan, then, my lord?"

Heard. He removed his hat, thinking over her comment quickly. She didn't seem to know that he had been there at Vauxhall when her husband was found. Which meant Sir had most likely not been here yet.

"I have," he said. "I've come to give my condolences and see if there is anything I can be of assistance with."

She stepped aside, a gesture for him to enter. He did, entering a small space packed with wash hanging from drying racks, baskets of waiting wash, minimal and cheap furniture, and gray, bare walls. The air in the entry room, which doubled as kitchen, dining space, and recreational area for the children, was hazy from coal smoke in the small brazier. But there were small signs of modest luxury: the wash consisted of new linens and clothing. One of Sir's younger sisters sat in a chair, peeling a small orange, of which there were several more in a bowl on the table. The other sister, slightly younger, held a porcelain doll that was certainly not secondhand. Lucy Givens herself brought the fine shawl she wore tighter around her, her fingers drifting over the still vibrant velvet.

Hugh's other rule for Sir had been that he must save at least some of his allowance for himself, and not spend all of it on his mother and sisters. But, of course, Hugh could not regulate that, and he also could not fault the boy for wanting to take care of his family. It seemed he had.

"I'm sorry for your loss," Hugh said, turning away from the young girls and lowering his voice.

"You know what kind of man my Harlan were," she replied, her voice tight and unemotional. "It were only a matter of time 'fore he riled someone stronger than him."

She turned away to sooth her youngest daughter, squirming in a highchair, her nose red and runny, tears sparkling on her long eyelashes.

"Do you know of anyone specific he'd angered lately?" Hugh asked.

She shook her head, lifting the little one from the chair and hinging her on the hip.

"He was working a steady job at a gaming hell," Hugh went on. "Did he ever speak of anyone he met with there who might have had a vendetta against him?"

Mrs. Givens bobbed the sniffling baby on her hip as she went to the slim window in the kitchen. She stared through it with a kind of wistful expression that Hugh couldn't make out. Not sadness exactly.

"He weren't just at the Seven Sins," she answered listlessly, eyes still on the window. "He had a few other jobs."

Hugh frowned. To have even one job was a feat for Mr. Givens. "Do you know where?"

"He wouldn't tell me a thing about it," she said. "Said he couldn't, that I might go and run my gob and then he'd be in for it. But he were acting strange the last few weeks. Never seen him so twitchy."

Audrey's vision came to mind, and how the two unidentified men who'd approached Givens had accused him of running his own gob. He'd known something. Something he shouldn't have.

"Do you have any idea what kind of work he was doing elsewhere? Security again?"

She closed her eyes as the child on her hip continued to squirm. An interrogation wasn't something the woman needed this morning. And Hugh wasn't on the murder case anyhow.

"Officers from Bow Street will be investigating," he said, curbing his questions. "I'm here to see if Sir—Davy—had been by."

She brightened a little, hearing her son's name. But the corner of her mouth tugged down. "No. Should he've been?"

Hugh hesitated, but then decided as Sir's mother, she was due the truth. Briefly, he explained how he'd been at Vauxhall at the time her husband's body had been discovered, and the unfortunate occurrence of her son coming upon the scene. Mrs. Givens took a seat at the table, her youngest whining and wriggling in her lap.

"And you haven't seen him since?"

Hugh shook his head. "I'd hoped to find him here."

The only other place he could think of where Sir would seek any comfort would be in Whitechapel, with his past acquaintances. The gangs of the East End were rife with boys his age and having quit the slums for a time to work for a toff, Sir might face opposition there. But at thirteen, Sir had grown headstrong and acerbic. Lately, even Hugh had been the target of his contempt.

Mrs. Givens set the wriggling child onto the floor, which only made her wails increase, and then got to her feet. "My boy knows how to mind himself out there."

He nodded, knowing she was right, and hoping that Sir's time with the beau monde hadn't polished away the grit required to survive on the streets.

Hugh took his leave and hailed another hack on Fenschurch. He had two more destinations in mind for that morning, the first of which was The Chesterfield at Portman Square. The former grand home had been renovated into subscription apartments for fashionable young men of means. But when the porter greeted Hugh at the front entrance, he was informed that a Mr. Travis Comstock did not lease any of the twelve apartments within. Furthermore, the porter, who had been in his position for seven years, had never heard of the man. Hugh thanked him and left, certain that Comstock had deceived Mr. and Mrs. Silas about multiple things regarding himself, and that he'd deceived Bethany too. If the young woman *had* eloped, she most likely did not know her new husband as well as she thought.

Another, shorter ride in a hired hack delivered him to number four Bow Street. Pangs of nostalgia and melancholy chimed through him as he took in the building's familiar façade. This place had been a second home to him. In fact, it had been his primary home, and Bedford Street a place to rest his head. Now, however, he had the baffling sensation of wearing ill-fitting clothes as he entered through the front door, nodding hello to the front desk clerk, Davis, who replied with an uncertain bob of his chin. He didn't stop

Hugh when he started in the direction of Sir Gabriel's office. The magistrate's court would be breaking soon, if they hadn't already, and the formidable knight, appointed thus for his service to the Crown during the Peninsula Wars, would be back in his office.

Hugh had spent the last few months sitting in Parliament, trying to find some cause to champion, to focus on. But for the most part, Parliament had appeared to Hugh as a bunch of blustering men arguing over topics that would in no way benefit the lowly masses they governed. They were sorely out of touch with the realities of the working class and working poor. Every time he attended a session, he left with more respect for Sir Gabriel's position. As magistrate, he heard evidence and testimony and was able to cast judgment quickly over whether a hearing from the Grand Jury was necessary or not. He was by no means the final authority on whether a man was found guilty or innocent, but he moved the wheels of justice along efficiently.

Sir Gabriel was a man of action. Of principle. And so, suspecting that he was the person Mr. Gye had convinced at Bow Street to stay mum about the two dead bodies found at Vauxhall disturbed Hugh. That Sir Gabriel also did not wish for his niece's disappearance to be investigated also warranted concern.

Hugh's fist came down on the door to the chief magistrate's office, bringing about the immediate customary bellow of, "*What is it?*"

He entered, and Sir Gabriel glanced up from papers on his desk to see who was bothering him. His annoyance slipped marginally, then snapped back into place.

"Neatham," he said. "I figured I'd be seeing you in here at some point today."

He shuffled his papers together, leaned back in his chair, and gestured impatiently to the chairs in front of his desk. Hugh remained standing. He could usually mask whatever emotions he was feeling, but Sir Gabriel knew him too well.

"Ach, come now, there's no reason to look like that."

"Like what?" he asked.

"Disappointed." Sir Gabriel sat forward. "I told Rebecca not to visit you about Bethany and for good reason. There's no mystery, no crime, except idiocy. The girl left with the intention of eloping."

"Do you assume, or do you know?" Hugh asked, again.

Sir Gabriel exhaled, took a moment to deliberate, and then opened a desk drawer. He presented a letter, folded, and dropped it onto the desk. Hugh took it, wondering why Mrs. Silas and Lady Rebecca had failed to tell him about the note Bethany left behind.

But as he started to read, he realized it was something else entirely.

"Hell," he muttered, dropping the letter to the desk once he'd finished.

"There is no way to know if Bethany is aware of these demands, but either way, she's ruined—utterly and thoroughly—unless she returns as Mrs. Travis Comstock. So, Mr. Silas has answered the demands of this blackguard bounder in the affirmative and is now simply awaiting their return from Gretna Green."

Sir Gabriel retrieved the letter, in which Comstock, writing in fanciful language, all but ransomed a generous yearly allowance on top of Bethany's modest dowry in order to see the elopement through. In no uncertain terms, Comstock threatened to return Bethany, unwed and scandalized, should his demands not be met.

"When did Mr. Silas receive this?" Hugh asked.

"The day after Bethany failed to return home from Vauxhall."

So, she'd been gone for one night; long enough to coax her parents into a panic.

"And why was her mother not made aware of this?" Hugh asked.

"Ignorance is bliss, Marsden. You of all people should know."

Hugh scowled. Sir Gabriel was surely referencing Hugh's own prior ignorance to the truth of his birth. He'd been heir to the viscountcy all along, not an illegitimate ward. The chief magistrate knew him well enough to know that he would trade it in for his old life in a heartbeat, if only it were possible.

"I'm surprised Comstock settled on someone like Bethany for his scheming," Hugh said, still bothered by the whole situation, and not just the deviousness of it. It was a unilateral union, at best. "Silas is landed gentry. A squire, just as Comstock is. Why not aim higher?"

Sir Gabriel stood, groaning as if his knees bothered him. "My brother-in-law is by no means a wealthy man, but he can afford the demanded allowance. He also has little power or clout to do anything more about it. As for Bethany herself, I don't wish to speak ill of my niece, but she is plain, and her charms are few. She would have been easy to persuade. Comstock chose his quarry wisely, as far as I'm concerned."

When put like that, Hugh found he agreed. That he'd

lied about having a sister, hired someone to stand in as the fabricated relation, and then also lied about where he was leasing rooms...it all spoke to his ultimate deception. Which seems to have gone off without a hitch.

Why, then, did the faintest of barbed friction remain just under Hugh's skin when he thought of Bethany?

"They should be returning within a day, I would imagine," Hugh said, having calculated the length of the journey to the Scottish border and back.

Sir Gabriel grimaced. "And I will be forced to give my congratulations, no doubt." He then narrowed his eyes further, deepening the crease that divided the bridge of his nose and his forehead. "You have also come here to discuss the happenings at Vauxhall, I am sure."

"*Happenings* is a mild description, one that might befit the society pages. These are *murders*, though no one in London seemed to know about them until this morning thanks to someone here at Bow Street."

The Morning Post had exclusively printed the story, and Hugh was certain a Vauxhall worker had tipped off the publication after last night's debacle.

Hugh held Sir Gabriel's darkening stare. He no longer answered to the knight. Respecting him did not mean he had to bow down to him or tuck his tail and flee.

The chief magistrate skirted Hugh's pointed comment. "I am aware you found the body at the Cascade."

A pert knock landed on the closed office door, cutting into the chief's agitated statement.

"What is it?" he bellowed.

The door opened, and a clerk stood aside to permit a visitor. Hugh raised a brow as Audrey entered the office. He should have expected to see her here.

"Your Grace," Sir Gabriel said, only slightly tempering his previous tone.

She gave the chief magistrate a placating grin; the one she reserved for those she thought were being petulant and hotheaded. She'd worn it a time or two for Hugh.

"I'm just in time, I see. Yes, Hugh found the body at the Cascade," she said. "We both did."

"Listening at doors, Your Grace?" The magistrate re-took his seat, but Audrey didn't quaver from the chastising.

"Hardly," she said as the door shut behind her. "Your voice is equal to the blast of a bugle, Sir Gabriel. I practically heard you shouting at the viscount when I stepped through the front door."

Well aware of his own aggressive reputation and booming voice, he laughed and invited her to take a seat. However, she stopped next to Hugh. The light floral scent of camellia and sunshine that he'd come to dream about warmed his blood.

"I'll stand, thank you," she replied. "Now, about the bodies at the pleasure gardens—"

"We've already been hounded this morning thanks to that article in the *Post*, but I cannot discuss it with members of the public, Your Grace. Let us leave it at that."

Hugh nearly choked on a laugh. The magistrate should simply give in now. Once Audrey had a question, she got an answer, no matter the route, and no matter how perilous.

"Harlan Givens was missing his left ear," Hugh said, deciding to help her along. "It looked to be a clean stroke of a knife."

Sir Gabriel glowered, accentuating his double chin as he tucked it. "What of it?"

"The other two were missing their ears as well."

Sir Gabriel sighed heavily. "Yes, the left ear."

"And their throats all cut?"

The magistrate nodded.

"So, then that means the same person killed all three victims," Audrey said.

With his cheeks turning florid, the magistrate had reached his limit. He gripped the edge of the desk and stood again. "Mr. Gye asked for our discretion, and I gave it, not because I give a damn about him losing money, but because announcing something like this would inspire a panic. And now, you can bloody well expect one, even though the general public is not in any danger."

"What makes you so sure?" Hugh asked.

"Tyne!" Sir Gabriel bellowed without warning, causing Hugh to wince and Audrey to jump.

No more than a moment or two passed before Tyne entered the office. The officer had to have been lingering in the corridor, likely drawn by word of Hugh's arrival. It was a petty thing to do, listening at doors, as Sir Gabriel had just accused Audrey of doing.

"Lord Neatham and Her Grace would like the particulars about the Vauxhall case, and they have assured me they will speak to no one outside this room of them, especially no reporters." Sir Gabriel's stare fired high as he turned it toward Hugh, then Audrey. "Isn't that correct?"

"Certainly," Audrey replied sweetly. Too sweet. But Sir Gabriel was not as schooled at her tones of voice yet.

The magistrate started for the door, grumbling, "I'm wanted at court."

Silence followed his departure as Tyne rocked back onto his heels, his nostrils flaring. Hugh waited for the man to speak. When he did, it was as though the words were struggling to form. "I take it you are joining the investigation."

Ah. Now he understood Tyne's bristling. He thought Hugh had come to take over. Stepping on Tyne's toes was the last thing he wished to do, even though he did take some pleasure in riling him.

"Not officially. My only interest is in Harlan Givens and why he was killed. If it's connected to these other murders, I'd like to know how and why."

The explanation did little to allay the officer. "I would think they would be beneath your notice, my lord." Again, the emphasis on the form of address smacked with scorn.

"They aren't," Hugh replied succinctly, leaving no room for more of an argument. Next to him, Audrey watched their exchange with interest.

"Who were the other two victims, Officer Tyne?" she asked. *The Morning Post* had not identified them by name, only that it had been a man and a woman.

"Madam Lee, a brothel owner," Tyne answered. His attention shifted to her, and the twist of his mouth led Hugh to believe he was taking pleasure in thinking he was shocking her. She did not so much as flinch.

"And?" Hugh pressed.

"Lord Stromburg, some Austrian count."

"In which order were the killings? Lee first?"

Tyne grimaced. "Stromburg first. Two days later, Lee."

"They were found in the early morning, before the

gardens opened to visitors, according to Mr. Gye," Audrey said. Tyne wrinkled his nose and gave her a look of annoyance. "But were they killed at the pleasure gardens, or were they brought there after the fact?"

"The lack of blood around Givens's body suggests he was brought there after he was killed," Hugh said, then turned to Tyne. "Did you make the same observation for the other two victims?"

His caustic stare had not abated. "I did."

"And where are you with the case? Do you have any suspects?"

He grimaced. "Not just yet, my lord."

Thinking he was being crowded out of his own investigation, Tyne was reluctant to give up his information. If he wasn't intent on being such an arse, Hugh might have taken pity on him.

"Which brothel was Madam Lee running?" Hugh asked instead, unwilling to back down.

Again, Tyne formed a smug smirk and directed his attention to Audrey. "The Red Lotus. Know of it?"

He was asking Hugh, of course, but keeping his eyes on Audrey was meant to fluster her.

"I don't," Hugh answered, beginning to change his mind about edging out Tyne and taking over the investigation. "However, I do know of Stromburg. I met him briefly at White's. He was visiting the Austrian ambassador, Anton Esterhazy. A prince of some sort."

Tyne snorted. "White's, is it?"

"Thank you for your help, Officer Tyne," Audrey said before Hugh could even consider a reply to the goading remark. "The viscount and I will be leaving now."

Before the pair of them could come to blows, no doubt. It had been a mistake to mention the gentleman's club. He should have known it would only nettle the officer. But what the Brown Bear was for Bow Street, White's was for Parliament.

The officer gave them a thin, mocking grin and left the office. Audrey took Hugh's arm, and only then did he realize how rigidly he was holding himself.

"I am going to assume Officer Tyne was one of the patrolmen who used to tease you by calling me *your duchess,*" she whispered as they left the magistrate's office and made their way toward reception.

Hugh opened the door for Audrey, and he breathed in deep as they came out into the afternoon sunlight. The weather was fair, the sky clear, and he was thankful to not have Tyne eyeballing Audrey any longer.

"He was," Hugh replied. "The man annoyed me then and does even more so now."

"At least he gave us some information to follow up on," she said as her driver Carrigan and footman, Travers, spotted their approach. Travers opened the carriage door. "A brothel madam and an Austrian aristocrat... How has no one reported Stromburg as missing?"

Hugh questioned that, too. Bow Street staying quiet on the deaths was one thing, but surely the Austrian ambassador would have noticed the disappearance of his visiting friend.

"I'll have to try and arrange an interview with Esterhazy," he said. "Though I have no idea how I can explain my interest in Stromburg without revealing his fate."

"What have they done with his body? Surely, they must need to return him to his family for burial."

"They could be preserving it while the investigation is on, but I can't see how they can cover things up for much longer, especially now that the three murders have been publicized." Hugh shook his head, irritated at Bow Street's silence, and Sir Gabriel's acquiescence to Gye's demands.

"If the bodies were transported to Vauxhall and left there, then it does stand to reason that visitors to the pleasure gardens are not in any danger," Audrey said, as though anticipating where Hugh's mind had gone. "Sir Gabriel was correct that inciting a panic would do no one any good."

"All right, yes, I agree. But the silence likely hampered the investigation. And I can't help but question if Tyne and Stevens are up for a case of this complexity. They don't seem to have gotten anywhere."

Her hand rested on his forearm, as if to stop his simmering agitation in its tracks. "You have other important concerns. Have you found Sir?"

He covered her hand with his own. "Not yet. He hasn't been to his mother's either."

"He'll turn up," she said. "Give him time."

Hugh nodded and was reluctant to see her into the waiting carriage. He held her hand against his arm for another indecently long moment. When they were married, he would never have to worry about such things again. It gave him a thought.

"I have news about Miss Bertram," Audrey said.

He welcomed the excuse to not have to part just yet. "You can tell me on the way."

She brightened with a curious grin. "On the way to where?"

He guided her into the carriage, and then climbed in

after her. "I would like to show you something. It's a short drive from here. Travers, ask Carrigan to go to 37 Berkeley Square."

The footman bowed and shut the door. Audrey peered at him, her keen curiosity bowing her lips in a way that made him want to whisk her into his lap and kiss her.

"What is at 37 Berkeley Square?" she asked.

"Patience, Duchess. Patience," he said, and from the driver's box, Carrigan urged the horses onward.

CHAPTER SIX

Audrey sank back into the squabs in the carriage. "The vile cad!"

Hugh had just described the letter Mr. Comstock had delivered to Mr. Silas, outlining his demands for two hundred pounds every year on top of the income from Bethany's dowry in return for a proper elopement with his daughter—and not depositing home a thoroughly ruined one instead.

"I'd be tempted to slip a little arsenic into his pudding next Christmas if I were Mr. Silas, but," Hugh shrugged and held out his hands, palms up, "it looks as though a trip to Gretna Green is to blame for Bethany's disappearance after all."

He didn't appear relieved, or even very convinced. His jaw grated, his narrowed stare trained on the window, since leaving Bow Street. The run-in with Officer Tyne had vexed him. Sir's unknown whereabouts weighed on him too.

Audrey had finished telling him about Flora Bertram's ruse to get her alone on the pavement outside her home, and the young girl's information. But the letter Hugh had read in Sir Gabriel's office wholly disputed her claims.

"Flora was certain it wasn't an elopement," Audrey sighed.

"She is what age, twelve?"

"Don't disparage her just because she is young. Children often have better opportunity than most to go unnoticed."

"I'm not disparaging her," he replied. "But she may have misinterpreted what she overheard."

Audrey granted that it was possible. "But what could the sanctuary be that Bethany and Gwendolyn spoke of?"

It was where Bethany had claimed to be going. Not Gretna Green, but the *sanctuary*.

"My guess is that Comstock tricked Bethany and lied to her about several things in order to see his plan through. The sanctuary, whatever it is, could be part of those lies," Hugh said.

The carriage slowed and turned. They'd been traveling west, toward Berkeley Square, and Audrey's desire to know the reason why continued to spike her pulse. She wasn't dressed for any society function. Gunter's Tea Shop was on Berkeley Square. He could be taking her there. Oddly enough, thinking about Bethany Silas and the mystery surrounding her absence soothed her in comparison to the mysterious outing they were currently undertaking.

"Why would Comstock demand so little?" she asked. "Two hundred pounds is nothing, really. Why not prey upon someone much wealthier?"

Hugh's attention again went to the window, as if he couldn't tear himself away from the streets and pavements scrolling by—and the chance that he might catch a glimpse of Sir. She'd wager everything that was what was truly bothering him. She held still on her bench, even though she wanted to join him on his and run her thumb along his cheek, smoothing the line there from his perpetual frown.

"Sir Gabriel argues that Comstock was wise to choose his target as he did. Why draw attention to himself with a young lady of higher social standing? Why curry hatred and distrust among those with more power?"

It was reasonable. But something simply didn't feel *right* about it.

"I still think we should speak to Gwendolyn privately, without her mother present. It may loosen her tongue," Audrey said.

Hugh didn't disagree, but he also was no longer focused on their discussion. Carrigan turned off Piccadilly, onto Berkeley Street, toward the square.

"When do you plan to tell me what we are doing here?" she asked.

They drove past the newly greening lawns belonging to Lansdowne House, the mansion set back at the north side of the square. Five blocks of townhomes occupied the east, south, and west sides, all of them well-kept and stately.

"When we arrive," Hugh answered as Carrigan drew them to the west side of the square, where number thirty-seven was located. Her driver stopped, and without waiting for Travers, Hugh opened the door and stepped down. He held out his hand and, even more nervous now, Audrey descended.

"Really, Hugh, I hope we aren't meeting with anyone. I like to be prepared," she started to say as he led her closer to the front entrance. She dug in her heels, and he stopped.

"What do you think?" he asked, peering up at the townhome.

Audrey followed his appraising gaze. "What do I think of what?"

He gestured toward the townhouse. "This place."

She blinked and again turned to view the home. Constructed of pale limestone, the Georgian rowhouse stood proudly alongside its neighbors. With three stories, large and numerous windows, it exuded understated elegance. A whisper of awareness stirred in the center of her chest.

"It is lovely," she answered, then cautiously asked, "Who...who lives here?"

Hugh took her gloved hand in his, uncaring of the ladies and gentlemen in the square, taking their ices from Gunter's under the shade of the maple trees. With his dark eyes now swallowing her, he replied, "If you like it well enough, I was thinking we could."

The pavement beneath her boots dissolved. It was only Hugh's hand on hers that kept her from sinking or falling backward. She stared at him, astounded, her lips gaping.

"Live here?" she said, her voice breathy. "Us?"

"Only if you like it." His brows lifted as he waited for her answer. Audrey peered at the townhome again, and this time, with a new lens. Hugh wanted this to be *their* home. Where they would live, together. Where they would build a family.

"I've had my steward looking at potential residences, and for whatever reason, I kept coming back to this one," he said. "It's half the size, if that, of Violet House, I know—"

"I never liked Violet House." She'd thought it blocky and ostentatious and too severe. She'd never felt at home there. But this townhouse did not give her those impressions at all.

She gazed at the exterior another moment, then turned to Hugh. He had been watching her, studying her reaction.

"Can we go in?" she asked, eager to see the rooms. He sighed.

"I brought you here on a whim, so I haven't a key. But I can arrange it."

She pinned her lower lip, suddenly nervous. "I think it's lovely," she said again.

"Lovely enough to make our home?"

"Yes, but...haven't we skipped an essential step?" She didn't quite know how to say it outright—that he had yet to propose marriage.

Hugh raised her hand and kept his melting stare on her as he kissed the satin ridge of her knuckles. "The part where I ask you to be my wife?"

She couldn't account for the blush that rushed to her cheeks. Or the flood of elation that left her limbs quivering. He had already stated in no uncertain terms that he would make her his wife as soon as her mourning was over. She'd been expecting it. But even knowing that, she still could barely breathe.

"Yes, that part," she answered as giddiness—a sensation that she was not wholly accustomed to—stole through her.

It mounted even more when Hugh arched a brow as if about to do something wicked. And then, he sank down in front of her, planting one knee on the pavement outside number 37 Berkeley Square.

Her breath gusted out between her lips as he kept her hand in his and, in full view of Carrigan and Travers and a handful of their future neighbors strolling by, said, "Audrey Sinclair, since the moment I met you, I've either wanted to throttle you, arrest you, or kiss you senseless. You drive me utterly mad, and I love you for it. I want nothing more than to be your husband. If you still wish to be my wife?"

She could barely see him through the veil of tears fogging her vision, but she gave a shaky laugh. "I want to drive you mad for the rest of my life, Hugh Marsden," she said, her voice just as tremulous.

He shot back up onto both feet and brought her closer, his lips lingering on her knuckles again. "I'll hold you to that."

Her heart gave a lurch. She'd never dreamed it possible to be this happy. When she and Philip had agreed to marry, it had taken the form of a business interview, absent of emotion, of nerves and uncertainties. For years, she and Philip had pretended to have a love match. But now, as her body and soul radiated with joy, she knew their act had been as thin as gossamer.

"I have a ring for you," he said, his thumb coasting over the left fingers of her gloved hand. "However, this was all spontaneous and so it isn't with me."

"You mean you hadn't practiced that little speech, telling me you've wanted to throttle me or arrest me—"

"Or kiss you," he cut in. "No, I hadn't. But I meant every word."

Audrey smiled, elated to know that this man would endeavor to make her laugh.

"I want to kiss you," she whispered. However, she was distinctly aware of how much attention they'd drawn, especially while Hugh was on one knee.

He groaned softly. "Soon, you may kiss me as much as you like. There won't be anything else for you to do anyhow since you'll be confined to my bed night and day for at least a week." His whispered promise sent an electric shiver up her spine. "Maybe even a fortnight."

Audrey missed being in his arms with a palpable ache. And to think—once they married, it would be perfectly acceptable. Expected even.

"How soon?" She didn't care if she sounded eager. She *was*.

Hugh pecked her hand one last time and then with a roguish grin said, "I have a special license."

She stared, astounded. "You do?" To obtain a special license for marriage, he'd have needed to appeal to the Archbishop of Canterbury. Hugh would have been required to name Audrey on the application, and the archbishop would have reviewed it to be sure they were both eligible.

"I visited the archbishop the day your mourning ended," he admitted. "I was the greenest and most impatient of bucks and the man practically chuckled as he signed the license, but..." Hugh leaned closer, and for a moment, Audrey thought he would kiss her and to hell with whoever was looking on. "We can marry tonight. Or tomorrow. Certainly, before you come to your senses and change your mind."

She laughed. "I will never change my mind. You already know how stubborn I am."

"I do. Mules look to you for inspiration," he said, and Audrey balked.

"It is part of my charm!"

"You have many of those," Hugh said, their lively banter making her feel light as air. His eyes raked her over in a slow, seductive manner that put her in mind of his promise to confine her to his bed. The rest of the world could fall away, disintegrate into mist, and she would be none the wiser. Nor would she care. However, even as those fervent and fanciful thoughts slid through her mind, her practical side stood firm against them. A few things needed resolving before the two of them could, without reservation, abandon the world for a time.

Audrey touched his shoulder, smoothing the fabric even though it didn't need it. "You realize, of course, that we cannot indulge in marital bliss for weeks on end, as you've so indecently described, until we find Miss Silas. And Sir."

He winced, and she regretted bringing up the missing boy. But it wouldn't be right to marry without Sir there. He formed a forlorn grin and nodded. "You are correct."

"Another one of my charms," she said, only wanting to lighten his mood.

He laughed, but this time it held a dismal note. "Then we best find a way to speak to Gwendolyn Bertram."

Across the newly greening gardens in the square, the front entrance to Gunter's Tea Shop bustled.

"I believe I have an idea," Audrey said.

CHAPTER SEVEN

The backs of Hugh's eyelids burned from lack of proper sleep. He'd spent a second night pacing his study until he could stand it no longer and had his driver bring the carriage around. He and a sleepy Norris had traveled the streets of Mayfair before bracing themselves and heading east, toward Whitechapel and Wapping. He'd kept his flintlock pistol primed and ready, as did Norris in the driver's box. But though he saw countless young boys around Sir's age loitering about, none of them had been him.

After a few hours, he'd taken pity on Norris and directed him to return to Bedford Street. Norris had likely dropped like a sack of turnips into his bed, while Hugh had been too wound up to do more than tip a hefty pour of whisky into a glass. But then, he'd dumped it out again.

During the autumn and early winter, he'd started drinking to excess, using spirits as a salve for the wounds Audrey's silence from the Continent had inflicted. He'd come home pickled most nights, and it had driven Sir away.

He already had a drunken brute of a father; he likely feared the same would happen with Hugh. Once he'd gotten that through his thick skull, he'd vowed to not use spirits to numb himself during some hardship, and he had followed through.

He now forced his brain to stay alert as he and Audrey waited at a corner table inside Gunter's Tea Shop, the hour hand closing in on three o'clock. It was cold inside the shop on Berkeley Square, which helped him in his endeavor to stay awake. The sweet scents of flavored ices permeated the air, but the tension that seemed to have taken up permanent residence inside his stomach had eliminated any desire to eat.

"She should be here by now," Audrey murmured, her spoon slicing easily through the pistachio sorbet that had already been melting when it was delivered to their table.

"She might have suspected the ruse."

Audrey put her spoon in her mouth and glared at him. He would have apologized for doubting her plan, but he was too entranced by the sight of her lips sliding the creamy sorbet off the curve of her spoon.

The woman was going to be the death of him. Especially if he could not marry her and make good on his promises of the previous afternoon outside 37 Berkeley Square. He'd sent immediate word to his solicitor, Mr. Potridge, to proceed with the purchase of the house, which was currently unoccupied.

"I believe Gwendolyn was rattled enough by my visit to believe it," Audrey argued.

She'd sent a note to Miss Bertram that morning, and with any hope the young lady would heed the brief message: *Come to Gunter's at 3 o'clock, alone. I need to see you.* She'd signed it *Bethie*, saying that was what Flora had called Bethany the day before.

"That might only be what Flora calls her," Hugh had cautioned when she'd outlined her plan. But it was worth the try.

They'd selected a table in the back, away from the front windows and from view of the conveyances lining this side of the square. Waiters were busily rushing back and forth across the street, receiving orders for ices, and delivering them before they could melt. As the weather had improved, some of the ladies and gentlemen were in the gardens of the square on benches, too. The buds on the trees were still young and compacted, allowing for a view of number thirty-seven, across the square. Another reason for his sleepless night and restless mind had been due to taking too much pleasure in imagining himself and Audrey, married and making their home there together.

He'd decided at the last minute to bring her around Berkeley Square and show her the house. Getting down on one knee and formally proposing had also been spontaneous, so he hadn't even had the ring. It was in his pocket now, of course, but there hadn't been a suitable moment to present it to her. A table at Gunter's certainly wasn't it.

The front door opened, and a young woman fitting the description Audrey had given of Gwendolyn Bertram entered. She was alone and seemed to be searching for someone. Hugh pushed back his chair and rose with his task while Audrey, her back to the door, quickly swallowed her sorbet and touched a napkin to her lips in preparation.

"Miss Bertram, I believe?" Hugh said as he approached

her. She went rigid with caution as she glimpsed him over. In any other place, it would have been unforgivably rude for a gentleman to approach and speak to a lady he didn't know, but at Gunter's, the rules were a bit looser. Men and women could meet here, unchaperoned, though in full view of society at all times.

"Yes?" she replied with appropriate wariness.

"Your friend is waiting for you. This way," he said, and then turned to lead her to the corner of the shop. From this perspective, Gwendolyn would not have a view of Audrey's face. So, it wasn't until she came to stand next to the table that she saw her, and with a flare of her eyes, put the pieces of the ruse together.

"This was a trick," she gasped.

"Please, Miss Bertram, do sit," Audrey said, but then, when the young woman continued to huff, added, "Causing a scene won't do if you don't want this getting back to your mother."

Hugh applauded her for the arm-twisting tactic. It worked. Gwendolyn Bertram sat in the chair that Hugh pulled out for her, her back straight and her reticule clutched in her lap.

"What do you want?" she demanded.

"The truth," Audrey replied.

Hugh re-took his own seat as Gwendolyn eyed him suspiciously. "And who are you?"

"Lord Neatham," he replied, and as expected, recognition spread over her tight expression.

"Oh." Her shoulders and spine stiffened again. "You were a Bow Street officer."

"I was. And we would like to ask you some more questions about Miss Bethany Silas's whereabouts."

Gwendolyn started to say something quick in return, but Audrey cut in. "We know she didn't elope with Mr. Comstock."

Hugh looked to Audrey, who had been stalwart in her belief that Bethany had not gone to Gretna Green, as Comstock's letter to Mr. Silas stated. He'd once told her to follow her instincts, and she was doing just that.

When Gwendolyn sealed her lips and raised her chin without making any argument, Hugh bit back a grin. Apparently, Audrey had been correct.

"What is the *sanctuary*?" she continued.

A sharp breath shuttled down Gwendolyn's throat as she gasped, and her coloring, flushed from being cornered, paled. She looked over her shoulder, toward the door.

"You shouldn't speak so loudly," she hissed.

"Who do you worry will overhear?" Hugh asked.

The patrons here were all upper class, mostly belonging to the peerage and landed gentry. Though most were having their orders delivered to their carriages or to the square, a handful occupied the tables inside.

"You aren't supposed to speak of it," she said in a raspy whisper.

"Of the sanctuary?" Audrey asked, and when the young woman winced as if in pain, decided to spare the girl and lower her voice. "Why not?"

Gwendolyn squirmed in her chair, and Hugh could see she was trying to formulate a way out of this undesirable situation. The only remedy for that was to keep the pressure consistent.

"Tell us," he said. "Miss Silas's mother is concerned for her daughter's welfare, and by the way you are acting, so are you."

The door to Gunter's opened, the bell chiming. Gwendolyn snapped a look over her shoulder, but only a waiter entered, transporting a tray of empty crystal bowls and dishes. With a small slump of relief, she closed her eyes a moment before saying, "It is the name of a society. I don't know much about it, I promise. Just that its members are all very prestigious."

Hugh sat back in his chair. London's upper crust had all manner of societies to which one could belong. Most had a common focus. Art, music, literature, science. At White's, Hugh had been extended a few invitations. He'd never taken up any of the offers. There were also secret clubs, those that delved into darker and more dangerous territory, like the occult. Of those, he'd only heard whispers. Never an invitation, not with his Bow Street background. He wondered what sort of society the Sanctuary was.

"And Bethany learned of this society through Mr. Comstock?" he asked.

She pressed her lips thin and nodded.

"That is where Bethany has gone?" Audrey asked.

A waiter came to the table then to take Gwendolyn's order, preventing her from answering. She sent him away with a shake of her head.

"I don't know," she answered after it was safe to speak again. "She was invited, and I know that she had planned to go." She still darted little glances around the shop with an edge of paranoia.

"When was this?" Hugh asked.

Gwendolyn frowned. "A week ago. The arrangement was for Mr. Comstock and his sister to fetch her for an evening at Vauxhall."

"He does not have a sister," Audrey said.

"But of course he does. Bethie met her. She said Miss Comstock was quite nice if a bit shy."

Hugh met Audrey's concerned glimpse. If Bethany had not known the truth about Comstock's lack of a sister, what more had she not known?

"Were they truly to go to Vauxhall? Or was the real outing to the Sanctuary?" he asked.

Gwendolyn cast her eyes down to the table, as if shamefaced. "The Sanctuary," she said, so quietly that Hugh had barely heard the words.

"Where is it?" Audrey asked, her impatience evident. Hugh felt the same; if this young woman had known all along where Bethany could be found, why had she stayed silent? To safeguard her own responsibility in the scandal?

"I don't know." At their mutual looks of disbelief, she leaned forward and more vehemently said, "I *don't*. It is secret. It's hidden and known only to members. Bethie didn't even know, but I expected her to tell me all about it the next day."

A streak of alarm tempered his annoyance with Gwendolyn. "You mean to say she did not plan to stay away?"

Comstock's letter, delivered to Mr. Silas, had arrived the day following Bethany's outing to Vauxhall. What had changed in those twelve hours or so?

"No, she said she would tell me everything over tea the next afternoon."

And yet, she had not returned. It was possible she had

changed her mind and decided to elope with Comstock when he proposed the idea, but Hugh's instinct—the thing he had always trusted, his inner compass—told him that she had met with trouble.

"I need to know absolutely everything you do about the Sanctuary, Miss Bertram. I believe your friend is in danger."

His curt order was met with twin looks of alarm. Gwendolyn's was touched with fright, Audrey's, with understanding.

"She...she said she would need to be blindfolded for the ride there."

Hugh's gut clenched. "What do they do at this society?"

Pink suffused the apples of her cheeks, and she dropped her gaze from his. It confirmed his guess.

"I don't know for certain," she began. "Bethie only said it was akin to one of the gentlemen's clubs, but that it was happy to admit women too. After an initiation."

Grasping her meaning, fury rippled through him.

"Initiation of what sort?" Audrey asked.

He stayed quiet, allowing Gwendolyn to speak, even though he was already certain of the answer.

She finally did, though blushing fiercely. "They...they must permit..." She shook her head, unable to finish her sentence.

"She had to submit," Hugh said, gritting his molars.

Audrey gaped at him, then at Gwendolyn as she comprehended. Blindfolded and led to a secret location, Bethany had been willing to pay the initiation fee into this society. A price only women were taxed with. Had she needed to submit to one man, or many? *Hellfire.* Was she still there?

"Why would she wish to be a part of such a vulgar thing?" Audrey asked.

Gwendolyn broke from her timidity to chuff a mocking laugh. "Tedium. Boredom. Why shouldn't she want a bit of excitement before she is tied to a husband who will become her ruler? You've been in society, Your Grace, you know the rules, all the restrictions. We are treated as if we are at first dolls for our mothers, and then broodmares for our husbands."

"And how has Mr. Comstock treated Bethany any better?" Audrey replied. "If what you say is true, he has used her most grievously. Mothers act out of love and care...most of the time," she put in, likely thinking of her own mother, who had never acted toward her out of anything close to love or care. "Mr. Comstock and his fellow Sanctuary members hide behind secret locations with only their own pleasure in mind. They don't care about Bethany at all."

Gwendolyn, properly chastised, sealed her lips thinly.

"Where did she meet Mr. Comstock?" Hugh asked. When she did not reply or even look his way, he pressed on. "The sooner you answer our questions, the sooner we may be able to find your friend. A friend who has been missing for nearly one week in part due to your silence."

Contrition undermined her stony expression. "They met at Vauxhall."

"He doesn't reside at The Chesterfield at Portman Square. Where does he live?"

"I don't know. Truly, I do not. I wasn't with Bethie when she met him for the first time at the pleasure gardens. But she told me that he next invited her to a gambling hell. One where the women needed to wear dominos. For anonymity."

"And she went?" Audrey asked.

Gwendolyn nodded, pallid again. Worried. As if this conversation had awoken her to the true danger her friend was in.

There were many gambling hells in London, and many that permitted women wearing masks to conceal their identities. Not that the concealment worked half the time. Audrey herself had once worn a domino to the Seven Sins, when she'd been on her quest to prove Philip innocent of murder. Hugh easily recalled seeing her across the gaming floor, her body encased in a form-revealing gown, her domino unable to trick him into confusion. His reaction then had been a heady cross between wrath and desire.

However, the mention of Vauxhall and then of a gambling hell had put him in mind of something else. Of *someone* else. His pulse quickened. He'd been puzzling over what Harlan Givens had been doing at the pleasure gardens, or how his body had come to be there. His flask had given Audrey a vision of him with two threatening men, and behind them, their conveyance—the door stamped with an inverted white cross.

"Sanctuary," Hugh murmured. Churches were often treated as sanctuaries. The universal emblem of a church was the Cross of Christ, and though the one on the carriage door had been flipped upside down, perhaps it was a commentary on the sinful behavior taking place in this *sanctuary*.

"Pardon, my lord?" Gwendolyn said, peering at him. Audrey was as well, but with a clever spark in her eye. She understood where his mind had led him.

He shook his head. "It's nothing. This gaming hell you

mentioned. It wouldn't happen to have been the Seven Sins?"

Gwendolyn's quizzical brow smoothed. "Why, yes. How did you know?"

CHAPTER
EIGHT

Philippa closed her fingers into a fist and gummed it, her saucer-like blue eyes gazing up at Audrey. The baby lay upon the carpet in the nursery, leftover tears from her earlier fit still sparkling on her long, thick lashes. Genie and Michael's little girl now babbled happily, all past distress forgotten. How easily that was achieved when one was only four months old. The most arduous thing little Pippa needed to work on was rolling from her back onto her front.

"You nearly have it," Audrey encouraged as Pippa kicked her tiny feet and wriggled. Philippa had completely stolen her heart. Little George had too, of course, but Audrey had spent more time with the new baby, considering that she was living under the same roof.

Though, not for much longer.

She grasped Pippa's bare foot and lifted it to her lips, giving it a kiss. The baby gurgled some more. Spending time with Genie and Michael's children was nearly the only thing Audrey enjoyed about living at Violet House, and she would be sorry to be parted from them. But the thrill she felt when she pictured the front of 37 Berkeley Square and how Hugh had dropped to one knee, obliterated any possible regret.

She'd been honest when she'd said Violet House had never felt like home. Not when Philip had been here and certainly not now. It was time to move on. And there it was again: the small twinge in her chest that had grown in size and strength over the last few months whenever she thought of Philip. She'd noticed it shortly after returning to London after the events in Dover, but it had taken a little while for her to understand the cause.

Lord St. John had designed his murderous plot with the intent of luring Philip out from wherever he'd gone on the Continent. With the Dowager Duchess of Fournier accused of murder at first, and then ultimately, going missing, the news was bound to reach into the country where Philip and Freddie Walker had absconded. St. John had been willing to wait months if necessary for Philip to return to England, perhaps under some disguise and with a new name.

But he hadn't. It had been four months since Audrey had sent St. John into the depths of the Dover harbor, never to resurface, while defending her own life. Four months since newspapers in France had printed the lurid story of the duchess accused of poisoning a fellow traveler on her packet ship, and then being involved in yet another murder in Dover, this time of a Baron of the Cinque Ports. She'd stewed with worry that he would hear about the trouble and try to return home, but now, she had started to hope he would at least write. He'd promised to send word once he and Freddie had settled. It had been a full year now. Wasn't that time enough?

There were moments when it struck her like a slap across the cheek that perhaps he had been placating her with that promise. That he'd never planned to write. That he was out of her life forever. And with his syphilis fevers, she worried some more. What if one had overtaken him? What if he could not get medical help?

Philippa grew blurry as her eyes stung and watered, the little girl utterly oblivious to the turmoil coiling inside her aunt. Everyone else had already spent a full year mourning Philip. Yet now that her official mourning was over, she had the oddest sensation that it was truly just beginning.

She thumbed away a tear that had slipped free from her lashes and rolled down her cheek. "Gracious, now I'm like you," she murmured to the baby, who only cooed in response.

With Michael and Genie attending a dinner party soon, it would be a quiet evening at Violet House. The time alone to sort out the last few days was much needed. A tenuous link had started to form between Vauxhall, Mr. Givens, and the disturbing new information in Bethany Silas's case. She'd been at the pleasure gardens with Mr. Comstock, who had then taken her to the Seven Sins, Mr. Givens's place of employment. Then, the strange carriage in Audrey's vision with the inverted cross...could it be linked to this patently *un*virtuous Sanctuary society?

Murder and a missing young lady weren't the only things that had sent her mind spinning off in all directions that day. Hugh's proposal continued to reduce her into a puddle of pleasure whenever it crossed her mind—and it did, often. He'd procured a special license. He'd searched for and found a home for them. This time next year, it was entirely possible they would have their own baby. As she reclined on one elbow on her side next to Pippa, she felt her heart squeeze with wonder. The idea of seeing Hugh holding a child...their child...it was overwhelming. What she needed to do was simply focus on right now, on finding Bethany Silas, especially if she wanted to enjoy her wedding night and the days following without any concerns niggling at the back of her mind.

"You are far away."

Audrey sat up, startled to see Genie standing within the entrance to the nursery. Her sister-in-law smiled at her as she continued into the room.

"How long have you been standing there?" Audrey asked.

"Long enough to suspect that infatuated grin of yours wasn't directed solely at my precious Philippa," she replied, giving Audrey a playful wink. Naming the little girl after Philip had been a sweet gesture, one that Michael had suggested.

Audrey had not mentioned the special license or the trip to Berkeley Square just yet. She and Genie were as close as sisters, but Genie would leap into action to plan the wedding for as soon as possible if she knew Hugh had officially proposed. Explaining that she and Hugh couldn't marry until this investigation concluded would not be received well.

Audrey stood up and brushed the seat of her skirt as Genie crouched to pick up the baby.

"Where is Tamara?" Genie asked.

"In the kitchen. I offered to look after Pippa for a short while."

The nursemaid had been grateful for the reprieve.

Philippa was already beginning to teeth and had been irritable for days.

"Are you quite sure you won't come with us tonight?" Genie asked. She was ready to depart for the evening, dressed in a lavish, pale green dinner gown of silk taffeta. With her blonde ringlets and ocean green eyes, the color was especially fetching.

"Lady Beauchamp was rather vocal about your invitation," she added. Genie had not yet informed the countess that Audrey would not be attending, still hoping she would change her mind.

"I'm sorry, I wish I wasn't so exhausted." It wasn't a lie; she *was* done in, and she *was* sorry that Genie would be disappointed. Genie sighed but was too good natured to continue complaining. Instead, she did what she usually did: thought of other people first. "Has there been any word about that young man, Sir?"

Audrey shook her head. "Not yet. Hugh is worried about him."

So was she. If only there was some clue as to where he'd gone, like there was for Bethany. Hugh had gone out the night before, into Whitechapel and toward the docks. He'd looked drained that afternoon at Gunter's.

"It is awful that the boy saw his father like that," Genie said as she bounced Pippa on her hip. Audrey quickly placed a linen over Genie's shoulder and bodice, to prevent any spit-up from landing on her gown. "And that his father may be connected to the other murders too... It is horrifying."

As expected, the other publications in London had latched onto the story in *The Morning Post* and had published their own versions.

"I am certain Sir will return to Lord Neatham," Genie said. "He is devoted to the viscount."

"And the viscount is devoted to him," Audrey replied. He would not stop trying to find Sir. He'd likely go out again tonight, to another part of London's underbelly, after he paid the Seven Sins a visit. He'd left her at Violet House earlier with a promise to inform her what he learned there about Mr. Comstock's and Miss Silas's visit—and with a firm refusal to bring her with him to the gaming hell. She had already been there once before, and in all honesty, had no wish to visit twice.

Tamara returned and whisked the baby from the duchess's arms just moments before Pippa hiccupped and spit up. Genie only looked longingly at her baby.

"I would love to stay home tonight, too. The dinner is going to be dreadfully dull with everyone discussing politics. And Cassie has her musicale to attend, so I will be entirely alone," she sighed. "Even the wives comment on politics, and I find myself feeling inadequate."

"You are not inadequate," Audrey replied, exasperated. This wasn't the first time her sister-in-law had confessed to feeling out of her depth as a duchess. Audrey always had as well.

"Perhaps I should have an opinion on what they are saying," Genie said as she walked back toward the door.

"I think any opinion should not be forced to the surface over some misplaced feeling of inadequacy," Audrey replied.

"I suppose. And the princess is so outspoken, I doubt I could get a word in edgewise anyhow."

Interest sharpened Audrey's attention. "Princess?"

"Prince Paul's wife, Princess Esterhazy."

She followed Genie to the door. "The Austrian ambassador?"

"You've met?" Genie asked, appearing surprised.

"Not quite." Audrey laced her fingers together, her mind charging forward. The slain Lord Stromburg had been visiting Prince Paul. Perhaps there would be a chance to speak to him at the dinner.

Audrey licked her lips. "I think I would like to go after all."

The change of heart was done without an ounce of polish, and Genie frowned at her. "I'm concerned as to why."

This time, Audrey at least tried to refine herself. With a light shrug, she said, "I should socialize now that I'm out of mourning, shouldn't I?"

From her raised brow, Genie didn't at all look to believe it. But as she'd gotten her way, she, too, shrugged. "Good then. You best get dressed, or we'll be late."

IN THE END, they were fashionably late to Lord and Lady Beauchamp's home, which was located just off Grosvenor Square, where Genie and Michael had lived before coming to Violet House. The drawing room was filled with guests when they were announced, and there was no mistaking the interest sparking off as heads turned and eyes sought after Audrey's named was called. She'd forgotten until they were already on their way to the earl and countess's home about the cartoon in the paper the previous morning, of her and Hugh strolling at Vauxhall with a body lain out on the path behind them. There had not been another cartoon, and there had been no mention in the society columns in any of the papers that day about Hugh's proposal on Berkeley Square, either. But it was clear that whispers had started to fan around society, and Lady Beauchamp, who joined them immediately, was not one to shy away from a direct question.

"Is it fair to say the Viscount Neatham is off the market, Your Grace?"

A light bloom of perspiration dampened the back of Audrey's gown—a vivid burgundy organza—when she considered it possible that a rumor had reached the lady's ears about the proposal. Next to Audrey, Genie and Michael wore twin looks of distaste for the countess's direct probing question.

"I have heard that the viscount has not been very active this Season," Audrey replied, attempting to skirt around an answer. And to prevent Lady Beauchamp from asking anything else, she said, "I have also heard Princess Esterhazy is in attendance tonight."

In her peripheral vision she saw Genie's glance. The countess also betrayed a look of surprise, though quickly followed it with a bright smile.

"I see," she said, drawing out the two words. Audrey wondered what, exactly, she saw...but then, at the countess's next words, realized her blunder. "An introduction to a patroness at Almack's is in order, especially now that you're out of mourning. Come with me, Your Grace."

Lady Beauchamp started through the crowd, expecting Audrey to follow. She did, though not without an inward groan of regret. Almack's Assembly Rooms were the highlight of the Season, where women of the ton—mostly debutantes—would go when they were entering the marriage mart. Admission to the balls at the assembly rooms was only granted by voucher, and those vouchers were given to select members of the ton by a handful of patronesses. These women, belonging to the upper echelons of society, were revered, though Audrey believed that was only because they alone could provide inclusion into London society, or exclusion from it. Princess Esterhazy was one such patroness.

As Lady Beauchamp led Audrey through the drawing room toward a large group, she began to feel slightly ill. By asking about the princess, she had insinuated that she wished for an introduction, and ultimately, a voucher to attend Almack's. And the only reason she would wish to attend Almack's, would be to seek a new husband. That she had mentioned the princess immediately after dismissing the countess's question about Hugh, also indicated her disinterest in the viscount.

Before the ball was over, that nugget of gossip would be known by every last guest. And it would surely find its way into the gossip columns in tomorrow's newspapers.

"Your Royal Highnesses," Lady Beauchamp said as she inserted herself into the closed circle surrounding the patroness. The conversation that had been underway was cut short, exacerbating the interruption. Audrey tried to tamp down the blush creeping up her chest, to her neck, and its ultimate destination—her cheeks—for all to see.

"May I present Audrey Sinclair, the Dowager Duchess of Fournier." The countess stepped aside, as an invitation for Audrey to come forward. She did so, albeit hesitantly.

The princess, Maria Theresia, assessed her with inquisitive, if icy, attention. With her short stature, dark eyes and lashes, black glossy ringlets, and full figure, she appeared doll-like and much younger than Audrey, though she knew her to be in her late twenties. In comparison, her husband, Prince Paul, stood much taller and was well into his thirties. He wore a somewhat more welcoming half-grin, but it was clear that they were guests of some honor here and held a good bit of social power. Though Audrey did not in any way wish for a voucher to Almack's, it was a believable reason for an introduction to the princess.

"Your Royal Highnesses," she said, addressing them both. "It is a pleasure."

"Am I correct that you are recently out of mourning, Your Grace?" the princess asked immediately, without allowing a single moment to pass after Audrey's greeting.

"That is correct," Audrey replied.

"My condolences to you," she said stiffly. "It must be gratifying to be out in society again. You visited Vauxhall of late." It was not a question. So, she had seen the lamentable cartoon, had she?

"I have," she replied, but was at a loss for what more to say. Not speaking of the body found would be seen as an attempt to conceal what everyone already knew. To speak of it would be inappropriate.

Thankfully, Lady Beauchamp swooped in and rescued her, although unknowingly. "Isn't it dreadful about the murders there? As I have always said, Vauxhall would be better served by following Almack's example. Letting in anyone at all only ensures a breakdown in civility."

Again, the princess spoke so quickly, she practically trod upon the heels of the countess's statement. "The commoners must have their entertainments too. I simply question why those of our set feel the need to share them."

It was a thinly veiled cut at Audrey for being at the pleasure gardens to begin with. The princess held her stare for another moment, to make sure it was received. She spoke as though she knew everyone was hanging onto her every word.

Audrey had not come to this dinner party to be scolded or spoken down to by the princess. Trading barbs was not worth her time. Some women in the ton thrived on these sorts of dramatics. Audrey loathed them. She'd come here to speak to the prince and finagle a way to learn more about Lord Stromburg, and so far, she was no closer to doing so.

Genie and Michael had been slow to follow Audrey, but they now stood among the circle of guests surrounding the prince and princess. They needed no introduction to the royal couple as they had met previously. Audrey used the protracted moment to change the subject.

"Perhaps Vauxhall is a destination one must see for oneself, at least once," she said, then turned to Prince Paul. "I hear an acquaintance from your homeland has been visiting London. Did Lord Stromburg wish to see the pleasure gardens?"

It was hardly an artful question, but after the prince's confusion over Audrey's knowledge of Stromburg's visit played over his features, he nodded slowly. "Why yes, indeed. I do believe Lord Stromburg enjoyed the pleasure gardens once or twice while he was here."

"He is no longer in London?" Audrey asked.

"No, he was called back to Budapest." His confused expression then cleared, and he turned to Michael. "Ah, yes, you met Stromburg once or twice, did you not, Your Grace?"

The new Duke of Fournier replied that yes, he had, but as she had before, the princess galloped over his reply and loudly complained of requiring another glass of wine. As the attention gathered back onto Princess Esterhazy, Michael slid his suspicious glare toward Audrey.

She pretended not to see it. Prince Paul and a few of the gathered men stepped into another conversation, taking Michael with them. That left Audrey and Genie with Lady Beauchamp, the princess, and two other women whom Audrey did not know.

"I was under the impression His Grace did not care for Stromburg," the princess said to Genie, one thick, dark brow arched over a shrewd eye.

"Really? The duke did not give that impression to us, did he?" Audrey said, imploring her sister-in-law with a widening of her eyes to go along with the lie.

To her credit, Genie gave a serene nod. "Indeed."

"I can't imagine what the duke would find off-putting about the prince's close friend, Your Majesty," Audrey went on. The topic of Lord Stromburg had seemed to put the princess off her stride. She sniffed.

"They are not as close as Stromburg would like to believe. Your Grace, I hope you will convince your duke to not seek out his company the next time Stromburg visits. His taste in vice is wholly disreputable."

Audrey held her breath as Lady Beauchamp and the other two ladies watched the exchange with voracious interest. Vice? It put her in mind of the gaming hell where Hugh was that very moment.

Genie blinked, taken aback. "Thank you for the advice, Your Majesty."

"My goodness," Audrey said. "Vice of what sort?"

Lady Beauchamp and the others now trained their fascination, touched by disapproval, onto Audrey. It seemed she'd pushed too far in her quest for information.

Princess Esterhazy leveled her with a censorious look. "Ladies do not speak of such things in detail. However, perhaps your curiosity is not entirely your fault. After so much exposure to scandal, one must find oneself prone to spectacles."

Audrey sealed her lips, properly rebuked. She would not expect that voucher to Almack's now. Nor did she want it.

"Your Majesty," Genie murmured as the princess gave them a dismissing nod and turned to seek a new conversation.

"You're going to have to explain yourself," Genie said as soon as they were alone. "Michael is sure to ask questions too."

As she watched Princess Esterhazy be absorbed into another throng of guests, her eyes connected with a man standing near them. He was already staring intently at Audrey, a grimace creasing his cheeks. He made no effort to alter his glowering expression as he lifted his drink to his mouth.

Audrey's pulse stuttered.

The man's cufflink stood in stark contrast to the crisp white shirtsleeve peeking out from the cuff of his black dinner jacket. The cufflink was a disc of black onyx inlaid with a white, inverted cross. Just like the coach door she'd seen in her vision of Mr. Givens. The two threatening men had come from that coach, she was certain of it. That symbol... Seeing it again, on these cufflinks, wasn't a coincidence.

"Who is that man?" Audrey asked Genie softly as she

turned from his targeted stare. "The man with the glass to his lips, the swallow tail jacket with velvet trim. Don't look at him directly."

Genie averted her eyes at the last moment; probably much too late.

"That is Sir Oliver Pendleton. What is going on here, Audrey?"

Though she considered making her way over to Sir Oliver and ingratiating herself into conversation with him in order to find out what he knew, the hostile glare stopped her. Had he overheard her conversation with the princess? Her questions about Lord Stromburg?

"I promise I'll explain, just not here," Audrey whispered to her sister-in-law. "For now, tell me what you know about Sir Oliver."

CHAPTER NINE

"If my membership is revoked tonight because you insisted on being an idiot, I will never take you anywhere again." Thornton thrust out his arm, barring Hugh from taking another step toward the front doors to the Seven Sins. "I am entirely serious."

Hugh pushed down his friend's arm. "I can behave myself when I want to."

Thornton had grumbled when Hugh turned up at his St. James's Square residence and laid out his plan for the evening. He was not a member of the gaming hell, but Thornton was. After a long-winded lecture on conducting himself better than he had the night Thornton had taken him to the opera, when Audrey had wanted to bump into Lord St. John during the investigation into Miss Lovejoy's murder, he'd agreed to sponsor Hugh for the evening.

"No stumbling around, pretending to be drunk, and lifting people's pocket watches," Thornton added, with a roll of his eyes. It was what Hugh had done at the opera; he'd pickpocketed St. John to give Audrey something of his to hold and read the way she could other objects. Unfortunately, Thornton had been far cleverer than St. John and had seen him do it. *It's possible evidence*, was all Hugh had said in explanation. His friend had glared balefully at him, not entirely believing it. But he hadn't asked more questions.

Not so tonight.

"What exactly are you looking for in here? Do you really think anyone is going to talk to you about Givens or Comstock? These types of places are notoriously private, especially about members, present *and* past."

"I'm looking for whatever I can find. That can't be done if I don't even try."

Thornton grumbled as the door to the Seven Sins opened, revealing a large, broad-shouldered porter. The man's lips turned down into a grimace.

"Gaming piece," he ordered. Thornton removed the opium locket from his pocket and held it out to the man. The porter took a long, close look at it. Then turned to Hugh, expecting his.

"I am sponsoring this gentleman for the evening," Thornton said, his lackadaisical tone intentional. He was a damn fine liar.

The porter held out his hand, and Thornton dropped the locket into his waiting palm. He wouldn't get it back until he and his sponsored guest left for the evening. Should anything untoward occur, Thornton wouldn't get it back at all.

They were permitted through, and as they climbed the curved stairs toward the main gaming floor, Thornton muttered, "Why do I feel that is the last I'm going to see of that locket?"

"Have some faith," Hugh replied.

The main floor opened before them, and the crush was impressive. Tables of poker, hazard, faro, and vingt-et-un filled the room, and the patrons crowding around them created a dull roar of noise. Thick cigar smoke hazed the air, muting the already dark interior of wine-red carpet and mahogany paneled walls and furniture. Ladies in masks of all designs mixed with the gentlemen, and there were a few who did not bother with a mask at all. They stood with the men at gaming tables, smoked cigars, lounged in laps, and laughed and spoke loudly. Hugh still recalled the bolt of fury and lust when he'd spied Audrey walking arm-in-arm with the Marquess of Wimbly. She'd been brave to come here, alone. Heedless and impulsive too.

Hugh's attention snagged on a deep green velvet curtain near the back corner of the gaming room. A burly guard stood next to it, arms crossed and expression stony.

"What is back there?" Hugh asked. Thornton followed his gaze.

"Your bride wouldn't be pleased if you entered the back of the house," Thornton replied.

Hugh glared at him. "I shouldn't have told you about the special license."

On the ride to the Seven Sins, Thornton had asked point blank if he'd proposed yet. Unable to settle on a good enough reason to lie, he'd admitted he had.

"What are you doing here with me when you could be marrying her, for god's sake?" Thornton asked.

Hugh tensed. He and Audrey had agreed to first find Miss Silas and, of course, Sir. But the more he thought about it, the more he felt something else was holding him back.

"She has just cast off her widow's black," Hugh said. "Waiting a few weeks would be more proper."

Thornton snorted. "Since when have you cared about being *proper*?"

"Since it will affect Audrey and how she will be received as my new viscountess. Not only is it a demotion in social rank, but let's not forget I arrested her first husband on charges of murder. I am tainted by scandal *and* the fact that I was working class. I don't want her to suffer socially because of me."

He exhaled—and having let it all out, felt lighter. He hadn't even admitted to himself these things until now. Audrey had never shown the slightest bit of care about the slip in her social currency. After so many scandals, she was undoubtedly less influential than she'd been after her marriage to Philip Sinclair.

"She doesn't care about those things," Thornton said. Hugh stopped next to a faro table and stared at him. Thornton laughed. "What is that look for, Marsden? She *doesn't* care, and you are well aware of that. What is really bothering you?"

Hugh couldn't answer. Not truthfully. There was something hanging over his head, continuing to darken the horizon, no matter how bright his future with Audrey. And it could not be shared.

He wished he could tell Thornton about Philip. But like Audrey's strange ability, it was something that needed to stay a secret. Thornton would never breathe a word to anyone, but it would be a burden on his shoulders. He wouldn't do that to his friend.

Hugh licked his lips. "I don't want to bungle anything up."

Thornton grinned. "I enjoy seeing you like this. Rattled. Worried." He ignored Hugh's scowl.

"I need to talk to someone about Givens," Hugh said, ready to be off the subject entirely.

Thornton gestured to a man near a billiards table. He was nearly as large as the porter, and his level attention drifted over the crowd.

"Talk to management and you'll get nothing except a boot in an objectionable place," Thornton said. "But Stokes over there and Givens were usually on the same shifts. He's muscle, but he's sharp."

Hugh started for the billiards tables.

"I'm getting a drink. Go easy," Thornton called after him.

Stokes's flat eyes noticed his approach. His brows narrowed as Hugh closed in.

"Good evening," Hugh said. The man remained stone cold. "I'm told you worked shifts with Harlan Givens."

Stokes nodded but made no attempt to speak.

"You are aware he was killed two days ago?"

Another nod. Hugh sighed. Men like this, the stoic, silent ones, had always been the worst to question. Despite their calm demeanor, they were usually spoiling for a fight. Thornton wouldn't forgive him too soon if he got himself tossed out on his ear after less than a few minutes of being here.

"I have reason to believe Givens was talking about something he should not have been," Hugh went on, thinking of the two men Audrey had seen in her vision and what they'd been saying.

The man gave no nod this time. Instead, his eyes swept the gaming floor, then came back to rest upon Hugh. "If you've got any brains in that skull of yours, milord, you won't keep talking."

Ah. At last, he'd been driven to speak. "I'm afraid I need answers."

Stokes stepped forward, coming toe to toe with him. "Then *I'm* afraid you'll go the same way as the lad."

Alarm shuttled up Hugh's spine. The gaming room disappeared from his peripheral vision. "What lad?"

"Harlan's boy."

Sir had been *here*? "Where is he?"

Stokes's lips split into a grin, revealing crooked teeth. "Got himself in a fair bit of trouble, coming here, whinging about someone knocking off his pop."

Less than a hand span separated him from Stokes. Hugh closed it despite the other man's advantage in height and weight. "I'll ask you once more. Where is the boy?"

Stokes's dumb grin faded. He backed up a step. "Tossed him out twice myself. Showed up tonight, too, so I brought him to Mr. Vance's office. He'll deal with him."

Lars Vance owned the Seven Sins, and his cutthroat reputation was credited for keeping his members in good form. Hugh's attention went again to the green velvet curtains shielding the back of the house. He side-stepped Stokes and started toward them.

Thornton fell in step beside him. "That didn't look like a friendly conversation."

"Sir is here. With Vance."

Thornton grabbed Hugh's arm to slow his charge toward the burly guard at the curtains. "Vance isn't a man you want to upset."

"Who says I want to upset him? I'm merely going to take Sir and leave."

"The thunderous look on your face says differently."

Only then did Hugh feel the scowl. He attempted to smooth it over with something less threatening as they reached the security guard. Like Stokes, the man's bland expression held a shade of menace.

Thornton cleared his throat. "My friend here would like to purchase a membership," he said, clapping Hugh on the shoulder with enough force to send him sideways. Purposefully, to be sure. "Is Mr. Vance in his office?"

The guard gave Hugh the onceover, then with a sniff of indifference, stepped aside.

"This is why I keep you around," Hugh said as they parted the curtains and found themselves at the base of a stairwell. They started up.

"I thought it was for my scintillating personality," Thornton replied.

Hugh snorted laughter but cut it short as muffled shouts came from the landing. He took the rest of the steps two at a time and found another security guard posted outside a closed door. A familiar voice, clear as day, reached through the wood: "I don't know nothin'!"

It was all the impetus Hugh needed. He charged forward. "Stand aside," he ordered the guard, who of course, did no such thing. The unmistakable sound of a hand smacking skin and the grunt of pain followed from within the room.

"Hugh—" Thornton called from behind him. But all Hugh could see was red.

He cracked his fist against the guard's jaw, and the man went down flat. The door wasn't locked, so he threw it open, sending it slamming against the wall. The tall and corpulent Lars Vance had Sir by the scruff of his collar. He swiveled to stare at the intruder. So did Sir. His lip had been split, and his eyes were red with tearful fury.

"Release him. *Now*," Hugh growled.

"Who the f—" Vance saw his guard sprawled on the floor. His hand went to the inside of his jacket, and he drew a snub-nosed pistol.

"Christ," Thornton hissed as he came in behind Hugh, his arms held up in capitulation. "Mr. Vance, this boy belongs to my friend here. We don't want trouble. Just the boy."

Sir struggled in Vance's hard and fast grip. "I don't belong to no one!" At the catch in Sir's throat, a murderous rage nearly overtook Hugh.

"Who is this man, Thornton?" Vance asked, still aiming his pistol at them.

Thornton lowered his hands and raked them through his hair. "Viscount Neatham," he sighed.

He was certainly not getting his opium locket back after this.

"Well, viscount, your boy has been badgering my employees about his dead father. I, and my club, have nothing to do with Mr. Givens's unfortunate fate." He gave Sir another shake when Sir tried to wriggle free. "He's been given his father's last wages and now he needs to go."

"To do that, you'll need to release him." Fire burned in

Hugh throat, scalding his words. Vance shoved Sir away, uncurling his fists from his collar. With the back of his sleeve, Sir wiped blood from his chin.

"What kind of man strikes a boy less than half his size?" Hugh asked.

Vance laughed but left the question unanswered. "Take your lad, viscount. And don't come back."

Sir hung his head, stormed across the office, and pushed past Hugh. He leaped over the guard, now stirring on the floor. The scrappy imp was moving fast, running again. But Hugh had questions for Vance, and after this, he wouldn't have another opportunity to ask them.

He turned to Thornton. "Follow him."

His friend eyed the pistol in Vance's hand and hesitated, but then swore under his breath. He left on Sir's heels.

Turning back to Vance, Hugh wasted no time. "Travis Comstock. You revoked his membership."

Vance glared. "What of it?"

"Was Harlan Givens associated with him?"

"I've already spoken to the *real* Runners who came here asking about Givens."

The waking guard pushed to his knees, then his feet. He slurred, "What do you want me to do with him, Mr. Vance?"

"Tell me what you know about the Sanctuary," Hugh said before the guard could receive his orders.

Across the room, Vance went utterly still. His scowl softened. But then, a hardness slid back over his features. He raised his pistol again with deadly calm. "Leave now. Make me say it again and you'll disappear."

The gaming hell owner had enough power and connections to make a reality out of the threat. Hugh held up his hands and backed toward the stairs. It was a wonder when he reached the main floor without a bullet lodged in his spine. Across the room, Thornton descended from view as he took the stairs to the entrance at a fast clip. Hugh ignored looks of alarm from the other patrons as he sprinted after him. Forgoing his coat, he rushed out onto the front step, into the brisk air. Sir was already halfway down the block, still running with Thornton on his tail.

"Sir, stop!" Hugh bellowed.

The boy ran a few more paces, enough for Hugh to begin sprinting again. He'd been searching for him for days; he wasn't about to lose sight of him now.

But then, all the sudden, Sir seemed to give up. He quit running and started to walk. Thornton reached him first, circling around in front of him while Hugh came close enough to snag his arm and jerk him to a halt.

"Where the hell have you been?" he shouted while also heaving for air.

Sir hung his head and wiped his nose. His clothing was dirty and stained; he'd changed into street clothes at some point. Patched trousers, yellowed shirt, threadbare sack coat.

He kept his chin tucked into his neck, the brim of his cap obscuring his face. But another sniffle and another wipe of his sleeve across his face, and Hugh realized he was crying. *Hell.*

"Thornton, could you get our things?"

The porter at the Seven Sins would still have their coats and hats and gloves. Hopefully they would be returned, even if the opium locket would not be.

"Never. Anywhere. Again," Thornton said, clipping each

word as he stalked back toward the hell's entrance. Hugh would try to find a way to make it up to him.

Once they were alone on the pavement, he drew a long breath. "It's been days, Sir. I was worried."

"You don't have to worry about me," he said, his voice constricted. He still stared at the pavement under their feet.

"Is that so? I just found you getting knocked around inside a gambling hell, so I would say I do."

Sir spared him a brief glare before turning away. At least he didn't try to run again. Even though he was furious with the boy for disappearing for nearly three days with no word, he was equally relieved. He was tempted to shrug it off and just be grateful he'd been found. But in the end, that would do Sir no favors.

"You're asking questions about your father's murder in a way that's going to get you hurt," Hugh said.

"I can take care of myself. I ain't a weak little baby."

Hugh pulled back, surprised by the force of the response. "I never said you were."

Sir scuffed his feet, his hands buried in his pockets.

"What is this about, Sir?"

He was silent for several moments. Hugh began to think he was being stubborn.

"I heard him, the last time I was home visiting my mum and sisters." Sir scrubbed his nose again. Hunched his shoulders. "He said he was doing something important, but he couldn't say what, because I was just a baby. He was always calling me a weak baby."

Repugnance for Harlan Givens and the way he'd treated his own flesh and blood was no new feeling for Hugh. But what was new, was what Sir had just revealed. Givens had been doing something important? Lucy Givens had said something similar about her husband the other morning. That he'd had a few other jobs, but he couldn't tell her about them lest she speak of it to others. He'd been acting strange and twitchy, she'd said.

"You aren't weak," Hugh said. "You are, however, angry, and anger can lead people to take unnecessary risks."

Sir glimpsed up from the pavement. "Like how you knocked that guard for six?"

Hugh groaned. "Yes. I should have expected to meet with a pistol when I threw open that door. But I was angry, you see. So, we are all culpable, adult and children alike."

His disdainful grimace returned. "I ain't a child."

"You're acting more like a child than you are a man. Running off like that, with no word. You're in my care—"

"Well then, I'll leave it!" His squeaky voice returned and bounced off the exterior of the building next to them. "Gonna need to soon enough anyhow."

"What are you talking about?"

He anticipated him saying something about becoming the man of the house, now that his father was dead. That his mother and sisters would need him. Hugh had already started thinking of how to respond to that and what he could offer, when Sir bowled him over.

"You're marrying the duchess, aren't you? Already got the ring and the license. Already got a new place picked out, too. She won't want me around once you're leg shackled to her."

Hugh's next breath stuttered, and his heart squeezed. He'd had no idea his plans to marry Audrey had fazed Sir, let alone worried him. It had been selfish not to think of it.

Blending their lives would not be without its many bumps and changes, but Basil and Sir were part and parcel to Hugh, just as Greer and Carrigan were to Audrey.

He cleared his throat. "Shows how much you know."

With Sir, the method of delivery mattered. He responded to challenges better than anything else.

Now, he crossed his arms and squinted up at Hugh. "I know plenty."

"Then you are aware the dowager duchess has asked which room is to be yours at 37 Berkeley Square?"

She'd done no such thing, but it wasn't a risky lie. Audrey would balk at Sir not coming with them to their new home.

Sir perked up. "She likes it?"

Hugh had taken Sir with him when his steward, a musty old man who'd been one of his father's, then Barty's, remaining staff, had shown it to him. As they'd toured the rooms, Sir had shrugged as if unimpressed.

"She does," Hugh replied.

"And she wants me to hang around?" His tone had changed from petulant and skeptical, to hopeful.

"We both do." Hugh held up a finger. "But if you ever run away like that again, you'll have to share a room with Basil so he can keep an eagle eye on you."

Sir choked on a half laugh, half groan. The tension between them eased as Thornton returned with their coats, hats, and gloves.

"I suppose there are other gaming hells in London," he said, tossing Hugh his belongings. "Mind you, none that I will ever take you to."

Norris came around the corner and pulled alongside the curb. Sir opened the door.

"One more thing, Sir," Hugh said as Thornton climbed in. The boy paused on the step up. "In Vance's office, I heard you say you didn't know anything. What had he asked you?"

"Oh, that. He wanted to know who my father was spying on. Can you imagine? Him, a spy?" He snorted in disbelief.

However, the two men from Audrey's vision had accused Givens of speaking out of turn.

"Did Vance say anything more about it?"

Sir shrugged. "No. But he didn't like when I called him dicked in the nob for believing my father was an informant." He touched his split lip tenderly then hopped up into the carriage.

Harlan Givens, a spy? Or at least believed to be one. It did seem highly unlikely. He'd been the furthest thing from discreet.

And that could have been why he ended up dead.

CHAPTER TEN

Audrey slept unexpectedly well after returning to Violet House from Grosvenor Square. Her spinning mind should have kept her awake all night, but it seemed nothing could compete with exhaustion, not even the realization that a member of the Sanctuary had been eyeing her with blatant menace all throughout the dinner party. The moment she'd lain down in bed, she'd been asleep. She couldn't even remember Greer taking her leave for the night.

Now, however, she sat on the sofa in her study at the back of the house, in her morning gown and robe, combing over the previous evening as she sipped her tea. After she'd first noticed Sir Oliver Pendleton glaring at her, she'd been met with several more of his hostile looks: across the drawing room, down the long dining room table, and just before he'd taken his leave, which had been much earlier than other guests. He'd been in a rush to depart.

Genie had only been able to tell her that Sir Oliver was a knight, had been granted the title for his service in the

Napoleonic Wars, was a partial owner of a few London newspapers, and that he sat in the House of Commons. Audrey hadn't drawn Genie's attention to the cufflinks Sir Oliver wore; she hadn't wanted to explain her interest in the inverted white cross emblem. However, on the way back to Curzon Street, she'd had no choice but to explain her interest in Lord Stromburg. Michael had, quite valiantly, resisted the urge to corner her before or after dinner and ask her what that nonsense with Prince Paul had been about.

"I will only tell you if you swear to secrecy," she'd replied in the carriage, earning an exasperated sigh from him. He'd leaned back his head and closed his eyes.

"What have you gotten yourself into now?"

Audrey told them a variation of the truth, stepping carefully around anything that had to do with her vision while holding Harlan Givens's flask. She'd explained that Mr. Givens wasn't the only body to have been found at Vauxhall.

"It appears Lord Stromburg was also found there," she said, then perhaps unnecessarily adding, "Deceased."

Michael's exasperation with her had severed. "I've heard nothing of this. It hasn't been reported."

"That is because Bow Street is handling the investigation quietly to avoid a public panic," she replied. "Mr. Givens, Lord Stromburg, and a third victim, a...brothel madame, were all found at the pleasure gardens, and all had their left ears removed."

Genie's loud gasp of horror rivaled Michael's exclamation of an obscenity.

"How are you involved in any of this?" Michael asked, but then shook his head and answered his own question. "*Neatham.*"

He said the name as if it abraded his throat. While the two men were civil toward one another, they were not exactly friends.

"He's investigating another matter, a disappearance, and it's beginning to look as if it could correlate to these killings."

Mr. Comstock's connection to the Seven Sins, and possibly Harlan Givens, was too loose for Audrey to be sure, but her mind kept coming back to it and sticking.

"I take it Sir Gabriel has asked Neatham to investigate," Michael said.

"Discreetly," Audrey replied.

"The man should know better than to involve a peer."

"Hugh wants to help," she argued. Her brother-in-law held rigid views on what peers should and should not do, and involving themselves in murder investigations was decidedly off limits.

"It doesn't matter what he wants. What matters is his duty. He should leave the investigating to the officers at Bow Street. He is no longer a part of that world."

Genie touched her husband's arm. "It can't be easy for him."

"Perhaps his duty looks different than yours, Michael," Audrey added, becoming frustrated with him. Anything that did not conform with society norms did not meet with his approval. Ever. It was one of the reasons why Philip had always felt apart from his brother. Why he'd never considered telling Michael the truth about his feelings for men, rather than for women.

"What about his duty to you?" Michael volleyed back. The carriage slowed, and they'd turned onto the half-circle in front of Violet House. Audrey had been eager to flee inside.

"I am not blind. I know he plans to make an offer," he added. "His interfering with criminal cases will affect you as well."

"Please allow me to worry about that." Or *not* worry about it. And she wasn't.

What the rest of the ton thought of her did not matter in the least. Some ladies would take to their rooms and sob if they didn't receive a voucher to Almack's. Invitations to balls or to tea were signals of acceptance, of importance. Audrey had never cared for those things. She'd never felt a passion for anything the way she did for picking apart a mystery with Hugh. Right then, finding Bethany Silas and bringing her home safely and arresting the person responsible for Mr. Givens's murder were the things she cared most about.

"You are still my family, Audrey," Michael had said, some of the fire leeched from his tone. "I care for you like a sister. I would like to see you happy and settled and for once, free from murder investigations."

They'd descended from the carriage, and she had kissed Michael's cheek as soon as Travers had handed her out of the carriage. Her brother-in-law did not mean to constrict her; he only wanted the best for her, and blustering about improprieties and safety was his method of choice. She admired his loyalty to her, even now that Philip was gone.

"I am glad to have you mother-henning me."

He'd scowled. "I am not a mother hen."

"Fine, then, papa-henning."

He'd not argued, and Genie had led him toward the front door with a knowing smirk.

They were likely still abed, as it was only ten in the morning. Unlike most married couples, Genie had shared with

Audrey once that Michael did not often use the bedchamber attached to her own. He preferred his wife's company. The notion that Michael's rigid and severe character turned to soft pulp when it came to his wife and children always made Audrey grin—and forgive him after he'd squalled at her.

She sipped her tea while turning the page in the *Times*, her legs stretched out on the cushion. There was nothing in the gossip column regarding her blunder the night before in all but asking the princess for a voucher to Almack's, but it was still early. A cartoon could still appear somewhere in a print shop window, or a pamphlet of *All the Chatter* could be published later in the day.

Greer bustled into the study.

"You've a message from Lord Neatham." She extended a folded and sealed note. Audrey let the broadsheet fall open on her lap and handed her cup to Greer in exchange for the note. She'd been eager to hear how his visit to the Seven Sins turned out.

Quickly, she read that although he'd learned nothing about Comstock or Bethany, he had found Sir, and that it was possible Mr. Givens had been an informant to someone regarding a sensitive matter. Hugh didn't elaborate, and Audrey wondered if that sensitive matter had anything to do with the Sanctuary. He signed off with a request to call on Violet House that afternoon.

Audrey folded the letter and bit her lower lip.

Greer freshened her tea and handed it back. "Is there anything amiss, Your Grace?"

"He's found Sir," Audrey reported, distracted.

"That's a relief," Greer said, but then cocked her head. "Isn't it?"

Audrey snapped out of her reverie regarding Mr. Givens and the Sanctuary. "Oh, yes, of course it is. I'm sorry, I'm just..." Her tongue went heavy and useless as she stared at a bold headline on the newspaper page open on her lap. She jerked forward and swung her feet to the carpet. Tea splashed from the rim of the cup and sprinkled the newsprint.

"Your Grace?" Greer said with alarm.

"Call for my carriage." Audrey's heart began to thrash. "I need to dress, right away."

She'd just found the elusive Mr. Travis Comstock.

HUGH CLIMBED into Audrey's carriage, latched the door, and pulled down the tasseled curtain in the window. He reached across to the other window and did the same, plunging the interior of the carriage into dimness.

"What are you—?"

Hugh sat beside her and with a forceful tug, lifted her from the bench and brought her onto his lap.

"Hugh!" His lips devoured her laughter as he kissed her. At the barest pressure of his mouth, she yielded, going soft in his arms. They wrapped around her, his hand bracing her back as he hinged her tightly against him.

"God, I've missed this," he murmured against her skin as his feverish kisses lowered to her jaw, then her throat. Audrey sighed and reveled in the pleasure. Sunlight seeped around the corners of the curtains, allowing a shadowy view of Hugh's face as she lifted his chin and kissed him.

"As have I," she said.

"I saw Greer in the driver's box with Carrigan and marveled at my luck."

"I don't think her sole objective was to give us time alone," Audrey said.

Greer and Carrigan spent their days off together, she knew, and this was another opportunity for them to sit and be together.

"Intentional or not, I don't look a gift horse in the mouth." Using his teeth, Hugh tugged at the tips of one of his gloves, and then flung it to the floor. His bared fingers undid the first button of her spencer jacket. "This must go."

She laughed again, even as he attempted to unbutton her spencer. "It cannot. We will be there within minutes."

The advertisement in the newspaper for a parcel of land in Essex, being sold by Mr. Travis Comstock, Esq. for the amount of one hundred pounds, pointed to an address on Gower Street near the University of London. A ten-minute carriage drive, at the most.

Hugh gave up on her buttons but didn't release her. "Then let us use those minutes to our best advantage." Her leg prickled when his palm reached under her hem and settled on her ankle. With his hand warming her through her stocking, Audrey's protests shriveled on her tongue.

She went to putty in his arms, sighing as his palm skimmed up her shin, to her knee, and then touched her skin where her stocking terminated. Her lips drifted over his forehead, her fingers raking into the dark, silky soft strands of his hair.

"I'm happy to hear about Sir," she said, thinking it entirely possible his playful burst of energy was due to his sense of relief.

"You wish him to stay with us, don't you?" Hugh asked, his finger hooking the lip of her stocking and brushing underneath. "Once we're married?"

She pulled back a little to see him. "Of course. Why do you ask?"

"He was worried we wouldn't want him around."

Her heart squeezed. "You set him straight, I hope?"

"It's what I seem to do on a regular basis," he replied with wicked smirk. The rough pad of Hugh's thumb brushed the weal of a scar on her thigh, compliments of a bullet grazing her leg last August. She shivered.

"The first chance I get, I am kissing this scar," he whispered. The promise brought a delectable image to her mind.

Audrey pushed her hand under the lapel of his coat and pressed her fingers against his shoulder. "Don't forget, I have one here too. That one will need the same attention."

She'd meant to make him smile, but after a flex of his brow, his hand stilled.

"What is wrong?" she asked.

He pressed his palm against her thigh, then released her, bringing his hand back out from under her skirt. She barely resisted making a moan of discontent.

"You've been in mortal danger too many times," he replied. "All in the name of an investigation. With me."

Audrey stared at him, half wondering if Michael had somehow gotten to him this morning.

"You cannot blame yourself. I would have investigated those crimes with or without you." He knew as much, too. He'd professed the need to join her, if only to try and keep her safe.

"I don't blame myself," he replied. "But I do blame my work. Take this case, for example. I've brought you into it."

"I want to be here."

"The trouble is, I want you here as well. You're good at this."

Audrey wanted to bask in the compliment, but sensed it was attached to something she wouldn't like at all. "I don't understand how that is troublesome."

She was sitting rigidly on his lap now, and though he still had his arms around her, the heat of the moment had fizzled.

"Because you will soon be my wife. And, I hope, the mother of our children. I cannot lose you. I cannot risk that."

He spoke softly, seriously. Audrey caressed his cheek, wishing she could take away his worry. Grant Thornton had lost his wife and infant years ago, and she knew his friend's loss had affected Hugh. He'd seen up close the devastation.

"You won't lose me," she said, though she knew it was a promise she didn't have complete control over. "However, I don't want to be treated like I am suddenly fragile just because I have the title of wife. Or the title of mother."

Hugh slid her from his lap, leaving her bereft. And a little perturbed.

"It is my duty to protect my wife. I take that seriously."

His duty? Gracious now he truly did sound like Michael. Audrey folded her arms, her temper rising. "You weren't serious about protecting me before?"

He moved to sit across from her, snatching up his tossed glove on the way. "Of course, I was."

She shrugged. "Then nothing has changed."

"Everything has changed," he said, his voice deepening

and rising. "You will be my responsibility. If you were to come to harm—"

"You would be at fault?" But then, another notion popped into her mind. "Or are you only worried that others will view it that way?"

Hugh tightened his jaw. His eyes flashed. "You know I don't care what other people think."

"Then what is this all about?"

He leaned forward, bracing his arms on his thighs as he pulled on his glove. "I want you safe. I don't want to have to worry that you'll be shot or abducted, for Christ's sake."

She felt her temperature increasing. "I don't want to worry those things will happen to you, either."

"They haven't happened to me. They *have* to *you*."

Audrey straightened, all electrical warmth from his hands and kisses now having vanished. "You've been stabbed," she pointed out, recalling how Delia Montgomery had plunged a blade into his forearm.

He rolled his eyes. "It was hardly deadly."

"It could have been!"

The carriage began to slow, and Audrey worried her exclamation had been heard by Carrigan and Greer. Frustration brimmed hot and fast. Why was he doing this? "You said we would be partners. In everything."

Hugh leaned forward and gripped her hand. "We are."

"But only if you think it is safe enough." She pulled her hand from his. "Maybe I'm not the right woman for you, if you want a wife who will simply sit back and do whatever you ask."

Hurt and then aggravation charged across his face. "That is not what I want. That's not what I'm saying."

"I don't know what you're saying."

"Clearly."

A soft cough came from outside the carriage. They'd drawn to a stop, she realized, and Carrigan was waiting at the door.

Feeling sick with disappointment, Audrey blinked back the sting of tears. "Yes, we're ready, Carrigan," she called to him, unable to look Hugh in the eye.

Her driver opened the door, flooding the interior with light. She took his hand and descended, her stomach curdling with regret.

CHAPTER ELEVEN

Hugh brought his fist down upon the door. There was a brass knocker provided for a more civil approach, but he wanted to hit something. Hard. Had he been able to flog himself without looking like a maniac, he would have.

How in hell had they gone from kissing, his hand slipping under her skirts, to Audrey questioning their engagement? When his fingers had slid over the ridge of the scar caused by a bullet, he'd wanted only to bring her closer. The bullet discharged from Robert Henley's pistol last summer could have struck her somewhere fatal. She'd been lucky. But when Audrey had reminded him of the other scar left behind by yet another bullet, which she'd received during their first investigation, a heavy weight had come down onto his chest.

When would her luck run out?

They waited at the door to the Gower Street residence, neither of them speaking. Or looking at one another. An invisible wall had gone up between them and it left him with an irritable, prickly sensation under his skin.

Footsteps approached from inside, and after the sounds of locks being slid back, the door opened to reveal a young woman in flowered muslin, a ruffled white cap, and pinafore. She bobbed a quick curtsey before saying, "May I help you?"

She looked to Hugh to reply, but Audrey beat him to it.

"We are here to inquire about the parcel of land listed in the *Times*. Is this Mr. Comstock's residence?" Her voice was tight and sharp. Angry.

Hugh ground his molars. It had been a long time since they'd argued in this manner. A long time since she'd been so damned stubborn. His only wish was to protect her from landing herself in dangerous situations. Why couldn't she understand that? It had nothing to do with wanting her to change.

The maid's eyes flared. Indecision stole across her plain features as she looked from Hugh to Audrey. "Oh. Yes, milady, this is Mr. Comstock's residence, however..." She tucked her chin, which then trembled.

"May we enter, miss?" Hugh asked.

She sniffled and stepped aside, allowing them in. The foyer was trim and neat. No decorative flounces, no touches of femininity. This was a bachelor's home, much like his own at Bedford Street. And near to the university, he thought it likely Mr. Comstock may have even attended there.

"I'm sorry," the maid said, touching the back of her hand to her cheek, as if to check for any wetness. Her eyes were red. She'd already been crying recently.

"Perhaps we've come at a bad time. Is Mr. Comstock not in?" Hugh asked.

The maid shook her head, more tears forming as her

composure quickly deteriorated. Foreboding chilled him as he waited for her to speak.

"Mr. Comstock is...he has died, milord." Her voice cracked. For the first time since leaving her carriage, Audrey's deep blue eyes slammed into him. Her lips parted on a gust of breath.

"When was this?" Hugh asked.

"Yesterday morning," she replied, dabbing at her eyes again.

"What happened?" Audrey asked. The maid started to speak, but then croaked on the first word before it could complete. She shook her head.

"I shouldn't say."

Had it been anything natural or blameless, giving the cause of death shouldn't have been an issue. Not doing so hinted toward the death being scandalous. Hugh calculated his approach. If pressed too hard, the maid's distress could lead her to show them the door. But if too gently coaxed, they would not uncover any answers.

He laid his hand on Audrey's back, between her shoulders, hoping to convey that a change of tactic was about to commence. And to go along with it.

"I apologize for our poor timing and our subterfuge, but we have not come to discuss the parcel of land. We came to ask Mr. Comstock about a mutual friend: Miss Bethany Silas."

Audrey crooked her neck to look at him. The maid cheeks went slack, and her expression revealed that she was cognizant of the name. Shutters quickly descended over that expression, but it was too late.

"I believe you know her," Hugh said, and then, with a

flicker of perception, took another chance. "You met her as Miss Comstock, I believe?"

Blood rushed to the tips of her ears and up her neck. Distress changed instantly to guilt. The risk having paid off, Hugh pressed onward. "But you are not Mr. Comstock's sister. What is your real name?"

She shifted her afflicted stare toward the door. "I...I think you should leave, milord."

"You are in no trouble," Audrey said. "Truly. Our concern is solely for Miss Silas."

The maid looked as if she might be considering bolting through the door herself in an attempt to escape.

"We know you were with Mr. Comstock the day he took her to Vauxhall," Audrey said, quickly adding, "However, no one else need ever know you posed as his sister. Surely, you were only trying to help him. How else was he to gain permission to take Miss Silas out for a carriage ride to the pleasure gardens?"

The maid nodded, bobbing her head shakily. "I never did feel right about it, but he said it would only be once or twice, and that Miss Silas wouldn't be upset once she learnt the truth. He said she'd think it romantic. Clever, too."

The pleading tone of her voice, and the close knit of her brows, displayed that she knew better now in hindsight.

"What happened once they reached Vauxhall?" Hugh asked.

She frowned. "I don't know, milord. Once we arrived at the coach field, Mr. Comstock told the driver to take me back here. It was never the plan for me to come along."

"And did he return later that evening?"

"Of course, milord."

Hugh crossed a glance with Audrey. Comstock had returned from the Sanctuary. Bethany had not. And now, days later, Comstock was dead?

"Miss...?" Hugh waited for the maid to provide her name. It took a prolonged moment for her to catch on.

"Clark. Miss Lavinia Clark." She curtseyed hastily again.

"Miss Clark, it's imperative that you tell us everything you know about his outing with Miss Silas. Did he say anything about her when he returned that evening?"

The maid shook her head, the lace trim of her mob cap fluttering. "No, milord. He was in a terrible state. I thought for certain he was in a high dudgeon because the young lady had spurned him. I didn't dare ask a thing."

"And his death, Miss Clark. How did it occur?" Audrey asked.

The maid's eyes welled again. Her chin quivered. "It doesn't make any sense, milady. I've been tidying his bedchamber for a year, and I've never seen the pill box that I found next to him in bed."

"Pill box? Do you mean to say he died of an opium overdose?" Audrey asked.

Miss Clark nodded. "They were painted gold," she said, still shaking her head. "I never saw anything like it."

Hugh had. The drug could be found in multiple forms. From the poppy seedpod itself, to powder, to liquid, to pills. The wealthy could afford gold-coated opium, while lower classes could spring for silver or uncoated.

"Did a physician come to determine if he'd overdosed?" Hugh asked.

"Just the constables, milord. They said they saw the gold on his tongue."

"Bow Street?" If they learned Comstock was dead yesterday, why the devil had Sir Gabriel not yet alerted Hugh? "Do you recall the officers' names?"

She shook her head. Hugh wasn't surprised. She'd been through a shock, and what did the officers' names matter to her?

"The body has been collected?" Audrey asked.

"Yes. Is Miss Silas asking after him? I swear, I meant no harm tricking her the way I did."

It appeared Miss Clark did not know that Bethany was missing. Hugh decided to keep it that way. "Miss Silas mentioned a place that your employer may have gone. The Sanctuary." Hugh watched for any alarm in her reaction, as Gwendolyn had showed. None came. "Do you know of it?"

"No, milord. Mr. Comstock never mentioned it." She was being truthful; there were no facial twitches or pauses in her speech, no apprehension in her eyes.

"Could we speak to Mr. Comstock's driver?" Audrey asked.

"There's no driver," she replied with a wince. "Mr. Comstock had to let Babson go a few months back."

The advertisement for a parcel of land started to make sense. If he was in need of funds, releasing servants, and blackmailing a man to increase his daughter's dowry, would be a way out of the River Tick.

"He took a hackney then," Audrey said, and as Miss Clark nodded, she reached into her skirt pocket. "Did the carriage that delivered your employer home have this symbol on it?"

She unfolded a piece of paper and held it out to the maid. On it was a sketch of the inverted cross.

"I couldn't know, milady. Mr. Comstock let himself in past midnight. I only heard him when he stumbled up the stairs."

Audrey nodded and folded the paper. She started to slip it back into her pocket.

"May I see it again?" Miss Clark asked. Audrey gave it to her, and the maid chewed her bottom lip. "This looks like what's on his favorite pair of sleeve buttons. He wore them often."

Audrey brightened as she took back the paper. "These sleeve buttons...would you allow me to take a look at them?"

Hugh knew what she was up to. She had that eager, ravenous look in her eye while biting her lower lip in anticipation. She wanted to see something useful in them. Miss Clark grimaced, confused as to why the lady would want to look at a pair of cufflinks but nodded before going upstairs.

"Sir Oliver Pendleton also wore cufflinks with this symbol last night at the dinner I attended," she said to him as soon as the maid was out of sight.

"What dinner?"

"It doesn't matter," she said impatiently, her eyes not meeting his. "I asked Prince Paul about Lord Stromburg, and Sir Oliver glared at me for the rest of the evening."

Hugh hinged forward as his muscles strung tight, forcing her to meet his eyes now. "You did what?"

She sidestepped his question, and him, as she moved to the other side of the narrow entrance hall. "The men accusing Mr. Givens of speaking out of turn had a carriage with this symbol. Sir Oliver and now Mr. Comstock both have cuff links with it. We know for certain that Mr.

Comstock took Bethany to the Sanctuary. The connection is there all around."

"What did you say about Stromburg?" he asked.

"Nothing about him being dead if that is what you are worried about. I'm not that much of a simpleton."

"I didn't say you were. However, finessing questions to make them sound natural isn't necessarily your forte." She was a bull in a china shop most times. "If this Sir Oliver fellow eyed you the rest of the evening, it's probably because he found your questions suspicious."

"Maybe because he knows Lord Stromburg is dead."

And now, so was Comstock. Hugh crushed the brim of his hat in his hand, uneasy with Audrey's request for the cuff links. He glanced up the stairs and lowered his voice. "You may see something horrendous when you hold them."

"Whatever I see, I will be fine," she retorted, still angry. "Do you want answers or don't you?"

"There are other ways."

"This is one of mine." At last, she speared him with a glare. "Or do you not approve of that either anymore?"

"Now you're just spoiling for a fight," he replied, his own hackles rising.

Before she could respond, the maid reappeared on the stairs. Audrey turned her back on Hugh and met her at the bottom.

"If you wouldn't mind, Miss Clark, might we take these to an inquiry agent at Bow Street? We have reason to believe this symbol is connected to Miss Silas's disappearance," she said.

"Oh, I'm not sure, milady, they were so very important

to Mr. Comstock..." the maid said, her eyes tearing up again as she looked at them, cradled in the bowl of her hand.

"Of course, I understand," Audrey began, her tone honey sweet. Hugh narrowed his eyes; she would never give up this easily. "We will send the inquiry agent here if you would prefer. That way, you can take the opportunity to explain about Mr. Comstock's involvement with Miss Silas, and how you stood in as his sister—"

Alarm poured over Miss Clark's expression, drying up her tears instantly. "No, no, milady, I wouldn't want to... Oh, but if you could take them and speak to the agent instead, and please, I never meant any harm. Mister Comstock said it would not amount to anything in the end..." The maid passed the cuff links into Audrey's gloved hands, her chin beginning to quiver again.

Audrey slipped them into her skirt pocket, the barrier of her gloves having prevented any visions. "You aren't to blame, Miss Clark. Truly, you needn't worry."

This time, at least, Audrey sounded sincere.

"Thank you for your time," Hugh said as the maid showed them out. "You've been very helpful."

Without a word or glance toward Hugh, Audrey walked swiftly back to the carriage. Carrigan handed her up, then sent Hugh an apologetic grimace, as though knowing he and Audrey were at odds. The driver stood aside and allowed Hugh to climb in. He secured the door, and Hugh took the bench opposite her. She wouldn't look at him. She also did not take the cuff links from her pocket.

Hugh sat back, his body strung tight. "Will you hold them here?"

Audrey hitched her chin, swaying with the rocking of the

carriage. "I don't think so. I...I think I would like to be alone. I can't think clearly right now."

Because of their argument.

"Very well," he said, hating the unexpected barrier between them.

He should have never opened his damnable mouth.

CHAPTER TWELVE

Audrey stood before the mirror in her room, watching Cassie pace in and out of the reflection.

"It is *my* inheritance. *My* fortune. If I choose not to marry, the income from it should rightfully be mine, shouldn't it?"

Behind Audrey, Greer quietly fastened the small buttons that closed the back of the midnight blue evening gown. Audrey had planned to spend the evening in, but after summoning the courage to seclude herself in her study and read the memories imbued in Mr. Comstock's cuff links, she'd sent a messenger to Bedford Street with an urgent request for Hugh to come to Violet House. The vision had made two things clear: the Sanctuary was located near Vauxhall. And Bethany Silas was in grave danger.

"If he's so bloody determined to dangle my dowry before any lord who comes salivating, so be it!" Cassie threw up her arms as she paced. "But the annual income from it should be mine to access. To live on. To do with as I please!"

With her sister-in-law burning a circle into the carpet,

and the sickening vision Mr. Comstock's cuff links had left imprinted in her memory, Audrey hadn't been able to think too deeply on her argument with Hugh. However, what she'd said to him kept echoing in her mind, making her cringe every time. *Maybe I am not the right woman for you.* She didn't want that to be true. But how could he ask her to stand aside so she could stay safe, up high on a shelf, when the whole time they'd been falling in love, she'd been right beside him on the ground, doing the things that mattered, even when they were dangerous? Hugh hadn't fallen in love with a coddled lady. And Audrey didn't want to be one.

At Cassie's sudden silence, Audrey looked again into the mirror. Her sister-in-law was watching her with an expectant look.

"Are you listening to anything I'm saying?" she asked.

"Every word," Audrey said.

Cassie had just left Michael's study, where another heated exchange had reached through the doors and echoed down the hall. She had attempted to discuss accessing the annual income from her inheritance early next year when she turned twenty-one. Cassie had every intention of still being unwed by then, and to no one's great surprise, Michael had not been receptive to the idea.

"This was your first discussion," Audrey said to her as she passed out of the mirror's reflection. "Give him time to adjust. Michael is a staunch traditionalist, you know that."

As a practice, unmarried women fell under the rule of their closest male relative. That male relative would legally oversee the dispersal of the lady's dowry and annual income. Cassie's inheritance was in a trust, and from what Philip had confided to Audrey, it was a tidy sum. Though she didn't dare say it aloud, especially with Cassie so incensed, the idea of handing her the entirety of the yearly income gave Audrey pause.

"He thinks he knows what is best for everyone," Cassie went on, her arms crossed. She then threw them out and up again as she exclaimed, "Why can't he understand that I have my own mind and that I'm capable of using it?"

Audrey bit her tongue. Cassie had always possessed a quick temper, but she'd yet to grasp that taming it would advance her cause far better than allowing it free rein.

"Have you considered a formal proposal for your income?"

Cassie halted and met her eyes in the mirror. "How do you mean?"

"If you know what you would like to do with it, how to employ yourself, perhaps your brother would be more willing to compromise."

It would also alleviate some of Audrey's own concerns. Cassie's only direction this last year had been to *not* accept any offers from suitors. A few had come in, and all were roundly rejected. Cassie would not deign even going for a stroll. Her icy demeanor had deterred many gentlemen, though many more were too tempted by her fortune to care.

She sat upon the chaise at the foot of Audrey's bed, arms crossed again, eyes distant. "I've been trying to think of something, but...all my life, the only thing I was instructed to plan for was my wedding. My marriage. Becoming a mother and running a household."

Greer placed a last comb in Audrey's chignon and stepped back and to the side. It was her signal that she was finished, and that Audrey should appraise her work. She nodded and smiled at her maid, who then took her leave.

"You have some months yet before Michael could hand you control of your fortune," Audrey said as she joined Cassie on the chaise. "Why don't you take that time to think about what you plan to do? You must have some purpose or else I fear you will be deliriously bored."

Cassie snorted. "And wives and mothers aren't deliriously bored too?"

She couldn't chastise her for the sarcastic remark. Not when she worried over the same thing. The truth was, while Audrey felt purposeful during an investigation, what gave her the most thrill was being with Hugh, having him as a partner. As her husband, he would be her partner in another sense. But would it be enough if she was made to curtail the other part of her life that gave her such satisfaction? And what if he continued to help at Bow Street? So many marriages she'd seen involved women living separate lives from their husbands. She didn't want that for herself.

Audrey placed her arm around Cassie's shoulders. "Michael is stringent, but it's not coming from a place of superiority or arrogance. It's because he loves you. Spinsters are simply not as secure in society as married women are. He wants only for your safety and protection."

Goodness. Now she was beginning to sound like Hugh. It gave her pause when Cassie again huffed and shook her head, as though rejecting the idea. She was blind to Michael's care. Perhaps Audrey was being blind to Hugh's point of view too.

The door to her bedchamber opened, and Greer reappeared. "Lord Neatham is in the drawing room, Your Grace."

Audrey stood, thankful he'd heeded her message and come so swiftly.

"I'll leave you to your beau," Cassie said with a flitter of her eyelashes.

Audrey envied her obliviousness to the true purpose of Hugh's visit. She needed to describe what she'd seen in the vision, and she hardly knew how she was going to eek the words out when she could barely stomach thinking them.

In the drawing room, Audrey found Hugh and Michael standing near the hearth, each with a whisky in hand. Hugh set his down with alacrity as soon as he saw her.

"I apologize for being a few minutes late," Hugh said loudly, setting his glass down. "We should leave if we want to get there on time."

"What do you—?" Audrey's words croaked to silence in her throat when Hugh's eyes widened in a meaningful way. He crossed in front of Audrey's view of Michael and continued to glare.

"Not to worry," she said, now thoroughly intrigued. It was obvious he wished to keep Michael in the dark about something.

"Give Sir Gabriel my regards," the duke said. Audrey raised a brow as she peered at Hugh. Apparently, they were going to dinner at the chief magistrate's home.

"Certainly. Good evening, Fournier." Hugh held out his arm for her to take. She did and bid Michael a hasty goodbye as Hugh all but whirled her from the drawing room. At the front door, Greer met her with her pelisse. Though it was spring, the night air still held a chill.

"What is this all about?" Audrey asked as they started for Hugh's carriage. The affable expression he'd worn in the drawing room had vanished. "I simply needed to tell you about the cuff links."

"You can. On the way to Tavistock Street," he said. "Yours isn't the only urgent message I've received. Sir Gabriel has sent one."

He handed Audrey up into the carriage, and then came in to sit across from her, latching the door behind him. As his driver turned out onto Curzon Street, Hugh's grim expression struck her. Premonition sent her skin prickling, and after the vision she'd received earlier, Audrey was certain she knew why.

"A body was found today in the Thames," Hugh said.

She shut her eyes. "No..."

"It is Bethany."

A pang of anguish cut through her. And with it came the flood of chaotic images that had barreled into her when she'd finally removed her gloves and held Mr. Comstock's cuff links: Travis Comstock in his bedchamber, face flushed, eyes red, undressing from full evening kit. Pushing back into the energy, Audrey had found Mr. Comstock in the confines of a coach, and through the window, the bright lamps lighting the Vauxhall coach field as they drove past were unmistakable. The same men from her previous vision, who had spoken to Mr. Givens on the street corner, sat across from Mr. Comstock, glaring at him, their mouths sealed. The menace they exuded had been palpable. When Audrey had pushed further, into grainier, weaker memories, the remaining gasps of the vision explained why.

Mr. Comstock was being dragged away from several black robed figures, all of them men, and all of them wearing elaborately grotesque masks. One mask, a red-painted devil face with a black snake's tongue protruding from an open mouth, stood out amongst the others. The man wearing it had a head of curled jet hair touched by gray, and his robe had red piping while the others did not. They were all gathered in a room, much like a library, though the edges of the vision were beginning to close in. The men encircled a table, covered by some animal pelt, and in the gaps between the robed figures, Audrey could see the white linen of a lady's shift, bare skin, and a woman's arm, hanging limp off the edge of the table. Overhead, a bird cage, disproportionally large, hung suspended from ceiling beams. One final push, and Audrey had found herself swimming in pure shadow.

"Audrey?" Hugh's voice dragged her back into the safety of the carriage. Her eyes were hot with tears. "Tell me," he implored, sitting forward.

She did. She forced the words out, detailing everything she'd seen, and as she spoke, Hugh's countenance darkened. He flexed his hands in and out of fists.

"The initiation was just as I feared," he said once she'd concluded. He sat back and scrubbed his palm over his cheek.

As they turned down another street, the setting sun blazed through the window, blinding her. She turned her head away, eyes watering. "We were too slow."

"Casting blame upon ourselves is not the answer."

She knew he was right, but still felt a sense of utter failure. Hugh held his hat in his hands, his gloved fingers passing the brim around and around, absentmindedly. He glanced at her, his expression desolate. She felt leagues apart from him right then, and she despised it.

"We should speak about earlier," she said after another

few silent moments passed. "Before we arrive at Sir Gabriel's."

"I don't want to argue." He sounded exhausted. Humorless. It suited the situation, but not him.

"Neither do I."

The carriage clattered on, turning them down streets toward their destination. Hugh spent the time staring out the window, brow pleated in deep thought.

Then, out of the silence, he said, "You are the right woman for me. You are the *only* woman for me." He turned away from the window and hinged his piercing gaze on her. It pinned her to the seat and slowed her pulse. "I am not a man who loves by half measures. I won't apologize for loving you intensely. For wanting to protect you."

Her breathing commenced again, though it was rough. How was it that this man could sear her to the bone with a hungry gaze and a few words?

"You don't need to apologize," she managed to say. "I only ask that you don't try to change me."

"I would never do that."

"By asking me to stand aside, you are." She gathered her mettle. "I will stand beside you. Or I won't stand with you at all."

He nodded, then again faced the window. Silence again consumed the carriage. Hugh's thoughts on her ultimatum remained locked behind his unyielding expression. When they arrived on Tavistock Street and were about to enter Sir Gabriel Poston's home, Hugh laid his palm on the small of her back. Though he said nothing, the touch conveyed a desire for a truce. At least for the time being.

"Rebecca has gone to stay with Caro for the night," the

magistrate told them after they joined him in his study. He looked undone—his jacket and cravat had been discarded, his cuffs rolled up. His silver hair, usually slicked back, fell around his forehead in a disheveled fashion. He sipped from a snifter of whisky, and by his red cheeks and hazy eyes, it wasn't his first drink.

"I should have started searching for her the moment Rebecca asked me to," he said, his words somewhat slurred.

Hugh went to the decanter and poured another whisky. He took it to Sir Gabriel, who finished the one in his hand before taking the one Hugh extended to him.

"The letter from Comstock was reason enough not to," he told the magistrate.

"You cannot blame yourself," Audrey added, which she realized Hugh had just said to her as well. It was futile to waste time laying blame upon anyone other than the person who had killed her. And from her vision, any number of men could have done so.

"Can you tell us how she died?" Audrey asked.

If she'd been found in the Thames, it was possible she had gone in on her own accord. But Audrey could not dispel the image of a woman's limp arm hanging off the table. Though she hadn't seen her face, it had to have been Bethany on that table. Not that she could share any of that with Sir Gabriel.

"It looks to be strangulation," the magistrate said. "There will be an inquest."

"So, nothing like the other bodies found at Vauxhall," Hugh said. The magistrate lowered his whisky.

"Why would it be? Without doubt, Comstock has done this deed. I have men searching for him now."

With an assenting nod from Hugh, Audrey explained. "We spoke to Bethany's friend, Miss Bertram. It appears your niece did not set out to elope. She set out to visit a secret society known as the Sanctuary. Mr. Comstock took her there the night of her disappearance. His maid confirmed that he returned to his home before dawn the next morning. Bethany, as we know, did not."

"Comstock delivered the letter insinuating an elopement and demanding a larger annuity when he was no longer even with Bethany. He was home," Hugh said.

"And his maid, as it happens, was the young woman who pretended to be Miss Comstock, his sister," Audrey included.

"But you can call back your men. Comstock is also now dead," Hugh said. "Of an apparent opium overdose."

The magistrate goggled back and forth between them. He shuffled to his desk and sat heavily into his chair.

"How is it that you did not know about Comstock?" Hugh asked.

"I have no idea," he rasped after taking another indulgent swallow of his whisky.

"I find it highly suspect that both he and your niece are dead a week after attending the Sanctuary together," Hugh said.

"The letter," Audrey began, her eyes on the carpet as she put something together that had been bothering her. "What if it was a diversion? When Bethany did not return home as she meant to do, Comstock knew she would be missed. There would have to be a reason for her absence, and he would be the first person that Mr. Silas would contact."

Hugh assented with a low groan. "Crafty bastard. Yes, I

think you're right. And as he'd already given a false address, Mr. Silas would not know where to find him."

"Why advertise a parcel of land in the paper then?" Audrey asked.

"A land agent or solicitor might have done it for him. A steward perhaps," Hugh answered. At the mention of a steward, for the briefest moment, she saw the edifice of 37 Berkeley Square. But then recalled their argument. She shook her head; now was not the time to dwell on that muddle.

It was also not the time to bring up the tenuous threads connecting Harlan Givens and Lord Stromburg to the Sanctuary. Audrey wasn't certain the magistrate could handle more complications just now.

"You mentioned this Sanctuary place before," Sir Gabriel said, raking back a hank of his silver hair. "A secret society you say?"

Audrey tensed her jaw and appealed to Hugh with a pleading look. He scrubbed the back of his neck and loosened his cravat before explaining to the magistrate what they had learned from Gwendolyn. Sir Gabriel stood from his chair, a vein in the center of his forehead beginning to pulsate.

"What in hell was Bethany thinking? Why would she do such a thing?"

"Excitement was the explanation we were given," Audrey answered, echoing what Gwendolyn had told them.

"Foolish, foolish girl," he seethed, coming out from behind his desk. "Why have I never heard of this despicable society?"

"I imagine it is because you are the chief magistrate at

Bow Street." Hugh's blithe answer earned him a scowl. "Whatever does happen there, it is likely not legal."

"I'd bloody well say so," he thundered, "if young, innocent women are strangled there!"

The scene around the table in Audrey's vision would support that theory. Bethany had been killed that evening, strangled during the initiation, the details of which Audrey did not want to contemplate. Mr. Comstock had returned home in a high dudgeon as the maid had reported, and the next day he began to formulate a diversion with the elopement ruse. Had he killed himself a few days later out of remorse?

"If the members are high ranking in society, they would stand much to lose if the activities they participate in there were made public," Hugh added.

Audrey thought of something and pulled out the sketch she'd drawn of the inverted cross. "This is the symbol connected to the Sanctuary."

Sir Gabriel whisked it from her hand. "*Mmmm*. It looks familiar."

"Sir Oliver Pendleton wears cuff links with this symbol. Mr. Comstock did as well. I think they might be something members wear to mark themselves," Audrey said.

The magistrate handed the sketch back to her. "I know Sir Oliver. I think a visit is in order."

Hugh stepped forward, his hand raised. "I wonder if you might hold there, sir. We don't want to tip off anyone that we are suspicious of the Sanctuary just yet. So far, any mention of it has been met with nervousness and hostility."

Sir Gabriel grumbled but relented and sat back down into his chair.

"We need to discover where the Sanctuary is located," Audrey said. "I say we follow Sir Oliver and see if he can lead us there. Then, we observe who else comes and goes."

"That is assuming he goes there on a regular basis," Hugh replied. "If he doesn't, we could be waiting for him to lead us there for quite some time."

"All right," she conceded, impatient but in agreement. "But so far all we know is that it is near Vauxhall."

Sir Gabriel grunted. "Bethany was found near the Vauxhall stairs. Her body was tangled in some fishing detritus. She'd been there for days..." He went quiet, his voice cut off under the strain of emotion.

"How long has Tyne been working the Vauxhall case?" Hugh asked.

"Since Stromburg was found dead. Why?"

Audrey thought she knew in which direction Hugh's mind had gone. "The brothel madame was found two days after Stromburg. And two weeks after that, Mr. Givens. Who, it's been suggested, had turned informant for someone."

Sir Gabriel got to his feet. "Informant for whom?"

Audrey understood now. "Do you think for Bow Street? For Officer Tyne?"

Hugh nodded. "If someone learned Givens was spying at the Seven Sins, nosing around about the Sanctuary and informing the police on what he heard, it would be motive for someone from the Sanctuary to want to silence him."

"Then what of Stromburg and Madame Lee?" Audrey asked. "Were they speaking out of turn about the society as well?"

"Madame Lee ran a specialty brothel that caters to wealthy men," Sir Gabriel said. "The Red Lotus."

And Stromburg, according to Princess Esterhazy, had possessed a disreputable taste in vice. At the time, Audrey thought only of the Seven Sins. But now, she crossed her arms with a twist of unease. "Specialty?"

She regretted voicing her ignorance when Hugh replied, "Certain brothels cater to different...proclivities."

"Oh, I see." She wasn't entirely sure she did, but it sounded rather indecent, and she didn't wish to continue the discussion with Sir Gabriel present. "If some of her clients were also Sanctuary members, she might have overheard things."

"And thought to profit from them," Hugh said. "In all his investigating, what has Tyne found?"

Sir Gabriel hitched his hands on his hips with a lowering frown. "Nothing to report."

Hugh exhaled, his skepticism about the officer's capabilities clear. "We do need to find the Sanctuary. We also need to know how Madame Lee and Stromburg connect to it. I have an idea on how we can see to both things tonight." He looked at Audrey. "It will mean splitting up. At least for a few hours."

A stone lodged in her stomach. She had a feeling she wasn't going to like his idea at all.

CHAPTER THIRTEEN

The brothel wasn't what Hugh had expected.

He was no stranger to businesses that catered to men's carnal appetites. For many, passion and violence danced along the thin edge of the same sword. He'd been called to a number of brothels during his time at Bow Street. When managed well, a house of ill repute could maintain a steady and lucrative business. It had usually been the poorly managed ones, where those in charge profited heavily and treated their workers like chattel, that Hugh and his fellow constables had needed to visit.

From the moment he set foot inside the Red Lotus, he knew he'd arrived at one of the better ones. Luxurious shades of pink, burgundy, and scarlet touched the silk paneled walls, satin hangings, and privacy screens. Potted palms offset the red, as did the black and gold carpets. The perfume of jasmine incense wasn't overbearing, but just enough to tempt those entering the front hall with sensual feminine promises.

Hugh stood unattended, except for the presence of a burly man in a black suit and red cravat near the draped entrance to another room. He merely observed Hugh and then tugged a bell pull, dangling from the wall behind him. A brass bell chimed within the house.

There were no half-dressed ladies rushing to drape themselves on his shoulder, but instead, a middle-aged woman wearing a high-necked gown of green satin emerged through the embroidered drapes. With a snap of her wrist, a hand fan unfolded, and as she sauntered toward him, she beat the fan languidly.

"We have not met," she said, her dark, keen eyes assessing him. She would surely be looking at the cut of his suit, his accessories, and even his bearing, to know whether he was acceptable as a client.

Hugh's jaw clenched. He had not come here to partake, of course, but to get the answers he needed. Sir Gabriel had agreed with the plan. Audrey's reaction, however, still stumped him. He'd expected her to protest, to balk at his visiting a brothel. Instead, she'd been strangely silent on the matter. *"Of course,"* she'd said after he'd laid out the proposal: He would visit the Red Lotus to find out more about Madame Lee, and Audrey would go toward Vauxhall in search of a carriage with the inverted cross symbol. She would not be alone. After what her vision had shown her, he was loath to let her go anywhere alone, ever again. Bethany Silas had been cruelly misused and someone at the Sanctuary who enjoyed the play of asphyxiation had taken things too far. Hugh had appointed Carrigan, Sir, *and* Basil to join her tonight.

As Hugh would never have considered taking Audrey with him to a brothel, and she would never have considered sitting at home idly while he was there, he believed it the best use of their time. Her easy acceptance should not have gnawed at him as much as it did.

"I have just learned of your establishment," Hugh said over the muffled tones of a pianoforte playing somewhere in another room. "Mr. Benedict Sterling, at your service," he added with a bow.

There was no flicker of disbelief from the woman at his false name. He only hoped he did not cross paths with another gentleman here who would know him. Then again, it was possible many clients presented themselves under false pretenses.

The woman snapped her fan shut. "I hope the gentleman who recommended the Red Lotus informed you of its area of expertise."

He bowed his head in a nod. Sir Gabriel had whispered the brothel's specialty as he and Audrey had been preparing to leave Tavistock Street. *"Flagellation,"* he'd said. *"Men who enjoy being subdued, shall we say."*

That close dance of lust and violence would be ever more potent in a place like this.

The woman held out her arm toward the cordoned off room. "Welcome, Mr. Sterling. This way."

She led him past the guard, through the pink silk curtains, and Hugh prayed that the low male voices murmuring on the other side belonged to no one he knew. Impressively, he found the room divided by hangings and privacy screens, positioned just so to create several private sitting areas. Hugh could not see the men ensconced behind them, and they could not view him either.

The woman led him through the fragrant brume of cigar and pipe smoke to one such enclosed area. The walls were formed of scarlet satin, hanging from ceiling hooks, and of a japonaise privacy screen. A table held a tray of whisky and snifters. She poured him a dram and then sat upon the only available sofa. He lowered himself to sit beside her.

"Your interests are more common than many might lead you to believe," she said.

"Thank you for your understanding, Madame Lee," he replied, his attention hinged on her face to see her reaction. He needed to prod her along and mistaking her for the former madame was one option.

Hugh had studied the newspapers over the last few days, and none had revealed the identities of the bodies found at Vauxhall. Bow Street officials were keeping that confidential, they said. Hugh was curious as to why the Vauxhall worker, who fed the secret to *The Morning Post* in the first place, had not also given the names. Whatever the reason, that information had still not come to light.

The madame tucked her chin and canted her head, her thin, dark brow arching. "I am Madame Knight."

Hugh pretended at confusion. "The Red Lotus has changed hands?"

Her lips and nostrils thinned. "Due to unfortunate circumstances, yes. However, the establishment itself has not changed."

He smiled as though that was a great relief to him. "And have you been here for some time, Madame Knight?"

"I have," she replied, though she wasn't comfortable answering the question. She proved it by launching a question of her own to divert him. "How did you hear of us?"

He sipped his whisky. "An acquaintance. Lord Stromburg."

Before parting ways for the evening, Audrey had informed him of Princess Esterhazy's complaint that the Austrian had a penchant for vice. She'd been curious if a link could be established between the count and Madame Lee.

Madame Knight blinked twice, and belatedly, she pushed on a tight grin. "Is that so? Very good."

Hugh didn't know if she was pretending to recognize the name, or if she truly did.

"I hope by naming my acquaintance, I have not lowered in your esteem," Hugh pressed, searching for more.

"Not at all. His lordship was a frequent and amiable guest of the Red Lotus while he was visiting Town."

Hugh finished his drink, toasting the accomplishment and looking forward to telling Audrey that Stromburg and Madame Lee *had* been connected after all. Madame Knight lifted a small handbell next to the tray and gave it a slight jingle.

"If you will follow Nanita, Mr. Sterling," she said as a young woman entered their small enclosure. He stood, though his stomach was slow to follow. It dropped as the pretty young woman, dressed in a gauzy white gown, hinged her intense eyes on him.

She turned to leave, and after a moment's hesitation, he followed as instructed.

He thought he now knew why Audrey stayed quiet when he'd suggested the evening's plans. Everything about this was untoward. Even in the name of an investigation.

In no way did he plan to follow through with an encounter with this young woman. Or any other offered to him. However, continuing to question Madame Knight about her predecessor would have only raised her suspicions. Questioning Nanita once they were alone could be more fruitful. He would make it clear to her straightaway that he only wished to talk. With any hope, she would not signal the alarm.

The upstairs of the Red Lotus was just as decadent and tasteful as the ground floor, but Hugh barely saw it before Nanita, a few paces ahead, opened a door and stepped aside to show him in. The bedchamber had been appointed in greens and blacks, and his attention caught and stuck on what first appeared to be a chandelier above the large tester bed. However, on closer inspection, he saw there were no candles or gas jets. Several ropes and ribbons of differing material hung from the ceiling fixture, reaching down to pool on the counterpane. With the specialty of the house in mind, Hugh imagined the ropes and ribbons were used in a variety of ways.

The door snicked shut behind him, and Hugh turned. The young woman was gone. She had not entered the room to join him, leaving him to wonder if his assigned companion would be sent.

Hugh tossed his hat onto a chair. It had not been taken from him at the door, nor his coat or gloves. He raked his hand through his hair. A curl of disquiet snaked its way through him, and he did not think it was merely due to his current location. The escalating sense that something was not right made the back of his neck sweat.

He'd turned to take up his hat when a door in the back corner of the room opened. He expected a young woman to appear, but when the burly man from the front hall entered instead, Hugh sighed.

"It appears I'm losing my touch," he said. Madame Knight hadn't been fooled.

The muscle came at him, giving Hugh only a fraction of a second to judge the man's skill. The way he lumbered forward, moving without finesse or economy, Hugh gaged him to be the sort of fighter who depended on brawn rather than dexterity.

Hugh sank down, dodging the man's fist. He wheeled to the side, out of the man's reach.

"Let's discuss this," he said, but the brute, of course, was not chatty. Madame Knight had given him a job, and he meant to do it.

He hurtled toward Hugh. Partially in thanks to his boxing lessons at Gentleman Jack's, but more so for his time defending himself against criminals as an officer, he dodged swiftly again. But the big oaf wasn't entirely without aptitude. His meaty arm hooked Hugh's middle as he was attempting to move out of reach, and he felt the floor go out from underneath his feet.

The man heaved him toward the floor, but it wasn't carpet that met his back. The breath was driven from his lungs as he cracked through as a low table. The thing crumpled like it had been made of sticks, whatever objects it had been holding, shattering too. Pain seared his back and the base of his skull. If Hugh's opponent had not been a man twice his size, with the sole desire to do him in, he might have taken a moment to catch his breath. The instinct to survive, however, drove him to roll to the side, just in time to avoid the man's fist coming toward his face.

Too slow to halt the punch, he ended up plowing his knuckles into the remnants of the wooden table. As Hugh rolled to his knees, his hand closed around the leg of the destroyed table. The man was starting to straighten when Hugh smashed the leg onto the back of his head. The man's knees folded, and then he dropped.

Hugh dragged in a breath, panting as he stared at Madame Knight's guard. He wasn't moving. Hugh threw down the chair leg and started for the door. Leaving was instinctive, but he stopped and fought against it. Madame Knight had sent this brute up here to either kill him, or just warn him—forcefully—to not come back. Had the mention of Madame Lee, or of Stromburg, decided it? He needed to know, or this trip would have been for nothing. He certainly would not be able to come back and try again.

Rubbing the growing knob on the back of his head where it had connected with the wooden table, Hugh peered at the ropes and ribbons splayed on the bed, suspended from the ceiling fixture. He selected the thickest hemp rope, rough against his palms, and brought them to the man's immobile figure. He tied his wrists together behind his back in as tight a knot as possible. With another line of rope, this one of sleeker, whip-like material, he bound the man's ankles.

Then, Hugh snatched up a silver candlestick that had been swept off the broken table, ripped out the candle itself, and backed up against the wall next to the door. He waited, allowing his heart rate to come back down. Less than a minute later, as expected, a slight knock landed on the wood. Then, the door opened. Madame Knight entered cautiously, coming to a halt as she saw her guard unconscious and bound among the detritus.

Hugh pressed the round opening of the candlestick against the back of her neck and kicked the door shut. The madame held still, and he could only hope she continued to assume the candlestick was the barrel of a pistol.

"He really wasn't the sort I was looking for," Hugh said.

"You are making a serious mistake," Madame Knight replied.

He ignored her warning. It had been a mistake to come here...*without his flintlock.*

"Tell me what happened to Madame Lee and Lord Stromburg."

"Who are you?"

"You are running out of time, Madame Knight." He hesitated. Then took a chance. "Someone from the Sanctuary will be here shortly if I do not get what I need."

She went instantly rigid. Her hands lifted to the sides, as if in surrender. "I want nothing to do with that place."

"Then answer my question. What happened to Madame Lee and Stromburg?"

On the floor, the man twitched. If he woke, he'd inform the madame that she was being held at candlestick point.

"Stromburg was a regular," she said, relenting. "He took to a certain girl. Opal. He liked her so much that he asked Minerva—Madame Lee—if he could bring her to a secret club. There were many members there that might enjoy the Red Lotus."

"And did she agree?"

"Yes. But then Stromburg returned in a fury. Another member had strangled Opal while initiating her."

Hugh nearly lowered the candlestick in surprise. Strangle? Like Bethany Silas.

"Minerva and Stromburg were in an uproar. They went to the police. And then...they both disappeared."

“When was this?” Hugh asked. The man on the broken bits of the table stirred again and moaned.

“Last month. When you mentioned both Minerva and Stromburg, I knew you must know something,” she said. “But I want nothing to do with the Sanctuary. I let every girl go, every guard who might have heard something about Opal, and hired new ones.”

He looked again at the moaning guard on the floor, and a memory of something Mrs. Givens had said struck him. “Was a man named Harlan Givens one of your guards?”

Sir’s mother had mentioned that he was working at more than just the Seven Sins as security.

“Givens? Yes. Why?”

Hugh was finished here. And by the increasing mobility of the man bound on the floor, in more than one way.

“Rest assured the Sanctuary will not pay you a visit. Now, I’m leaving. Am I going to meet with any trouble as I go?”

Madame Knight turned her head far enough to display her hateful glare. “Just get out. And do not come back.”

“With pleasure,” Hugh said. Then, lowering the candlestick, he slipped out of the bedchamber.

CHAPTER
FOURTEEN

Shortly before nine o'clock, Carrigan parked the barouche-landau at the edge of the coach field outside Vauxhall, along Kennington Lane. The position gave them an unobstructed view of the other conveyances coming and going. There weren't many. In the few days since a body had been found at the pleasure gardens, Mr. Gye's concern that such a thing would frighten off visitors had come to fruition. The papers were reporting that the sale of entry tokens and season's passes had decreased, and the nearly vacant coach field supported it.

It had been over an hour since Carrigan had parked them, and not one of the carriages that had arrived or departed had possessed an inverted cross stamped on the door. With every passing minute, Audrey found it more difficult to suppress her urge to stamp her foot and groan in frustration.

Hugh would be at the Red Lotus by then. It made perfectly good sense that she could not go with him to such a place. And if they were to close in on the Sanctuary and discover who had killed Bethany Silas, it also made perfectly good sense that they should split up. Divide and conquer, as it were.

But every time she pictured him walking into a house of ill repute, a vibration of anger and envy shook through her. It was absurd, and she despised the reaction. She was more mature than that. Too confident in Hugh and his morals. And yet, logic failed to disperse the feelings.

Sir leaned on the ledge of the open window, his cheek digging into his palm. "I'm getting hungry."

"You just barely finished the biscuit that was squirreled away in your pocket," Basil replied.

"That only made me hungrier."

The two had been bickering since they, along with Carrigan at the reins, had driven away from Violet House. Hugh's valet had become increasingly more dramatic with his sighs of boredom and annoyance too. *I am a valet*, he'd muttered several times, *not an assistant inquiry agent.*

Sir teased him about just missing his nightly tea and crumpets while he read romantic novels in bed. When Basil had denied the accusation, Sir had whipped out a copy of *A Romance in the Forest* by Ann Radcliffe from his own coat pocket. "Then what do you call this?"

Basil had tried snatching it away from Sir, complaining that the little pickpocket had no respect for privacy. The bit of levity had only lasted until Basil had finally succeeded and stuffed the book back into his own pocket. Then, they returned to watching for any sign of the inverted cross on passing carriages.

Audrey sighed. "This isn't working." Sitting still, in one spot, was entirely ineffective. She thought again of her idea to watch Sir Oliver Pendleton's home, and to follow him should he leave. She probably did not possess the patience for that endeavor either.

"Maybe this Sanctuary place isn't even around here," Sir suggested.

"It is," she replied. The vision she'd had of Mr. Comstock in the coach with the lights of Vauxhall's coach field in the background had proved it. But as Hugh was the only one who could know of that, she ticked off the reasons she was certain. "Miss Silas met Mr. Comstock here for the first time. He took her here the day she disappeared. Her body was found near the Vauxhall stairs in the Thames. And the other bodies that were found—" She swallowed her next words. Sir kept looking out the window, as if unaffected, but she knew he wasn't.

"I'm sorry, Sir, we won't speak of it."

He shrugged. "It's all right. We've got to if we're going to figure out who snuffed my father."

"We *will* figure it out." She raised her voice. "Carrigan?"

"Yes, Your Grace?" He had remained seated in the driver's box, just as many other drivers with the thankless task of waiting for their charges were.

"Can you take us around the streets here, relatively close to the pleasure gardens?"

He whistled and shook the reins and the carriage rolled from its spot.

"What are we looking for now?" Basil asked.

"The cross symbol and term 'sanctuary' puts me in mind of a religious element," she said. "What if the secret society is being held inside a church? Or near one?"

"One that's been shut up, you mean," Sir said.

With a nod from Audrey, Sir doused the lamp in the carriage. It allowed them to see better into the dark streets as Carrigan started to drive a wandering route along one street to the next. The horses ambled slowly, giving them plenty of time to look. There were lampposts along the streets in most places, and people were out. But most of the buildings were residences.

"So, you and Lord Hugh are getting leg shackled soon, right?" Sir's question startled Audrey from her peering through the window. Carrigan was taking them around the Oval off Devonshire Place.

"Hush," Basil said. "That is none of your business."

"It's quite all right, Basil," she said, then to Sir, "I believe so."

She and Hugh had argued, yes, but she could not face the possibility that they would part ways because of it. Audrey had already given some thought to the blending of their staffs, but in truth, Sir wasn't a servant. He was more along the lines of Hugh's ward. Which meant that he would be her ward now too.

She wondered how Sir felt about that. He was so accustomed to only having to follow Hugh's edicts. Audrey wasn't sure what her role would be. Sir already had a mother, one he cared for, and who cared for him as much as she possibly could. Like so many other women of her class, Lucy Givens had limited resources when it had come to protecting her son from her abusive husband. But now, she was a widow, and with three children younger than Sir.

Perhaps now that Mr. Givens no longer stood in his way, Hugh would be able to extend his generosity toward her too.

"Over there," Basil said, interrupting Audrey's half-formed idea of taking Mrs. Givens and her daughters from the East End and placing them somewhere nicer. Safer. And closer to Sir.

"What do you see?" she asked. But then, she saw it too. A stone church with a tall spire, and its front door boarded up. It looked to be in disuse.

"Carrigan, stop here," she called. And when he did, she opened the door. Sir darted out first and held out his hand.

"Thank you," she said as she let him guide her onto the pavement. A lamppost a dozen paces away shone, reflecting off the church's lancet windows. A few were missing, and some scaffolding at the corner also appeared in shambles.

"I'm going to take a closer look," she announced.

"At this ghastly place?" Basil asked.

"Someone should go with you." Carrigan started to rise, but Audrey held up her hand.

"Stay with the carriage," she said. "I'm not going far."

"I'll come," Sir offered. She gave him a thankful grin, and then the two of them approached the church together.

With the front door boarded up, any entrance would have to be found at the side or back. She went toward the abandoned scaffolding. The shabby look of the church could be a deterrent, a disguise for passersby. And perhaps the Sanctuary operated out of the vaults of the church, curbing the emission of any light and sound. It would suit the room from her vision, which had been candlelit.

But as they started down the narrow alley flanking the church, any feeling of certainty shriveled. There was nothing here. No sign of people. Certainly, no inverted cross.

"Never mind," she said, coming to a stop. "Let's return to the carriage."

Just then, a square-sided coach clattered past the opening in the alley behind the church, where a lamppost gave off yellow light. Stamped onto the coach's door, a white inverted cross flashed into view, then out again as the coach went by.

Audrey held still. But then, she realized what she'd seen, and she dashed toward the alley opening, and the street running behind the church.

"Your Grace!" Carrigan shouted.

"Sir, hurry! That coach that just went by—"

"Had a cross like you said!" Sir finished for her.

They exited the alley and came into the street under the lamppost, just in time to see the back end of the coach carrying onward, past a cross street. There was no time to go back to Carrigan and Basil. She started after the coach on foot, with Sir at her side. He quickly overtook her, his flat-soled boots far more suitable for running than hers with their little heels. She could only hope that Carrigan would come looking for them in this direction.

Her breaths sawed in and out as she tried to keep up not just with the coach, but with Sir. The stays she wore dug into her ribs as she sucked in air, and water splashed up onto her hem as she darted through puddles. A handful of people out walking gasped with alarm as she and Sir flew past them.

The coach, visible by its guiding lanterns, turned right down another street and disappeared. Audrey's feet began to bruise, her lungs burned, and yet if she slowed to tend to herself, she knew she'd feel crushing disappointment. Digging into a well of reserved determination, she reached the cross street only a few paces behind Sir. They both drew to a stop, breaths heaving. The street was empty. Not a single carriage was in view.

"But that's impossible," Audrey panted as her pulse continued to charge.

The carriage should have been somewhere along the long street stretching before them, considering the short length of time since it had turned.

"It must've gone down some alley," Sir said. He walked briskly, and Audrey followed, ignoring the stitch in her side.

The alleys they passed were dark, and even though she considered dipping down into a few of them, good sense vanquished out the idea. Hugh had accused her of being heedless before, and that it often led to danger. She hated to admit he was right, and with Sir with her, she had a responsibility for him. Leading him into some alley would not do.

A few carriages passed them, but none had the symbol. After a few minutes, she slowed. "The carriage must have turned off this street."

Sir stopped and waited for her by the opening of yet another dark alley, this one gated. The tall iron bars were set on hinges attached to a stone arch marking the alley entrance. The gates were open, and as Sir held still, waiting for her to catch up, two men came through. They were walking quickly. One knocked into Sir's shoulder as he came around the corner of the gate.

"Watch it now, rat," the man said as he kept walking.

"You're the one who knocked into me," Sir shot back.

The two men quit moving and turned to confront him. Audrey hurried forward.

"What's that you said, rat?"

Both men were twice Sir's size, and paired together, they circled him like vultures.

"That is quite enough of that," Audrey said as she

reached them. She slid around the taller of the two men and placed herself at Sir's side.

"That's enough of that, is it?" the man parroted back, mocking her. He stepped closer. Close enough for her to see his face. The gaslight from the nearest lamppost was just strong enough to illuminate him.

Audrey's knees turned to jelly.

It was the man from both of her visions, the one who'd been warning Mr. Givens, and who had been seated across from Mr. Comstock, glaring. Breathing thinly through her nose, she shifted her eyes to the other man. She hadn't seen him fully in the visions, but she recalled the slimmer build and beard.

She clutched Sir's arm. He flinched at her touch.

"We have no quarrel with you," she replied as evenly as she could. "It was an honest mistake."

The man scratched his thumb across his chin. The motion, as benign as it was, appeared threatening. As if he was preparing for a brawl. "He should watch where he's standing."

"You should—"

Audrey cut Sir off. "Very good. We will be sure to do that. Good evening, gentlemen."

She tugged Sir's arm and began walking away from the two men. Her back prickled with the press of their stares, and she worried they were going to overtake them and obstruct their path away. But after several strides, and no resistance, Audrey allowed herself to breathe again.

"What was that?" Sir yanked his arm free. "Those two deserved a mouthful of knuckles."

"They were dangerous men, Sir." She sealed her lips

against the truth that Sir could not have possibly bested both of them—whether they deserved a mouthful of knuckles or not.

She stared ahead. Gracious, where was Carrigan? They hadn't run very far. He should be driving the lanes nearby in search of them.

Sir grumbled but none of his words were audible. She imagined he was embarrassed about being led away from a fight by a woman. Hiding behind a skirt was surely emasculating. But if Sir's anger was the price she must pay for avoiding the two men from her visions, it was worth it.

She tossed a look over her shoulder. They hadn't followed. The gated entrance to the alley was now closed and the men were gone. The steady clatter of wheels and tack lifted her spirits, and when she faced forward again, she saw Carrigan driving straight toward them. Basil threw open the door once Carrigan had drawn to a stop.

"That was entirely too reckless," the valet said.

"Awe, stuff it, Baz, we saw the white cross and had to follow. It's why we're out here to begin with."

"Where is it now?" Basil asked.

"Who knows? We lost it," Sir grumbled, still peeved.

She cast a look back toward the stone arched gate. "Actually, Sir, I don't think we did."

CHAPTER FIFTEEN

Pain seared Hugh's scalp as the cloth came down onto the gash there. He winced and swore and ripped the alcohol-soaked cloth from Thornton's hand.

"I can do this part myself," Hugh said, carefully dabbing the back of his head, where his friend had just placed four sutures with far too much enthusiasm. Had Hugh been able to stitch up the gash he'd received at the Red Lotus himself, he would have done so. However, Thornton had been all too happy to assist.

"That lip could use a suture as well."

"It is fine," Hugh grumbled. He hadn't even realized his lip had been split in the fisticuffs until he was on his way to Thornton House.

Thornton stepped away, his hands raised in concession. "Something tells me Audrey won't think it is *fine* when it comes time in the wedding ceremony to kiss her groom."

"I will be healed by then," Hugh replied, wishing he'd

kept his mouth shut about her accepting his proposal. Thornton would find any opportunity to rib him now.

The physician rolled down his sleeves. "Not rushing to use that special license, I see."

"Finishing up this case first." Hugh pulled away the cloth and sighed at the blood there.

"And things look to be going so well," his friend said dryly.

Hugh lobbed the cloth at him and stood from the table in Thornton's home surgery. "Thank you for your tender care, but I think I would have received better from Basil."

Mentioning his valet made him think of Audrey. He wondered where she was now, and if her evening had gone any better than his own. He'd discovered the connection between Stromburg, Madame Lee, and Harlan Givens, and why they might have all been silenced, but there was still no proof of anything.

Hugh reached for his coat, the collar spotted with blood. Basil would have a fit of the vapors when he saw it.

"Can I be of any help?" Thornton asked before Hugh could reach the sliding pocket doors closing off the surgery. By the changed tone of his voice, the offer was genuine, and his apology clear.

Hugh's muscles ached from exhaustion and from the scuffle he'd been in at the brothel. Bruised and tired, Hugh tossed aside his coat. "You could pour me a drink."

Thornton did. A generous one, which Hugh forced himself to sip slowly after sitting in one of the club chairs before the hearth.

He'd informed him about the night's events while Thornton had been sewing up his scalp, along with the discovery of Sir Gabriel's niece's body. Though he was in deep with the demimonde and other more risqué areas of society, Thornton had not heard of the Sanctuary.

He took a seat in the other club chair. "A sex society where women are only invited if they are willing to sleep with the members. And now, two such women that you know of have been strangled in the act." Thornton swirled his whisky but looked too ill to sip it. "It makes me see red."

"And those who speak of it have their throats cut and ears lopped off," Hugh said, his whole skull throbbing dully.

"Why their ears?" Thornton asked.

Hugh shrugged. "Maybe because they heard things they weren't supposed to." He sipped slowly. "Just the left ears, mind you."

That was important, he knew, and discovering the answer as to why would surely bring him more answers.

Thornton looked away from the flames in the hearth that he and Hugh had been staring absently at. "I've read that business is thin for Mr. Gye."

"He could not expect to keep the discovery of three mutilated bodies a secret from the public forever. One of his workers was bound to feed the story to some rag for his own gain."

And now, the backlash he'd feared had come to pass.

"Why wait?" Thornton asked, arching a brow.

"How do you mean?"

His friend shrugged. "Why would this anonymous worker wait until the third body turns up? Why not spill to the papers after the discovery of the first?"

"Perhaps they thought it was beginning to get out of

hand. They might have disagreed with Gye about keeping it from the public."

Thornton took a swig of his whisky. "You're probably right."

Hugh knew that tone. "But?"

"*But*...have you given any thought about why *Givens* was left to be discovered when the gardens were busy, but the other two were not?"

Hugh had given that some thought, though admittedly not enough. Not until now.

"If the Sanctuary is behind the deaths, as we believe, they might have grown impatient with the lack of publicity. Givens changed that," Hugh said. "And then, immediately after, someone tipped off *The Morning Post* about the other two bodies."

The new thoughts began to unravel with more speed. He sat forward. "What if it wasn't a Vauxhall employee, but someone associated with the Sanctuary?"

"Why would the Sanctuary wish for their deeds to be made public?" Thornton asked. "One would think they'd want to keep things hushed, just as Gye wanted."

"Gye wanted to keep things running smoothly at Vauxhall." Hugh's thoughts picked up speed. "What if the Sanctuary wanted the opposite? What if they wanted the pleasure gardens to suffer?"

"It certainly is now," Thornton said with a nod. "Do you think the Sanctuary could have some vendetta against Vauxhall? Or Mr. Gye?"

It was something to find out.

"I'll pay him a visit tomorrow, to see if he has any enemy in mind," Hugh said, setting down his still full whisky.

"I'll come with you. You may be concussed. And by the way, you mean *today*," Thornton said, standing to see him out. He tapped the face of his fob watch. "It's nearly two in the morning."

Hugh's eyelids drooped shut on the ride back to Bedford Street, but when Norris called to the horses and the rhythmic sway of the carriage slowed, he snapped awake.

The lamps were still lit inside the residence, and when Whitlock answered the door for him, he'd barely handed the older man his coat and hat when he heard the sharp intake of air from the entrance to his study.

"What happened to you?" Audrey rushed toward him, her eyes scouring his face. "Your head is bleeding."

"The Dowager Duchess of Fournier is here, my lord," Whitlock languidly intoned.

"I can see that, thank you," Hugh said, then dismissed his butler. The man moved at the pace of an elderly snail and spoke just as slowly.

Hugh led Audrey back into the study, where they both turned to one another and said simultaneously, "Tell me what happened."

She crossed her arms and waited for him to answer first. She'd made herself at home, it seemed. A small glass of sherry had been left on his desk, along with an opened book. He pictured her as she'd likely been, reclining in his desk chair, her legs tucked up underneath her. It was a delectable image, one he wished he could have seen. It was then that he remembered they'd parted on tense terms.

"I got into a bit of a scrape at the Red Lotus, but I am fine. The important thing is that I now know how the three Vauxhall murder victims were connected."

He went to his desk and sat in his chair, groaning at the ache of his muscles as he did. Audrey eyed him with concern but didn't press him about his injuries.

"How?" she asked, remaining on the opposite side of the desk.

"Mr. Givens was working as security at the Red Lotus when Madame Lee and Stromburg were both killed. The two had decided to go to the police about the strangulation of one of Madame Lee's girls, whom Stromburg had taken to the Sanctuary for initiation."

"Strangulation," Audrey echoed. "Like Bethany."

"Yes."

Her expression darkened at the mention of the young woman. "Do you think Mr. Givens heard them discussing it and thought he might profit by turning them in to the Sanctuary?"

Hugh shook his head, though only once. It hurt too much. "No. Givens would have no access to such an exclusive, well protected society club."

"Then who did he tell?"

"If he was an informant, it was more likely for the police. He knew his way around Bow Street. Knew that officers paid people like him for information. Information that could lead to an arrest."

"He told the *police* about Madame Lee's strangled employee? How would that benefit him?"

"It wouldn't," Hugh answered. "I don't think he told the police anything...not until *after* his employer and Lord Stromburg mysteriously disappeared."

Hugh suspected Givens had figured out some benefit to being an informant for Bow Street. He'd fed the investigating officers what he'd overheard about the strangled girl and the Sanctuary, aiming for a monetary reward should any of it pan out.

"But then, how did the Sanctuary learn that they'd been betrayed by Madame Lee and Lord Stromburg in the first place? How did they know to silence them?"

That was the question Hugh had kept coming back to. The answer he'd come to accept curdled in his gut and made him feel turned inside-out.

"The men from your vision," he said, "knew Givens had been talking out of turn. If that was the case, and he was an informant for someone at Bow Street..."

"Someone at Bow Street told someone at the Sanctuary," Audrey finished.

Lead ballast slid into his stomach. "Most likely, yes."

"A Bow Street officer is part of the Sanctuary? But only wealthy men are invited as members." She went still, the most plausible answer paling her complexion. "You don't think Sir Gabriel...?"

He had thought it. But instantly dismissed the ridiculous notion. "No. Never. He's not corrupt. And Bethany was his niece."

"He didn't want you to investigate. And he agreed with Mr. Gye to keep the murders from the press," she pointed out, playing devil's advocate. But he wouldn't be swayed.

"No, it's someone else. My guess is Tyne."

"But he's working class," she said.

"Who better to bring into the fold, offering luxuries and pleasures he could never access normally, in exchange for protection?"

The more Hugh thought on it, the more convinced he became.

Audrey uncrossed her arms. "If that is the case, Officer Tyne may tell the Sanctuary we are investigating."

He had thought of that as well. "Nothing is going to happen to you."

"Me? I'm not the one with a split lip and bloody head."

Hugh remembered his swollen lip and gingerly touched it. He winced. Audrey sighed and came around the desk, to stand behind his chair.

"What are you doing?" he asked, flinching when she reached for his head.

"Sit still," she admonished. Her fingers delved tenderly into his hair, but even then, his scalp stung. "This looks serious, Hugh."

"Thornton declared me hale and hearty, though possibly concussed."

Her fingers continued to probe around the wound. "Gracious, what did they strike you with? You could have been killed."

Hugh reached up and back and wrapped his hand around her wrist. Gently, he dislodged her hand from his hair and swiveled in his chair, still grasping her wrist. He kissed the tips of her fingers. "I am fine."

Some of the rigidity went out of her shoulders and arms. Hugh didn't want to release her, so he adjusted his hold on her wrist, taking her hand instead.

"I'm sorry," he whispered. "For earlier. Our discussion—"

"It was an argument," she corrected.

"Which I would rather not do again any time soon."

She gave a soft nod, and at the tamping of her ire, he gave a tug on her arm. She easily came down into his lap. His bruises protested, and he grunted.

"You're too hurt," she said, starting to rise again. He flexed his arms and brought her down harder. He swallowed the grunt this time.

"I am far better with you here," he told her.

A little grin of satisfaction touched her lips. But then it flattened out. "We can discuss our argument later. First, I should tell you that I think I know where the Sanctuary is."

He pulled back. "Where?"

"If I'm correct, it neighbors Vauxhall, on Burdick Close."

She quickly told him about her and Sir's foot chase after a carriage like the one from her vision, then of running into the two men from her visions—in a literal sense.

Hugh straightened in the chair, sparks igniting in his chest. "You came face to face with them?"

"They were exiting an arched alley with an open gate...I think because the coach had just turned through it."

"They are murderers." And she'd *spoken* to them. More of the same familiar agitation, like what had inspired their earlier argument, built up underneath his skin.

"Most assuredly, but that isn't the point. The point is that this is very likely where the Sanctuary is located."

He suppressed the instinct to point out how much danger she'd put herself in, chasing after the marked coach. It would only anger her.

"Well done," he said instead. "Now we must determine what to do with that information." So far, even speaking about the Sanctuary could be deadly. Stepping foot inside, uninvited, was surely just as perilous.

He leaned his head back. It was nearly three in the morning. His whole body throbbed, and he needed sleep. And yet he wouldn't have dislodged Audrey from his lap unless the whole house caught ablaze, forcing them from their cozy nest. He rubbed small circles on her lower back, where he braced her.

She traced her thumb over his injured lip. Then dropped her hand back into her lap.

"What kind of place was it?" she asked. Then, more faintly, "What specialty?"

Hugh had wondered if she would ask. He'd seen the questions in her eyes when Sir Gabriel had mentioned it.

"It's untoward," he replied.

"As we are to marry," she shifted position in his lap and drew her legs up so that her knees rested against his abdomen, "we can speak of untoward things together, can we not?"

That suggestive reasoning made him want to toss her over his shoulder and carry her up to his room.

"We are still marrying, then, even after our argument?" He wasn't too proud to admit that he'd wondered if she would change her mind.

"Only if you can accept that I won't change. And that I won't always do exactly as you wish."

"Even if all I wish it to keep you safe?"

"Even then."

Hugh ran his palm up her leg, to her knee, over the muslin of her gown. "I don't want you to change. Ever. But I *will* tell you if I think something is dangerous. Or if you're being rash."

She hooked her arms atop his shoulders and linked her

hands around his neck. "Very well. Now, tell me about the Red Lotus."

As discomfited as he'd been while inside the brothel itself, discussing it now with Audrey brought his blood up. "Flagellation."

She frowned. "Being struck?"

"Pain in general. There are men who enjoy it, and places like the Red Lotus cater to them."

Audrey's fingertips curled around the hair at his neck. "What other kinds of specialties are there?" Hugh shifted his position in the chair, and she pinned her bottom lip. "Do you have any interests?"

The little minx. She knew what she was doing to him, even if she was genuinely innocent regarding the topic.

"My interest is solely in you," he answered.

She leaned closer and brushed her lips against his, though she avoided his lower lip, mindful of his injury. The slow, languid kiss, even if only concentrated to his upper lip, made him coil inside. But then, she pulled away.

"I'll go," she said, beginning to slide from his lap. He hauled her back into place.

"No, stay. I've missed you." He kissed her again, uncaring of his painful bottom lip. Spiced notes of sherry lingered on her tongue, and during the next several minutes, Hugh's hand renewed its earlier pursuit under the hem of her skirt. No argument interrupted the seeking of pleasure this time. He kept his mouth adhered to hers, swallowing the soft, decadent sounds she made. However, delighting in the full scope of his future bride would require leading her upstairs.

But even as he made the request, he knew she would not agree.

"I can't. Carrigan is waiting outside. Besides, we both need rest if we are going to the Sanctuary tomorrow."

He'd been nuzzling her neck, but now went still. "This is what I meant by too rash."

"Not alone," she insisted, pushing off his lap and out of his arms. She swept into the front hall. "We need to bring some Bow Street men. Who do you trust?"

Hugh followed, only to find Whitlock snoring in the porter's chair. He shook his head and fetched Audrey's pelisse and hat himself.

"Other than Sir Gabriel?" he said, thinking. "Stevens."

"But he's Tyne's partner."

"Yes. But Tyne is a bully, and something tells me Stevens would be happy to see him gone." Hugh helped Audrey into her pelisse, but as he did, he turned her to face him and gripped her shoulders. "Finding the Sanctuary is only a small part of this. We need a suspect and evidence against him. At this point, we have nothing."

"Bethany's last known location was the Sanctuary. It should be enough for Sir Gabriel to insist on questioning someone there, especially now that we know where it is."

Hugh nodded. "All right. I'll visit Sir Gabriel first thing tomorrow." He recalled his plan to visit Mr. Gye with Thornton as well. However, right then he was far too exhausted to explain what he and Thornton had theorized, about the Sanctuary having some vendetta against the pleasure gardens.

She opened the front door. "And then we will go to Burdick Close. Don't bother to argue about my presence. The sooner we figure this out, the sooner we can marry, and that means the sooner I can discover what your specialty interest *really* is."

Audrey then whirled through the front door, shutting it behind her. Hugh stood in the sudden silence, speechless.

"What's your specialty interest?"

Hugh turned. Sir was on the stairs, arms and ankles crossed as he leaned against the wall.

"How long have you been standing there?" He glimpsed the opening to the study, wondering about the view from there. Thankfully, his desk and chair weren't in sight.

"Long enough to suspect she's always going to get what she wants."

Hugh locked the door and after a snort from the sleeping butler, started back for his study. "Go to bed, Sir."

CHAPTER SIXTEEN

The shouting coming from within Michael's study was growing to a fevered pitch, and Audrey worried that soon, people walking past on Curzon Street would even hear it.

She hesitated at the bottom of the stairs. Privacy was a sacred thing. Just because she lived under the same roof as Michael, Genie, and Cassie, it didn't mean she needed to be part of every conversation. Or in this case, dispute. However, she'd not heard Michael bellow this significantly in a long time. Perhaps ever.

Once again, he and Cassie were quarreling over the release of her inheritance once she reached her majority. Genie was with them, but her voice was so low and calm, it was barely audible through the closed doors. Her usual pacifying presence did not seem to be having much of an effect.

Earlier, on her way to the front hall, Audrey had heard raised voices in the study. She'd been checking with the footman at the front door, to be sure no message from Hugh had been forgotten in the salver. Hugh said he would go to see Sir Gabriel first thing, and she'd been dressed and ready to hear the outcome for two hours. It was noon and she'd yet to hear from him. Passing back through to the stairs, she'd only intended to listen outside the study doors for a moment, but now minutes had passed.

Cassie would come straight to her afterward to divulge the argument in its entirety anyway, so for efficiency, it would be better to simply join them. She drew a breath and pushed open the study doors.

"...you are not equipped for such a thing!" Michael was saying before all eyes skipped toward Audrey.

Cassie and Genie beseeched her with pleading looks. Cassie, wanting Audrey to come to her defense, and Genie, wanting her help in diffusing the argument. Michael tossed up his arms at the addition of another female.

"Unless you would like the neighbors to discuss your private matters, I'd advise you all to lower your voices," Audrey said. "Excepting Genie, of course."

Cassie crossed her arms tightly. "He refuses to listen."

"She refuses to see good sense," he shot back. "If you refuse to ever marry, you will find yourself set apart in society."

"Maybe I wouldn't mind that very much," she said.

"There are precious few options for unmarried women, Cassie, even heiresses." Michael looked undone by the argument as he tugged at his already drooping cravat.

"Why should I be content with marrying some man just so I might be able to mingle better in society? I want more than that out of my life, thank you."

Genie, who stood between the brother and sister as a kind of buffer, turned toward Cassie. "And you should want more than to just marry *some man*. You should be able to marry the man of your choice, and Michael is not saying otherwise."

Audrey wished Genie's good sense would be taken to heart, but she knew the mulish cast of Cassie's expression too well.

"I have yet to meet anyone who I would even wish to take a stroll with, let alone marry."

"Perhaps you would, if you would give any suitor an honest chance."

Cassie deftly swerved away from Michael's cutting observation. "This discussion isn't about whether I marry or not. It's about receiving the inheritance our father settled on me."

"As I have already stated, you are not equipped to manage such a fortune."

"Equipped?" Cassie balked.

"Yes, equipped—with good sense!" Michael roared, his patience visibly breaking. "One only need look at the debacle with Renfry to prove it!"

Audrey winced, and Cassie's face turned to stone as she stared at her brother. Even Genie appeared stunned, her hand settling over her lips.

"How dare you throw that into my face?" Though she spoke softly, Cassie's vehemence filled the suddenly quiet room.

Michael seemed to realize his blunder but, in his stubbornness, wouldn't be moved toward contrition. "You were foolish. Too trusting, too naïve."

"Michael," Genie started to say, but she didn't appear to know how to continue.

Audrey went to Cassie's side and took her hand. Her

fingers were slack, though, as if too stunned to grip hers in return.

"You've been sheltered, Cassie," he went on. "Coddled and spoiled and you've no idea the realities of managing more than your pin money."

"That is unfair," Audrey said, feeling the cut even though he hadn't made it toward her. "She hasn't been given the chance."

He turned his incisive eyes toward her. "And you think I should give her that chance with an income of nearly two thousand pounds a year?"

"Yes, because it is mine, not yours," Cassie replied. "You cannot withhold it from me."

"Legally, I can, as it is in a trust, and I am the holder of that trust. Besides, what would you even do with it?" Michael asked.

Cassie ripped her hand from Audrey's. "Maybe I would use it to help other women like me to escape from the overbearing men in their lives!"

He rolled his eyes. "Like you?"

"Yes, I was foolish. I was trusting. I believed the lies of a man because all my life I had been taught to trust them, depend upon them, know that they are honorable. Well now I know they aren't."

Audrey tried to re-capture her hand. "Not all men are dishonorable, Cassie."

She moved away, toward the study doors, leaving Audrey grasping at air.

"They want only two things: money and pleasure. I know I'm not the only woman who's been taken for a fool." She stopped then and turned, her eyes bright. "Maybe I will use my fortune to help other women like me. Women who have nowhere else to turn."

Michael threw up his hands. "You speak as if you don't have anyone to support you."

"Is this what you call being supportive? I am living under your thumb, brother, and unless I agree to replace your thumb with some other man's whose only interest in me is my money and my body, then you will withhold what is rightfully mine."

"You are being vulgar."

"And you are being a tyrant!" she returned. "Very well. If you don't wish to give me my inheritance, I will find a way to make my own living."

Cassie seemed to sway with the statement, perhaps realizing the enormity of the threat. But then she turned on her heel and stormed out.

All was quiet for a few moments in the wake of her departure. Audrey was glad she'd joined them. She hadn't been an ounce of help, but at least now Cassie wouldn't have to work herself up into a froth by retelling the story to her later.

"You are being too stringent with her." Genie's tone was gentle but unyielding.

"If you don't meet her in the middle on this," Audrey agreed, "I fear she will land herself into some trouble."

Not the same sort of trouble she'd found herself in two summers ago, when she'd allowed the roguish and charming Lord Renfry liberties and ended up needing to go away to give birth to a child in secret. She would have been ruined had anyone ever learned of it, especially since Renfry had so cruelly posted the banns to marry an exorbitantly wealthy heiress. At least he had never learned of the pregnancy.

Michael sat down heavily into a chair. "I only want what is best for her."

Genie slid her hands over his shoulders. "You must allow her the chance to determine what that means for herself."

He laid his hand on his wife's and squeezed. "I'm a blind man when it comes to Cassie. Philip would have known what to say to her."

Guilt flayed Audrey's chest when the duke and duchess took a silent moment to acknowledge their loss. These moments continued to sneak up on her, and she was always left questioning if she would ever stop feeling like a fraud.

The study doors reopened, and their butler, Barton, entered. He held a shallow silver tray in his gloved hand, and within it was a folded note.

"A messenger has just delivered this for you, Dowager Duchess."

Finally, she thought, eagerly taking the note. But even before breaking the wax seal, her hopes foundered. It wasn't from Hugh. The handwriting addressing Audrey was unfamiliar.

"Excuse me," Audrey said to Michael and Genie, who were looking on with curiosity. She left the study, reading the note as she went. It was from Flora Bertram.

Please come as soon as you can. My sister has not been home in a day, and I am frightened that something has happened to her, as it did to Bethie.

Audrey stopped in the middle of the hall, the breath driven from her lungs. Gwendolyn had been missing? For a day?

"Are you leaving?" Cassie was suddenly standing right in front of Audrey. She had not gone running to her room as expected. "I'm coming with you if you are. I need to get away from this house and my insufferable brother."

Audrey's heart re-started, and she folded the note, stuffing it into her pocket as she made a decision. She signaled a footman and requested a carriage be brought around, and quickly.

"I need you to wait here for Hugh," she told Cassie.

She scowled. "For Hugh?"

"He is due to send word or come here himself, only I'm not sure when. But it's important that when he does, you tell him that I've gone to the Bertram residence on Fitzroy Square. Tell him Gwendolyn has not been seen for a day."

She followed on Audrey's heels to the front door. "Who is Gwendolyn? What is this about?"

Another footman hurried to open the door for her, and she was grateful she'd already been dressed and ready to depart at a moment's notice. "I can't explain right now, but Hugh will understand. Please, Cassie, this is important."

"Very well, I will tell him, but Audrey." She grabbed her hand before she could dart outside. "Be careful."

Flora was sitting in the front window of her house when Audrey arrived. As soon as she stepped from her carriage, the girl jumped up and pointed to the left. Her motions were animated, and Audrey read the instruction clearly: she didn't want Audrey to knock on the front door but to go around to the back of the house. Mrs. Bertram had not summoned her, and likely did not know that Flora had. The young girl disappeared from the window.

"Carrigan, wait here." Audrey started for the corner of the house, where a narrow lane cut back to a mews.

Within a minute, Flora opened a gate and slipped out onto the pavement. With one eye on the windows of her home, she motioned for Audrey to come stand with her behind the screen of a trellis, cascading with purple wisteria.

"I'm so glad you've come, Your Grace," she said, her breaths quick and words rushed. "No one will listen to me."

Her eyes were swollen and red from crying, and her voice was hoarse.

"Tell me what you know," she encouraged Flora. "I'm listening."

"After we learned Bethie had...died," she stopped to take a quivery breath, "Gwen became frightened. She kept telling me to stay out of the windows and draw the drapes."

"Did she think someone was watching the house?" At Gunter's, she'd been worried about being seen and overheard.

"She would only say that the less I knew, the safer I would be. But yes, I think someone was."

With the sensation of being elbowed in the stomach, Audrey closed her eyes. How could she have been so careless? She should have thought to call on Gwendolyn after news of Bethany's death arrived. At Gunter's, any of the posh ton taking their ices in Berkeley Square might have witnessed her meeting with Audrey and Hugh. Though, they had only spoken of the meeting with one person: Sir Gabriel.

"When did your sister disappear?" Audrey asked after

pushing away the disenchanting thought that Hugh might have been wrong about the magistrate.

"Yesterday. She went to Bond Street with Mama, and while Mama was in with the milliner, Gwen went into a bookshop. Mama said she came back to the carriage and waited fifteen minutes before going into the shop herself, looking for her. But the bookseller said Gwen had left at least twenty minutes before that."

"Did the bookseller say if she left with anyone?"

Flora shook her head of dark curls. "I don't know. Mama was too flustered to ask, I presume."

Gwendolyn had been taken on Bond Street, in full daylight? And no one had noticed.

"Mama returned home in such distress. Now she's in a complete panic. She thinks Gwen must have run off to elope, the way Bethie had..." Flora choked on her words and went quiet.

"You said no one is listening to you," Audrey reminded her. "What did you mean by that?"

Flora sniffled, then firmed her quivering chin. "A carriage. I saw it a few times before Gwen told me to stay out of the windows. It was strange."

"Strange how?"

"There was something on the door. It looked like a cross, but it was—"

"Upside down." Audrey went cold as Flora nodded vigorously.

"Yes! But how did you know?" Her amazement wilted as she seemed to understand. "You've seen it too."

"Yes."

If someone from the Sanctuary had been driving past her

house, and then she disappeared from Bond Street... Gwendolyn was in danger.

"You were right to send for me. What you've said is very helpful, Flora," she said, not wanting to distress her any further. "I will send word to you as soon as I can."

She started away, and Flora fell into step beside her. "Will you help find her, Your Grace?"

Making promises that Gwendolyn would be safely returned could be premature, and Audrey didn't want to lie to her. She turned Flora back toward the gate. "I won't stop until I do. But you must stay here."

If anyone learned Flora had been speaking of the Sanctuary, she could also be targeted. Audrey gave her a little nudge. "Go inside your home. Please."

She whirled around and ran back through the gate obediently. With any hope, she would stay put. On the way back to her carriage, Audrey observed the square and the conveyances nearby, looking for a coach with a cross. She didn't see one. However, she did see a phaeton drawing up behind her carriage. Sir was at the reins in the front seat. Next to him was Hugh, and in the back seat were Thornton and Cassie. Her sister-in-law waved. "I wouldn't tell them where you'd gone unless they brought me with them."

Thornton's irritated expression confirmed her claim.

Hugh hopped down from the phaeton, but before he could inquire, Audrey explained what Flora had revealed. He swore under his breath.

"Damn it. I've just come from Bow Street. Sir Gabriel won't send men to Burdick Close with so little evidence to go on. He can't just storm into a private home because we *think* it might be the Sanctuary."

"If he knew Gwendolyn was now missing, he would have to do something, wouldn't he?" The knot in Audrey's stomach tightened. "And if he doesn't, then we must ask ourselves why. Hugh, he is the only person we spoke to about Gwendolyn's information on the Sanctuary."

He shook his head. "He may have told Tyne."

There wasn't time to argue with him. She turned to Cassie, still in the back seat of the phaeton. "I'm glad you've come."

"You are?" Cassie peered at Thornton smugly. "See, I told you she wouldn't mind."

The physician looked as though he wanted to make a snapping reply, but Audrey spoke up first. "Yes, you and Sir can go with Carrigan in my brougham to Bow Street, to inform Sir Gabriel that unless he takes his men to Burdick Close right now, another young woman may die."

Cassie paled, her haughty expression falling.

Sir threw down the reins and stood. "If this has to do with whoever killed my father, I'm not wasting time at Bow Street. I'm going with you."

It wasn't for her to say yes or no. It wasn't for Hugh to approve either and he seemed to know it. He nodded to Sir, though with reluctance.

Hugh handed Cassie down to the pavement, her pleasure now visibly reduced. "What if Sir Gabriel does not listen to me?"

"Perhaps I should go with you," Thornton said, starting to stand. It was all Cassie needed to instantly find her poise.

"Don't be absurd, I am perfectly capable." She quickly pecked Audrey on the cheek, then went to Carrigan, who tipped his hat.

"Be careful, Your Grace," was all he said before seeing Cassie into the brougham.

Hugh held out his hand to Audrey. "To Vauxhall then?"

She took his hand and looked to their driver. "As fast as you can, Sir."

CHAPTER
SEVENTEEN

The coach field at Vauxhall held paltry few conveyances when Sir parked the phaeton. That it was early in the afternoon didn't signify. The pleasure gardens should have been bustling, even at this time of day. Children, families, and anyone who did not enjoy the crush of dinner revelry and entertainment would come to the grounds during daylight. The quiet of the coach field didn't bode well for the proprietor at all.

"There is no benefit in stopping to speak with Mr. Gye," Audrey said. "We should go directly to Burdick Close."

Hugh could understand her desire to leap into action, and she'd been consistent in her opinion ever since Hugh mentioned going to the Vauxhall proprietor's building first, to see if the owner was in his offices. But Hugh wouldn't relent.

"If he can provide any information on the Sanctuary at all before we go charging in, it will be worth the delay," he explained. *Again*.

After combing over the discussion that he and Thornton

had the previous evening, it seemed entirely likely that Mr. Gye had an enemy, one tied to the Sanctuary, and who might wish to damage him. Dumping bodies at his place of business would certainly do it. It was also entirely possible the man himself was a member of this secret society.

"I agree," Thornton said as he stood from the seat. "It pays to be prudent."

Her glare scorched the physician, even as she took his proffered hand and descended to the grass.

"Sir, stay with the phaeton," Hugh said.

Surprising no one, Sir scoffed. "I'm not going to sit here on my arse. That ain't helpful."

"It helps if you prevent my rig from being stolen. I just bought the bloody thing," Hugh said. "We'll return shortly."

He wasn't entirely sure they would, but if it kept Sir in the coach field for a little while, the lie would be worth it. If they were going to be making their way to Burdick Close, he didn't want both Audrey and Sir there to divide his attention. Already, his muscles were strung tight with the knowledge that Gwendolyn was in danger. Perhaps already dead. He should have thought to check on her. It seemed she'd had good reason to be afraid at the tea shop after all.

They entered the proprietor's house and learned Mr. Gye was, in fact, in. An attendant led them to an office overlooking the entrance pavilion in the gardens. The windows were open, inviting in a breeze, though the proprietor himself was flushed as he stood at his desk, bracing himself over a stack of papers. Several crates were on the floor around the desk, some lidded and others open. Mr. Gye looked to be packing.

He glanced up from the papers, wearing a deep frown.

"Your Grace. My lordships," he said, an insincere grin attempting to stretch its way across his lips. "To what do I owe the pleasure?" His attention jumped back toward the papers that he'd been staring daggers at.

"We've caught you at a bad time," Hugh said. "It appears as though you're moving."

"Selling," he said grimly. Mr. Gye reached behind his stock and rubbed the back of his neck.

"Already?" Audrey asked. "You've only been leasing Vauxhall for a year or two, haven't you?"

Mr. Gye appeared green at the gills at the reminder. "Yes, and it appears I am finished here. Profits are plummeting, people are staying away, and I cannot count how many articles there have been calling me corrupt for trying to hush up the murders."

Hugh sealed his lips. Those articles might not have been very far from the truth.

"If these are not signs from above that I should wash my hands of the place, I should call myself a fool," Mr. Gye concluded.

Through the window overlooking the pavilion, the lack of people strolling demonstrated his concern.

"People are frightened to come here," he said, following Hugh's gaze.

It begged the question, yet again, as to why the Sanctuary had left the bodies here for discovery. Why not throw them into the Thames, or dump them out into a street gutter? There was a reason. Perhaps it had to do with Gye himself.

"Is there anyone you can think of who might want to damage your business here?" Hugh asked. "Anyone who dislikes you, or who might wish to make things difficult for you?"

The proprietor scoffed. "Not a soul. I don't have any enemies."

"Every businessman has enemies," Thornton argued. "People you've passed on the way up, maybe never even noticing them."

"I resent that," he snapped. "I'm not some power-hungry ogre. I'm on good terms with all my workers. It is this dead body business that is ruining me."

"The bodies were left at your establishment for a reason," Hugh said. "There is purpose behind it. We're trying to figure out what that is."

Mr. Gye sighed and started back for his desk and the pile of papers that Hugh now suspected were letters of sale. "The Bow Street Runners say it is but a prank. One of the men I had posted on night security must have accepted a bribe. I've dismissed the lot of them, hoping to ease the sale of the lease, and hired a whole new detail, but I fear it's too little too late."

"Where is the Sanctuary, Mr. Gye?" Audrey's question cut straight through, to the reason for their visit. Her unswerving focus on finding Gwendolyn overrode everything else. Even the smallest thread Hugh now had the impulse to pull, regarding the lease for Vauxhall being up for sale.

Mr. Gye screwed up his face. "Come again? What is the...what?"

"The Sanctuary," Audrey repeated.

There was no flare of his eyes or nostrils, no loss of color in his cheeks. Only a grumble of impatience. "Is that some sort of church?"

Hugh peered at him, askance. "You've never heard of it?"

"I have not," Gye said, patience ebbing. "Does it have to do with these murders?"

"Possibly," Hugh answered.

Gye tossed his hands upward. "Why would a church want to kill people and leave them at my pleasure gardens?"

"It isn't a church. But maybe the intent was to drive you out," Hugh said, pulling at that thread. "Owning Vauxhall's lease could be highly profitable, I imagine."

Gye wrinkled his brow with a meaningful look, one that confirmed Hugh's presumption. "It is also very costly," he added. "I know it has only been a week since attendance fell off, but I pride myself on my business instinct. Recovery is not ensured, and this is too good of an opportunity."

Hugh frowned, not understanding his meaning. Thornton, however, did.

"Opportunity? Do you mean to say you have a buyer?" he asked.

Mr. Gye brightened. "I do. As it turns out, my steward is still interested and quite flush."

"*Still* interested? He wanted to purchase it before?" Audrey asked.

"Yes, there were several bids last year when the Tyers-Barretts put up the lease," Mr. Gye said, shuffling through the papers. "But Vauxhall needed a true businessman at the helm, someone who would revive the place. I did exactly that." He sighed as he set the papers down again. "For a little while at least."

Hugh recalled the steward's reaction to Mr. Gye on the night Givens was found, when Mr. Gye had tried to trundle

Audrey off with him, believing the scene of a crime was no place for lady. His name escaped Hugh, but he did clearly remember the look of animosity he'd given the proprietor.

"If I recall, you said your steward had worked for the Tyers-Barretts?" Audrey said.

"Yes, that's correct. And his father and grandfather before him. Their family residence even abuts the property. Fine man. Very efficient. But to be completely honest, his temperament isn't entirely conducive to the job. He's not, shall we say, particularly solicitous to our guests. Far too serious. And this is a pleasure garden!" He opened his arms theatrically toward the windows.

Hugh's pulse slowed; everything around him seemed to decelerate too.

"Your steward's residence abuts the property?" Audrey asked Mr. Gye. "It is connected to Vauxhall's grounds?"

"Of course. It's imperative that he have access to the grounds at all hours. Now, if you don't mind," he said, looking about the office, "I do have quite a bit to manage here. If you've asked all your questions...?"

Hugh held up his hand, recalling the man's name. "Was Mr. Hammond upset that his bid wasn't chosen last year?"

"Not at all. He completely understood. And Hammond is his Christian name. His family name is Abbey."

The small hairs on the back of Hugh's neck stood up. Audrey whirled so fast to face him, her skirt billowed.

"Abbey!" she exclaimed.

"Known to be a sanctuary for nuns and monks," Thornton said, then with a low whistle, "The man has a twisted sense of humor."

"It's a play on his name," Audrey said as Hugh's mind and heartbeat began to race again.

He turned to Mr. Gye. "Where is he?"

The proprietor peered at them quizzically. "Not here yet, I'm afraid. What is this about?"

"Does he live on Burdick Close?" Audrey asked, overruling his question.

"Yes, that's right. Now, I must insist, what is—"

"Where is his access to the grounds?" Hugh cut in. When Gye sealed his lips and looked to vacillate, Hugh closed in on the man until he loomed over him. "Bow Street officers are on their way. There is a young woman missing, and we've every reason to believe she is with your steward. Now, we need to know—where is his access point?"

Gye only wavered another second or two before capitulating. "In the southeastern corner of the grounds, near the Firework Tower. It's a door set into a stone wall. It leads to a tunnel that runs to his house."

The Firework Tower, Hugh knew, was secluded on the grounds, far from the main entertainments near the orchestra and supper boxes.

"Is the door locked?" Hugh asked.

Gye opened a desk drawer and with slightly shaking fingers, retrieved a ring of keys. "I think this is the one." He fumbled to get one of the several keys off the large ring. He then placed it into Hugh's waiting palm.

"Good. Audrey," he turned to her. "Go to Sir. Tell him everything, and then go together across the bridge and signal the first foot patrolman you see. I don't trust anyone on the south side of the Thames. They could all be in Abbey's pocket."

As he'd been speaking, she'd been visibly bristling, and he was ready for the coming dispute.

"I'm staying with you." She said it more calmly than he'd expected. She then addressed Mr. Gye. "There is a young man in a phaeton in the coach field. He answers to the name Sir."

Gye balked as he understood her intent. "Your Grace, you must be in jest. You want *me* to go across the bridge and signal a foot patrol? Viscount, surely, I would be of better assistance to you. I will show you where the door is."

Audrey pinned Hugh with a stare, waiting for his reply. Although he would have rather had her and Sir both safely away from Burdick Close and whatever was unfolding there, he could not keep pushing her away, if only to shield her from harm. Audrey had already proven to be keen and competent under duress. In fact, Mr. Gye's offer to assist fell vastly short of what Hugh knew was needed: Trust. Allegiance. The ability to read his thoughts. Just because Gye was a man did not mean he'd be a better partner when faced with some dire situation.

Hugh clenched his jaw. "We'll find the door, Mr. Gye. It's imperative you help by alerting the young man in the phaeton as to what is happening and sending patrolmen to Abbey's residence as soon as they've gathered a number of men. One or two alone won't help."

Audrey beamed at him for a few glowing moments as the proprietor accepted his task and took up his hat. She shifted her countenance to one of grim determination as she, Hugh, and Thornton took an open terrace door that led directly out into the gardens.

"You have your pistol?" he asked Thornton.

His friend lifted his coat to display the polished black handle of his flintlock. “I’ve learned that when I’m with you, I tend to need it.”

CHAPTER
EIGHTEEN

The Firework Tower was within sight, and still, Hugh had not relented.

"I would have been more use fetching a foot patrol across the river than I will be standing guard," Audrey groused, keeping her eyes peeled for the access door Mr. Gye had told them about.

The door Hugh had commanded she stand next to while he and Lord Thornton entered and pursued Hammond Abbey. *On their own.* It had certainly tamed the bubbling of elation she'd felt after discovering who was behind the Sanctuary: Hammond Abbey, the sour-faced steward she'd briefly met the night Mr. Givens had been found at the Cascade. He'd been easy to overlook, with nothing much remarkable about him, other than his obvious dislike for his employer. Not that Mr. Gye had noticed.

Now, however, the man wearing the devil mask in the vision the cuff links had imparted, *did* resemble what she recalled of the steward. Black, curled hair with streaks of gray. Tall and lanky. A pronounced curved stoop to his shoulders.

"We need someone on this side of the tunnel unless there is trouble, and also to direct the foot patrols, should Gye direct them this way," Hugh replied as they passed a pair of marquees built to house onlookers for the firework displays.

"I know what you are doing," Audrey said.

He did not stop his march toward the boundary of the gardens to look at her. "I told you that I would always say when something was too dangerous, whether you wanted to hear it or not. This is one of those times."

Audrey balled her hands into fists, then noticed an arched wooden door set into a tall stone wall. She swallowed her reply as nerves prickled her skin. The door was half hidden behind some hanging ivy, but closer, Audrey noted the ground next to it had been worn down to smooth dirt. This entrance was used often.

Hugh inserted the key into the lock and twisted. It gave and the door swung open, revealing an arched wall and ceiling constructed of pale brick leading into a darkened space.

"There must be something else that I can do than just stand here," she said.

Thornton stepped into the tunnel but didn't go far. Just far enough away to give Hugh a moment with her.

"Audrey." He took her by the shoulders and cocked his head, waiting for her to look at him. "We have no idea what we will meet with in there. We are going in blind. If Gwendolyn is still alive, I need to be able to help her. If you are with me, no other person in the world is going to matter to me. I will choose to protect *you*, not her."

She despised the feeling of being left behind—and of having to admit that what he said wasn't wholly unreasonable. Audrey did want him to concentrate on finding and rescuing Gwendolyn, not her. She crossed her arms.

"Very well. But Hugh..." She ran her palms down the front of his waistcoat. "You must be careful."

Hugh took one of her hands in his, kissed it, and then stepped into the tunnel with Thornton. They partially closed the door behind them, and Audrey let out a groan as she faced the grounds. The parkland was quiet and serene, while she felt nothing of the sort. She kicked at the dirt, frustrated. And worried. What if Gwendolyn had already been silenced? She dreaded the idea of having to see Flora Bertram again and telling her that she'd failed to save her sister.

Audrey walked a few paces, turned, and then paced some more. There was nothing to do. Nothing but stand and wait, and she'd never been any good at that. It made her muscles bunch tightly, her skin uncomfortable. Backing up from the stone wall a bit, she was able to see the rooftop peaks of a house. A weathervane topped one ridge, and she held her breath. Instead of an arrow pointing the direction of the wind, the decoration was a wrought iron cross. The brass had oxidized over time to a pale green. Did that indicate that the Sanctuary wasn't anything new?

How long had it been operating? If Mr. Abbey was flush, as Mr. Gye had said, the money he made with the Sanctuary had to be exorbitant. Places like White's and Brooks's, and even the Seven Sins, were only available to those who could afford the high membership dues. And if the Sanctuary offered up uniquely perverted pleasures, the singularity of it could come at a much higher premium.

If he took over Vauxhall, Mr. Abbey could tie his society to the pleasure gardens. Expand his empire. Already, the entertainment grounds were known for its seedier side, where trysts and hired companionship could unfold in the remoteness of the parkland at night. Audrey felt ill thinking of the young women who might be lured to the Sanctuary the way Bethany had been.

"Your Grace."

The voice came at her back, and she leaped as she whirled. But then, she let out breathy laugh. "Good heavens, Officer Stevens. Where did you come from?"

The Bow Street officer had come upon her without a sound. He held his hands clasped behind his back. He narrowed his eyes. "I didn't expect to see you here, Your Grace."

He was alone, without his partner, Officer Tyne. For that, Audrey was grateful. Especially if what Hugh suspected about him was true.

"I didn't expect to be here either," she replied. "You've gotten here rather quickly. Did you meet with Mr. Gye?"

Stevens nodded, but it was a sad, almost regretful motion. And then, he unclasped his hands from behind his back to bring them forward. Gripped in one hand was a small pistol.

"I did. My apologies, Your Grace, but I'll ask you to do as I say."

Though he did not aim the barrel at her, her next breaths shriveled in her lungs. "Stevens..." She couldn't continue. Couldn't understand. But then, with paralyzing fury, she did.

"It isn't Officer Tyne. You're the Bow Street man that belongs to the Sanctuary."

Stevens raised the pistol slightly in a gesture for her to move. "Into the tunnel."

"How could you?" she asked. "Hugh trusted you!"

"I don't want to have to do this here," Stevens said.

"You don't have to do it at all."

He shook his head. "That isn't an option. Into the tunnel. Now."

With the pistol now aligned with her chest, Audrey saw not just Stevens, but Mr. Fellows as he'd aimed his gun at her while she'd been trying to escape his houseboat. And Mr. Henley, as he'd leveled his weapon on her and Millie as he'd been taking them away from Greenbriar. Both men had fired their shots. Both had struck her. She'd been lucky those times, but something told her she would not be so lucky now. Not with Stevens exposing his duplicity to her. He didn't plan to let her live long enough to breathe a word about it to anyone. Eager to delay him, Audrey did as she was told and stepped into the tunnel. Stevens closed the door behind him, and she heard the click of a lock being bolted into place.

"What did you do to Mr. Gye?" She raised her voice, hoping the tunnel would carry it onward, toward wherever Hugh and Thornton were. If they were even still in the tunnel.

"Hush up," Stevens barked. But then answered, "Gye's perfectly fine. For now, at least. I came out here after Marsden saw Sir Gabriel this morning, talking about Burdick Close."

"You knew he'd figured out where the Sanctuary was," Audrey said, again risking Stevens's anger by throwing her voice.

"I said quiet," he spat.

Audrey stumbled over a rise in the tunnel floor. She caught herself, and realized it wasn't totally dark. Small openings in the ceiling bricks, evenly spaced apart, let in dappled light; looking up, Audrey saw blue sky. There had to be a walkway running right over the tunnel, interspersed with grates.

"I saw Gye outside the proprietor's house. He said Marsden had ordered him to fetch more foot patrols. That his steward was in some trouble."

"We know everything," Audrey said. "And there will be foot patrols and officers and even Sir Gabriel himself here soon."

"Maybe there would've been, had I not told Gye to go back inside and that I'd take care of everything." The point of the pistol nudged her in the back, between her shoulders. "Move faster."

Ahead, the grates in the ceiling let in sunlight, revealing where the tunnel branched.

"Go right," Stevens instructed.

"What is to the left?" she asked.

"Nothing for you to see." He pushed her again from behind, and she followed the right branch.

Which way had Hugh and Thornton gone?

At the base of a staircase, he barked, "Go up."

Unless she chose to grapple with him here, she had no other choice. Wherever the stairs led, she might have access to something to defend herself with.

She climbed, her mind racing, her heart beginning to thud out of its usual rhythm. She couldn't panic. Not now. The stairs led to a long passageway, and as Stevens urged her onward, she passed several doors and the base of a stairwell. After turning down another twisting passageway, Audrey finally entered a vast hall with parquet flooring polished to a gleaming shine, beamed ceilings inset with murals, a long table with at least two dozen chairs surrounding it, couches and chairs, and a massive fireplace. And in front of that fireplace, tied to one of the dining table chairs with blood smearing his face, was Lord Thornton.

Standing over him was the burly man from her visions, the one who'd tried to pick a fight with Sir outside Burdick Close. He brought his fist across Thornton's chin, and more viscera arced through the air.

"Grant!" Audrey started forward. Stevens caught her arm and hauled her back. She wrestled to toss him off, but he only dug in his fingers harder.

"Ah. The Dowager Duchess joins us, at last."

Another man stood from a chair near the fireplace where he'd been watching the brute beat Thornton. He turned to greet them.

"Hammond Abbey," Audrey said, recognizing Mr. Gye's steward.

He cut a grin, but she could recall seeing the grotesque devil mask with its pronged, lolling tongue.

"Let her leave, Abbey. She's nothing to do with this," Thornton slurred, his mouth glistening with blood. His nose looked broken, and a gash ran alongside one eye.

The rest of the great hall was empty. Where was Hugh?

"When a lamb walks into the Sanctuary, we don't just let it leave." The steward strolled forward. "Well done, Stevens. Taking the initiative, I see."

"Gye knows about you," the Bow Street officer said,

practically shouting in Audrey's ear. "She says foot patrols and the magistrate will be coming."

Mr. Abbey's slick grin fell off. "Is that so. Well, Stevens, why are you still standing here? Go head them off. Or else what use are you to me?"

Stevens released Audrey's arm and darted her a look. The barest trace of guilt and indecision lingered in his expression. He must have been the one to inform Abbey about Lord Stromburg and Madame Lee's visit to Bow Street. Had he also given up Harlan Givens as an informant for Officer Tyne? And now, he was leaving her to her fate. She rubbed her arm, where he'd held her in his bruising grip.

"You are nothing but a coward," she told him.

Stevens averted his eyes, and then hurried from the room.

"You are correct, Your Grace. He is a coward," Abbey agreed. "But a useful one."

"What should we do, Mr. Abbey?" the man standing over Thornton asked. When Abbey twitched his head, turning his ear sharply toward him, the man repeated, louder now, "Mr. Abbey, what should we do?"

Audrey stilled her hand. The bruise on her arm went numb as she blinked and gaped.

"You're deaf," she said, and when Abbey didn't respond or react, she raised her voice. "You're deaf in one ear, aren't you?"

He heard her this time. He seared her with a glare before it flashed over to humor.

"The left ear," she added, thinking of which ear had been taken from the three bodies left in the pleasure gardens.

"Clever. Stevens told me you were a shrew, but I didn't quite believe it. My mistake."

Audrey heard the telltale sound of his deafness now. His vowels and consonants weren't fully formed, something that would be a challenge for anyone who was unable to fully replicate speech.

"Why cut off their ears?" she asked.

For a moment, she thought Abbey might gesture for his brute to grab her and take her away. He could easily turn on his heel and leave the room, ignoring her question. Instead, he strolled across the hall toward her. Instinct demanded that she back away from him, but she held firm to her spot on the floor.

"So many people think that because I am deaf here"—he touched his left ear—"I am also deaf here." He touched his right ear. "When someone betrays me, I like to demonstrate how, even with just one working ear, I know everything that is said about me or my Sanctuary. When I cut off their ear, I tell them they are about to die. By the look in their eyes, they hear me perfectly well." He grinned. "Even with just one working ear."

At that deranged grin of his, her tongue went heavy and useless. She'd met criminals. Killers. This man, however, seemed to take such pleasure in what he'd done. He frightened her as no one ever had before.

But he seemed to enjoy talking, and for the moment at least, she was still breathing.

"What have you done with Gwendolyn Bertram?"

"You should concern yourself with what I'm going to do with you."

Fear chilled her veins. Cassie had been tasked with sending Bow Street patrols to this place, but what if they weren't fast enough? What if Sir Gabriel dismissed Cassie?

What if Sir was still completely clueless as to what was happening, and Mr. Gye had gone back to his office to continue packing? Or what if Stevens was able to head any constable off as he'd been ordered to do?

She needed time to find some way out of this. Keeping her wits, and keeping Mr. Abbey talking, was one avenue—even if she didn't know where it would lead.

"All this because you wanted the lease to Vauxhall?" she asked.

Mr. Abbey laughed. "And you have derived that as well. Impressive. No, it was merely a good opportunity that arose out of the need to keep order. Members know the rules. Including the punishment for crossing them."

"Gwendolyn isn't a member," she said.

His chilling grin resurfaced. "After tonight, she will be. And she will not be able to speak of it without suffering the consequences."

Audrey let out a breath of relief. She was still alive, then.

Thornton, his head drooping forward, arms bound behind the chair backing, gurgled a laugh through his bloody nose and mouth. "You won't make it until tonight."

Mr. Abbey rolled his eyes and swished his finger through the air. "Martin?"

The man standing over Thornton drew back his fist and brought it down across his jaw again. Audrey winced as Thornton grunted.

Where was Hugh? Abbey had made no mention of him yet. Neither had Thornton. Audrey met the physician's eyes as he spit blood, and he gave the barest shake of his head. A signal to stay quiet about Hugh, she deduced.

"Bethany Silas," she said, wanting to keep Abbey talking. "What happened to her?"

She was nearly afraid to hear the answer.

"Unfortunately for her, she befriended Comstock," he replied with a blasé shrug of his shoulder. He inspected his nails. "She was a willing aspirant."

Aspirant. The word made her stomach roll.

"Why would she ever wish to join a club like yours?" Disgust drenched her words, and by the slipping of his easy, amused expression, Abbey heard it. That smirk was his mask, she realized. His true countenance was the one he'd worn while glaring at Mr. Gye at the Cascade. One of bitter hatred.

"The Sanctuary is no *club*," he said. "This is a brotherhood, one my father founded. It has been building in strength for decades, operating out of sight, protecting its brothers *and* its sisters—"

"You call passing young women around for some twisted initiation and strangling them *protection*? You are deranged."

Martin moved away from the bleeding physician and came toward Audrey. But Abbey raised a hand to stay the brute.

"Most members can restrain themselves. Sadly, Comstock was not one of them." He kept strolling toward Audrey, the firelight from the hearth glowing over the black superfine of his jacket. She stood a few strides away from the dining table, which was dressed for dinner with silver cutlery and china plates. Audrey pretended to scuttle back, away from him in fear, and she went in the direction of the table.

"Things tend to become heated during our initiations," Abbey said, stalking her. She made a show of backing up into a chair at the table and being startled by it. If she reached behind her, she could close her hand around a fork or knife.

But Abbey must have foreseen her plan. He grabbed her wrist and tugged her to him before she could grab for a utensil. He spun her so her back sealed to his chest and wrapped an arm around her, pinning her arms into place at her side. His other hand closed around her throat.

"Comstock had a penchant for asphyxiation," he said, his lips at Audrey's ear.

"Release her, Abbey!" Thornton shouted, but Martin only struck him again.

The fingers around Audrey's throat closed with slightly more pressure. "I gave him a second chance after what happened with Stromburg's initiate." *The woman from the Red Lotus,* Audrey thought as her pulse began to throb in her ears. *Comstock* had been the one to strangle her. And then, he'd strangled Bethany too.

"But we must weed out troublesome members before the rot sets in," Abbey whispered into her ear. "You, Your Grace, are very troublesome. As is the Viscount Neatham. Where is he? Oh, I know he would never allow you to come here all on your own."

Her ears were pounding now, her breaths constricted. But elation still managed to weaken her legs. They may have captured Thornton, but not Hugh.

"He's about to bring Bow Street down on your head," she rasped, her words barely able to form for the pressure on her throat.

Air shuttled into her lungs as Mr. Abbey released her and shoved her away. She fell to her knees, lightheaded from the sudden influx of oxygen.

"The viscount is here, I am certain of it now," Abbey said. "Martin, put her in with the other. Then send Trunchett and Boggs to search the rooms and passageways. Don't overlook the stables. He could have come in through there."

Martin hauled Audrey to her feet, her vision tipping. Thornton thrashed at his bindings in the chair as she was dragged out of the hall.

Abbey was right. Hugh was here. Somewhere.

Audrey only prayed that he had a plan.

CHAPTER
NINETEEN

Thinking it better to split up and cover more ground, Hugh and Thornton agreed to part ways at the branch in the tunnel.

"And if one of is apprehended?" Thornton said.

"Pretend you are Sir Galahad, come to rescue the fair maiden, and are entirely alone, of course," Hugh replied.

"Or I could sell you out to save my own hide," his friend had muttered as he'd taken the branch leading right.

"If you do that, I will tell your father all about Dr. Brown in Whitechapel," he'd tossed back.

Thornton had been running a charity clinic in the slums for a few years now under the pseudonym of Dr. Brown. If the Marquess of Lindstrom were ever to learn of it, Thornton's generous annual income would surely be slashed. That clinic and his devotion to it was the one glaring flaw in Thornton's otherwise impeccably drawn character as a devil-may-care rake. And it was why Hugh knew his friend would lay down his life before selling him out.

The left branching tunnel had gone on for another

minute of twists before finally emptying out into what looked to be an underground stable. Several horses and coaches were stored there, and sure enough, the door of each coach had been emblazoned with the inverted cross. He was in the right place. The Sanctuary. That didn't give him much relief, only the vindication of being correct.

The stable was quiet; no grooms were attending the horses, nor drivers present for the coaches. At so early an hour in the afternoon, perhaps they weren't needed. The Sanctuary, Hugh supposed, would be active at night, when coaches could come and go without much notice.

Members might even access their society via the tunnel, after first spending time at Vauxhall. Operating a pleasure den right next to another source of entertainment was, Hugh had to admit, ingenious business sense. However, he could only imagine the trouble Hammond Abbey would be required to go to in order to preserve the secrecy of it. Slashing the throats and lopping off the ears of suspected informants was one way to do it.

In the silence of the stable, the echo of a voice brushed his eardrums. He cocked his head back toward the tunnel opening. The voice had only been a sound. No clear words, or even an indication of if the speaker was male or female. Audrey would not have followed him into the tunnel. He'd seen comprehension soften her angry glare when he'd admitted that he would choose to protect her over Gwendolyn. She wanted the young woman brought to safety too much to risk it.

The muffled sound might have been Thornton's voice, but there was nothing he could do about that now. He kept moving across the rough cobbled floor. The doors to the stable were shut and barred, but adjacent to them was an opening to a stairwell. The steps led up. A few horses snuffled as he passed them, perhaps sensing his tension. He had his double flintlock in hand and primed. With only two shots available, he'd have to be prudent.

After listening at the base of the stairs for any footfalls or voices, Hugh took the steps. At the top, he entered a narrow passageway. Empty, thankfully. But only a few paces along, approaching voices had him diving through the nearest open door, into what appeared to be a storage room. Hugh crouched behind a few stacked crates, taming his breaths. Bottles of wine and port lined shelves, beeswax candles filled several open crates nearby, but it was the long shelf of folded black cloaks, a feather-decorated domino atop each one, that captured his interest. Audrey had described the members of the society wearing these costumes, standing around what may as well have been a sacrificial slab. At the thought of Bethany Silas's purpose for being here, as well as Opal's from the Red Lotus, he resisted the urge to pummel something.

Had someone entered the storage room right then, he'd have gone toe-to-toe with them with a surge of ferocity. But that would only draw attention to his presence. And he needed to find Gwendolyn Bertram. If she was still alive.

The voices passed the storage room, sounding as if they were heading in the direction in which Hugh had come. After several more moments, the voices faded entirely. Hugh came out from behind the stacked crates and lingered at the exit to the room, listening again. He glanced back toward the shelf of cloaks and masks. There was no guarantee that he would not meet with someone once he left this room. Quickly, he took down one of the cloaks and drew it around his shoulders, bringing up the hood. Then, pulled on the domino. The mask concealed everything but his mouth and chin. The disguise would not get him very far, but it might at least give him a few extra moments of anonymity should he come across any of Abbey's men.

Hugh followed a narrow passageway, stepping lightly. The cloak billowed behind him. Within a dozen more paces, the sounds of weeping greeted him. A woman's sobs. He increased his speed, toward an open door ahead. Stopping to peer around the corner, he saw it was a large study. Dark wood paneled the walls, the windows draped with black silk, shutting out daylight. The only light at all came from a fire leaping in the hearth and from several lamps set around the room. With its leather chairs and gaming tables, it resembled the billiards room at White's. With one exception: three large bird cages hung suspended from the ceiling beams. Audrey had described a cage from her vision. The wrought iron enclosures were large enough for a human to fit inside. The cage nearest to the door, and the one at the back of the room were empty, but the middle cage was filled with the huddled form of a young woman. Gwendolyn Bertram.

Hugh moved before thinking. Only after entering the room did he see a tall man in an evening suit. He peeled off from the black marble column that he'd easily blended into.

"What are you doing in here? How'd you get in? The Sanctuary don't open for hours."

There was no question that he was hired muscle.

"Mr. Abbey has allowed me early entry," Hugh said as he continued forward, his hand gripping the flintlock under the cloak.

"Boss don't allow anyone early entry." The man squared his shoulders. "Take off the mask. Who are you?"

In her cage, Gwendolyn had come out of her hunched position. She moved, causing the cage to sway. Underneath the cage was a long table covered in a brown bear pelt. Audrey had described that table too.

"You wouldn't know me. I'm new," Hugh said without slowing. The man shook his head and reached for a tapestry rope hanging next to the column. A bell pull, which would alert others.

He slammed into the man, pushing him sideways, but not before his hand had grazed the rope. Whether it signaled on the other end, Hugh didn't know. Nor did he care when the man's elbow cracked back into his jaw. Gwendolyn screamed as Hugh staggered. He threw off the cloak and brought out his flintlock, but the man was already running. Hugh swore. He couldn't shoot a man in the back. He chased after him instead, and when he was within reach, clouted him on the back of the head with the stock of his pistol. The man collapsed, and for good measure, Hugh clobbered him again. He went still.

"Help me!" Gwendolyn threw herself against the bars of her cage and peered down. Hugh ripped off the domino. Gwendolyn gasped. "Lord Neatham!"

"How did they get you up there?" he asked even as his eyes followed the chain holding the cage to a pulley set into the ceiling beam. From there, the chain ran the length of the study ceiling, joining with the chains from the other cages.

"There, over on the wall by the other door." Gwendolyn stuck her arm through the bars to point. Three crank levers were set into the wood paneling across the room. With no time to lose, Hugh rushed forward, dodging chairs and tables, but fell short of the wall when the door near the levers opened.

He stared, dazed. "Stevens. Bloody hell, how did you—?"

"He's one of them!" Gwendolyn screeched, but not before Hugh saw the snub-nosed pistol in the officer's hand.

"Lower it, Marsden," Stevens said. With his stomach sinking toward his ankles, Hugh did. "Toss it aside."

"Stevens, you rat. I swore it was Tyne."

"That's what the duchess said too."

Alarm seared his spine and fired out along his arms. Hugh stared at the officer, his finger tensing on the trigger and nearly sending one of his two shots into the floor. "What have you done? Where is she?"

He'd thought she would be safe at the tunnel entrance.

"Toss it," Stevens repeated.

"Not until you tell me where she is."

"With Abbey."

Hugh raised his pistol, uncaring that Stevens had one trained on him. The knowledge that Audrey was with that madman stole away every ounce of fear for himself. When the officer didn't squeeze off a shot, Hugh knew he'd achieved the upper hand.

"I was only coming for the girl," Stevens said. "We can let her go, and if she cooperates, tells the foot patrolmen she ran off and nothing more, it will head them off."

"There is no 'we', Stevens. It's too late. I don't know how you got involved here, but it ends now."

"I don't want to kill you, Marsden."

Hugh saw the truth of that in the man's eyes. He'd dug himself in too deeply with this place, with Abbey. He was trapped. "You're not a murderer. Put your weapon down. I'll speak on your behalf, explain that you helped free Miss Bertram."

He shook his head, panicked laughter erupting from his throat. "I'll end up like Givens."

"You'll end sooner than that, with a bullet in your chest, if you don't put down that pistol."

Beyond the room, a woman's voice sounded. It streaked through him like a bolt of electricity. *Audrey*. She was shouting to be released.

"But if you help me, Stevens," Hugh went on, his pulse rising as he realized Audrey was likely being led to this room, to the cages. "If you can be the officer I know you truly are, I will use all my leverage to make certain you don't hang. You have my word."

The officer looked torn, his nerves shredded, as his eyes skipped between the other door, the cages, and Hugh.

Before he could give any answer, the coming commotion surged through the door across the room. A brawny man dragged Audrey behind him, wrenching and thrashing to free her arm from his grip. She saw him and went still.

"Hugh!" she cried.

Stevens swiveled on his heel. "Martin, let her go." He aimed his pistol toward the man—and at Audrey.

"Don't shoot, you idiot!" Hugh shoved the officer's arm aside. But Stevens's had already fully cocked the hammer, and at the slightest pressure of his finger on the trigger, the pistol went off.

A mirror on the wall shattered, and Gwendolyn screamed as the man holding Audrey flinched and crouched. Audrey, however, did not. Using her captor's distraction to her benefit, she swept her arm across a table and gripped a metal candelabra holding three burning tapers. Hot wax extinguished the flames as she bashed the man in the head and tumbled out of his grip.

"Audrey, get down!" Hugh shouted, and she did—throwing herself back out through the door just before Hugh fully cocked his flintlock and fired off his first shot. The man swiveled from the impact of the bullet and crashed onto the floor.

"Stevens—" Hugh turned toward the officer, but he was no longer there. The coward had fled.

"I knew you were here somewhere, Neatham."

Audrey reappeared in the study, her arms up, her hands splayed. Hammond Abbey practically stepped on her heels, his pistol trained on her back. "Your doctor friend wouldn't say where, not even when I broke his fingers. True loyalty, that."

Thornton. *Damn it.*

"You bastard," Hugh seethed. A strange, new feeling of futility and doom closed in around him. But he couldn't allow it to gain traction. If he did, he would be finished. And not just him, but Audrey, Thornton, and even Gwendolyn.

Abbey pulled an aggrieved face. "Our erstwhile Bow Street officer. Couldn't leave the detecting behind. Toss your weapon aside, if you will."

Audrey's eyes filled with an expression he couldn't read. He thought it might be regret. Maybe even fear. But when she rolled her eyes up, to look at the empty cage hanging above her and Abbey, and then pointedly shifted her attention to a spot behind Hugh, he realized she was plotting something. He presumed that she was looking at the panel of levers. What was she thinking? All he knew was that Audrey hadn't yet given up. So, neither would he.

Hugh kept his grip on his pistol. "I don't think so, Abbey. Release her."

Abbey scoffed at the suggestion and urged Audrey forward a few more steps, using her as a shield.

"How bored you must be as a lordling if you would rather continue to play at inspector," he said. "My members here understand that dead feeling inside. You have it all, and yet nothing just the same. Excitement, that's what they want. You're not unlike them."

"I am nothing like them," Hugh gritted out.

"No, you're not, are you? Stevens said you're the kind that wouldn't bend, even under a steel hand."

"Stevens isn't the traitor you think he is," Audrey said. "He tried to shoot Martin."

Abbey laughed. "That weasel? I never would have expected it of him."

"If he isn't heading off the police, how much time do you think you have?" she pressed on, her eyes again going to the levers and then the cages behind Hugh. His muscles tightened in anticipation of something, though he didn't know exactly what was going through her head.

Abbey sighed. "I have no fear of the police. Do you have any notion of how many powerful men my Sanctuary caters to? Every one of them have sold their souls to me, and to keep their names unspoken, their reputations unsullied, they will protect me." Abbey reached forward, his hand curling around Audrey's chin. Fury boiled under Hugh's skin as the steward put his lips to her ear. "So, in answer to your question, I have all the time in the world. A good thing, I think, since I'm not quite finished with you yet."

"Yes, you are. Now, Sir!" Audrey shouted before sinking her teeth into Abbey's hand, which he'd made the mistake of putting too close to her mouth. He roared in pain and ripped his hand free as the sound of chains suddenly rattled overhead. Audrey threw herself aside and Hugh raised his pistol.

"Oi!" a familiar voice screeched as the empty cage above Abbey came down fast.

He twisted to leap aside, but the base caught his shoulder, knocking him down. However, it failed to pin him.

Abbey staggered to his feet and wheeled, his pistol aimed toward Hugh. The percussion of two pistol shots filled the room. Pain bit into Hugh's shoulder, but he remained standing. Abbey did not. He dropped to the floor, a groan of anguish ripping from his throat.

"Hugh!" Audrey was at his side in the next second, her attention riveted to his shoulder.

"I'm only grazed," he said, though he kept that arm tight to his side and reached for her with his other arm instead.

Pea whistles pierced the air as Abbey, blood expanding through the fabric of his waistcoat, tried to crawl for the door. Shouts and commotion erupted in another part of the house. Bow Street had arrived. "In here!" Hugh shouted.

"Oh, thank god," Audrey said as he gathered her to him. "Have I ever told you that you have excellent timing?"

He pressed his lips to her forehead. "A time or two." He then noticed she, too, cradled her arm close. "You're hurt."

"No, only bruised." Her body quaked with shivers. "Sir! Lower the middle cage."

Only then did Hugh see the boy at the panel of levers.

That's what Audrey had been looking at over his shoulder. Sir. He'd left the coach field and somehow sneaked his way in. Sir tipped the brim of his hat and began to crank the middle lever at a more cautious pace. Gwendolyn broke into fresh sobs as her cage began to lower.

"You aren't mad I left the phaeton, are you? I saw that shifty bloke, Stevens, and figured I'd follow him at a distance," Sir said as the cage came to rest on the floor. Hugh and Audrey joined him there.

"Considering you just saved our hides," Hugh said, grinning, "I'll give it a pass."

Several patrolmen entered the room then, their eyes going wide at the scene before them. And then, Sir Gabriel Poston entered on their heels. He pulled up short and stared down at Hammond Abbey. The steward had given up on his escape and sat against the wall, bleeding heavily from the wound in his side.

"Glad to see you made it," Hugh said, earning a scowl from the magistrate.

"I take it this is the man that needs arresting?"

Hugh nodded, his shoulder beginning to throb now. "I'd hurry up about it. He might not be breathing for much longer."

Sir Gabriel stared down at one of the men responsible for the death of his niece. "With any hope, he won't be." The magistrate snapped his fingers, and the patrolmen got to work.

CHAPTER TWENTY

Audrey reclined in her copper tub, the hot, scented water massaging her aching muscles and sore arm. Greer had drawn the bath while Audrey had been in the drawing room, going over the tumultuous events of the afternoon with Michael and Genie, who'd been shocked and horrified as she'd explained about Mr. Abbey, his secret society, and his penchant for violence to keep tongues from wagging about his foul club.

On her way back to Violet House, she'd considered keeping her lips sealed about everything. It would only stir Michael's temper, and he'd already been furious once that day, with Cassie, earlier in his study. Gracious, it seemed like ages ago, rather than just a handful of hours.

However, the duke would have certainly heard about the commotion at Burdick Close the next day. If not from Cassie, who had arrived with Carrigan shortly after Sir Gabriel, then from the city's newspapers, all of which were sure to ink the story onto front pages.

Although Hugh had dispatched Audrey and Gwendolyn Bertram from the Sanctuary as soon as possible, there was always the chance that they'd been spotted leaving the scene—or that some newspaper editor had a Bow Street patrolman on their payroll. So, Audrey had decided it would be better for Michael to hear it from her first. In an unexpected twist, her brother-in-law had simply stood there, listening. His lack of a reaction had, oddly, been one of the larger surprises of an already astonishing day.

"Are you going to say anything?" she'd finally needed to prod after a few moments of quiet once she'd finished speaking. Cassie and Genie, too, had watched him with concern.

Michael had gone to the window and looked out at the street and the greening boughs of Hyde Park. "It isn't that I don't trust in your capabilities, Audrey. Or in yours, Cassie." He'd sounded thoughtful and calm. "In fact, I'm quite impressed. Audrey, if not for your persistence and your... your bravery," he'd said, selecting the word after a moment's deliberation, "a young woman would have likely died. And Cassie, you were integral in convincing the magistrate to get to where he needed to be."

Cassie had gaped at him, as had Audrey. It was enormously difficult for Michael to speak like that, from the heart, and they all knew it.

"Rules are safe. Order and stability are safe. And after losing my brother, I thought if I could only keep you all safe..." He tugged at his stock and cravat, unable to finish his thought. He needn't have finished it. Audrey knew what he meant.

He cleared his throat. "A single woman in possession of a large fortune is a target, and I have already failed you once before, Cassie. I didn't protect you from that blackguard, Renfry. I will never forgive myself for that."

Cassie had stood up, called him stupid, and then crossed the room to throw her arms around him. There, they'd remained in an embrace, and Audrey had seen herself out of the drawing room, letting them have their moment. Michael's wish to protect Cassie, and to advise Audrey and protect her, wasn't so unlike Hugh's desire to do the same. It was driven by love, not a desire for control. The difficult part was stepping back and admitting that love wasn't about restriction. It was about loosening your grip and trusting that the other person would continue to hold on.

She'd climbed the stairs to her bedchamber, her legs heavy with exhaustion. After leaving Burdick Close, Audrey and Cassie had returned Gwendolyn Bertram to her home on Fitzroy Square. Sir Gabriel had given his word to her that he would do everything in his power to limit the mention of her name in regard to the case of the Sanctuary and Mr. Hammond Abbey. Should she be tied to any part of the scandal, it would be a death knell for her reputation. Audrey had only stayed long enough at the Bertram's to inform Mr. and Mrs. Bertram of Sir Gabriel's intent. She would let Gwendolyn explain the rest to them as she saw fit. On Audrey's way out, however, Flora had followed her and thrown her arms around her waist. She'd hung on for just a moment before peeling her arms back, curtseying, and then running back to rejoin her sister.

If only Bethany Silas had received the same safe homecoming. *Safe*. Michael's paramount concern did not seem so unreasonable when viewed in that perspective.

Greer had helped Audrey out of her clothes, gasping in

alarm when seeing the bruises on her arm, inflicted when she'd been dragged around the Sanctuary. However, her bruises were nothing in comparison to what Lord Thornton had suffered.

As Audrey led Hugh through the halls of the large, rambling Burdick Close residence back toward where Thornton had been left tied in the chair, they'd come upon him. He had already been found and released by a few patrolmen. He'd looked ghastly with his bloodied nose and lips, eyes swollen and bruised, and he'd been cradling his left hand close to his chest.

"I should have taken the tunnel to the left and given you the right," he'd said in greeting.

Hugh had shored him up with his shoulder, and they'd made their way to the front entrance. By then it was swarming with police, as well as with Carrigan and Cassie. Her sister-in-law's eyes had blown wide at the sight of the physician, whose two fingers had indeed been broken by Abbey. But Thornton insisted it was because he'd insulted Abbey's overuse of gold in his décor and that it had nothing at all to do with protecting Hugh.

"You bloody idiot," Cassie had said. "You need a doctor."

"Do you know of a good one?"

"No," she'd replied, but Audrey had heard the wobble in her voice and seen the concern in her eyes as she'd tried to dab at Thornton's split lip. He'd waved her off, insisting he was fine and that he only needed to return to his home so he could set his own fingers and clean up.

"He is infuriating," Cassie had complained once they'd dropped Sir and Thornton at the coach field, from where Sir would drive him back to St. James's Square in Hugh's phaeton.

Audrey had long suspected her sister-in-law's feelings toward Thornton went deeper than pure annoyance. It worried her. She liked Thornton immensely, and his devotion to Hugh spoke volumes to his good character. But he was at least ten years Cassie's senior, and Hugh had made it clear that Thornton had not overcome the loss of his wife. He wasn't capable of anything serious. Like Michael did, Audrey wanted to protect Cassie from men—even good ones—who might break her heart.

But she also knew she had little control over the matter. She could no more tell Cassie what to do than Michael could.

With a long sigh, she now settled further into the hot, jasmine-scented bathwater. It was so decadent that Audrey decided she would stay there until she became a prune. There was nothing to see to now. Nothing pressing to do. They'd been unable to bring Bethany home, but they'd saved Gwendolyn, and solved a handful of connected murders. She felt no pity for Mr. Comstock. He'd been a murderer himself, and he'd most likely been forced into an opium overdose—one of Abbey's clean-up jobs, to protect himself and his secret society. A society that had given him a sense of power and authority. Her mind could have gone on all night, picking apart the potential reasons behind the society, why anyone would wish to be a member of such a thing. But it was all so twisted and dark, and she didn't want to allow it to consume her.

"Your Grace?" Greer entered the boudoir, thankfully severing her thoughts. Audrey opened her eyes and sat up a little in the water. "This came for you earlier." Her maid set a letter on the dressing table.

"Thank you, Greer." When the maid continued to stand still, hesitating, she asked, "Is there something else?"

Her maid came forward. "There is something I would like to speak to you about, if you don't mind."

"Of course, I don't," she said, though not without a twinge of worry. It sounded serious. "I'll dry off and dress, and then you can tell me what it is."

With regret, she abandoned the bath and stepped into a robe, and soon enough, Audrey was seated at her dressing table, with Greer toweling her hair.

"Why do I feel as if you're about to give me some horrible news?" Audrey asked.

Greer stilled the towel. "Eamon has asked me to marry him."

Audrey twisted in the chair, agape. "Eamon? Oh! Carrigan." She grasped Greer's hands, still holding the length of toweling, and beamed. "That's not horrible news at all! I'm thrilled for you."

One of Greer's rare smiles cut through her worried expression. Though only for a moment. "I know everything will be changing soon, Your Grace. You'll be leaving the duke's household."

Audrey nodded. "Yes, I will be."

She thought of the home on Berkeley Square and Hugh's proposal, and her heart skipped. They would be marrying soon. There was no need to post the banns either since he'd acquired the special license. With a jolt of excitement, she realized they could wed as soon as *tomorrow*. Greer was right: she'd be leaving this room, Violet House, her life as dowager duchess. Everything *would* be changing. She rubbed her sore arm absentmindedly, her palm a little damp.

"Are you leaving service?" Audrey asked. "I imagine you'll want to start a family with Carrigan—I mean, Eamon." She felt wretched that she had not known Carrigan's given name. That Greer's last name was Babson was a distant memory too.

"Oh no, I'm much too old for that," Greer said. "We both are."

"Surely not." She was in her early thirties, at the most.

But her maid shook her head tightly. "We've discussed it and agree. We'd like to stay on with you, Your Grace, if you and the viscount will allow it."

Audrey stood. "I couldn't imagine my life without you, Greer. Or without Carrigan. I know the viscount will feel the same. Of course, you will stay with me. You both will."

Knowing her maid would only stiffen at an embrace, Audrey merely took her hands in hers and squeezed. Greer's eyes filled, but she sniffed and straightened.

"I'll fetch you a gown," she said, back to her usual no nonsense self. "The viscount is waiting for you downstairs."

Audrey brightened, eager to see Hugh and learn what had happened at Burdick Close after she'd left. And perhaps even discuss what would happen now. Her stomach flipped as Greer went to the wardrobe to select a gown, and Audrey sat again, reaching for her hairbrush. But seeing the letter Greer had brought in, she picked that up instead. The seal was unfamiliar. A dark burgundy pressed with an olive branch. She released the wax wafer with her nail and unfolded the letter. But as soon as she began to read, she knew what the letter was. With every word, every sentence, a chiming in her ears grew louder. Audrey couldn't breathe. She tried to stand, but her knees went soft, and she came down again, into the chair. Her elbow knocked something aside with a clatter.

"Your Grace?"

Audrey turned to her maid. "Bring Lord Neatham at once."

HUGH PACED THE DRAWING ROOM, oddly nervous. The day had been no better than one belched up from hell, and yet he wasn't tired in the least.

After leaving Bow Street, he'd stopped briefly at his home to change before setting out for Violet House. He had needed to see Audrey. Needed to be certain she was well. Everything had unraveled so quickly after Abbey had been taken into custody, his injuries severe from the bullet in his side. He was alive, for now. If the bullet wound didn't kill him, once convicted of the murders, he would surely swing. Rightfully so.

With Abbey and his henchmen in custody, the Sanctuary was shuttered. But what of its members? In their search of Abbey's belongings, Bow Street might find a list of names. They would be questioned, of course, but belonging to a club wasn't a crime in and of itself. And what was to stop someone from forming another society like the Sanctuary?

"Where there is one, there is bound to be another," Sir Gabriel had said when Hugh posed the same question to the magistrate. "We won't be able to dismantle them all."

Hugh could only hope that the names of its members

might find their way into a newspaper article, bringing them exposure and shame. But that wasn't for him to decide.

Neither was Stevens's fate.

While the officer had claimed to have never taken part in any of the rituals, he'd admitted that protecting the Sanctuary had been lucrative. When Lord Stromburg and Madame Lee had come to Bow Street, it had been pure luck that Stevens was on duty and able to take the complaint about Opal. He'd never filed it, but instead, went to Abbey, who in turn had silenced the pair of them. And when Harlan Givens came to Bow Street claiming to know something more about the bodies found at Vauxhall, Officer Tyne had brought him on as an informant. Givens was to learn as much as he could about this Sanctuary that he'd heard of through the Red Lotus. Stevens had, of course, tipped Abbey off to that as well.

As for Comstock, the constables that Miss Lavinia Clark mentioned had indeed filed the report of his death; Stevens, however, pulled the record and misfiled it to keep the news from ever reaching Tyne or Sir Gabriel.

The Bow Street officer would lose his post, but since he hadn't done the murders, he would likely only spend a little time behind bars. Of course, Newgate wouldn't be friendly to a former officer of the law.

"Let it be a lesson to any officer thinking of doing the same," Sir Gabriel had said, feeling no pity for the man.

Hugh crossed the drawing room at Violet House for what might have been the fiftieth time. He'd already proposed to Audrey, and she'd already accepted, but now… Now it was time to make arrangements. His hands began to sweat. It was absurd. It was a wedding. Not a march to the gallows.

The door to the drawing room opened, and Greer appeared, her eyes slightly wild.

"Her Grace needs you, my lord," she said, breathless.

She started away immediately, and Hugh followed.

"What is it?" he asked, taking the stairs after Greer, his pulse beginning to pound. "Is she hurt?"

"No, my lord," she replied, rushing through the hall upstairs. "Hurry."

His mind reeled as Greer led him into a bedchamber, where he saw Audrey in her banyan robe, pacing the carpet. Her hair was loose and damp; she looked to have come straight from a bath. Clenched in her hand was a sheet of paper. She turned to Hugh, and he saw that her cheeks were wet, her eyes glistening.

"Audrey? Christ, what has happened?"

She held up the paper, creased in the fashion of a letter folded for posting. He could see handwriting through the thin cotton. "It is him," she whispered.

Hugh stared at the letter again as a strange weight settled over him. His pulse skipped, and it throbbed an echo in his ears. *Philip*. He'd told Audrey he would write to her one day. And it seemed he had. Dread poured through Hugh as he forced himself to move toward her, his legs heavy.

"What does it say?"

That he was coming back? That he'd changed his mind? Even as the instant fears fed into Hugh's mind, he knew it couldn't be so. Philip could not return. In his heart, Hugh knew that. But Audrey's tear-dampened cheeks worried him.

Greer left the room, shutting the door behind her, and

Audrey took a seat on the divan at the foot of her bed. Hugh lowered himself rigidly next to her.

"Will you read it to me?" he asked.

She nodded, the motion rough and shuddering. "Dearest Audrey," she began, her voice constricted. She coughed and started again:

Dearest Audrey,

I have started this promised letter to you a dozen times, and a dozen times I've thrown it to the fire, questioning if it should be sent. But when I realized it had been a year—a full year—I knew I must complete it. By now, the person I suspected you loved, and who loved you, will have asked for your hand. Knowing you, before accepting, you will have confessed to him everything. While I cannot claim to know him well, I do believe he is a man of honor. He will keep your confidence. So, I suppose this letter is to you both.

Let me start by saying I am sorry. For the burden I've placed upon you, for my selfishness, for the guilt you have undoubtedly shouldered this last year. You've unwillingly given me the greatest gift I will ever receive: the chance to be who I want to be, and with whom I want to be with. In return, I can only assuage my conscience by hoping that I have given you the same gift. Do not be afraid to open it, my darling.

This will be the last you hear from me. When this letter reaches you, we will already be crossing the ocean for a distant corner of the globe. There, we will become who we were always meant to be—for however long a time we have left together. I still struggle with my malaise, and though the illness may be advancing, I plan to keep fighting. You, too, have your own life to live and fight for, and my deepest hope is that it be full and happy and long. Goodbye my dearest friend. I will forever carry you in my heart.

Audrey lowered the letter to her lap. Hugh's throat cinched tight. His eyes burned. He'd never liked Philip Sinclair. He'd been arrogant and aloof, privileged and, at times, churlish. On more than one occasion, he had been tempted to drive his fist into the man's chin.

And then, he'd left. He'd given up his life, faked his death, and as his letter had just acknowledged, left Audrey to pick up the pieces. He'd expected her to uphold a lie that had caused grief for people she cared for, and that had caused her no shortage of guilt. For that alone, Hugh had wanted to track him down on the Continent and put him in the ground, in truth.

And yet, had the duke not been a selfish prig and abandoned his life, Hugh would not be here, with the woman he loved. He would still be stuck loving a married woman with no hope of ever being able to declare himself. Philip's decision had damned them as much as it had freed them.

"He's gone," Audrey whispered, her voice cracking. "This whole year, I tried so hard to convince myself he would never return, but I always feared maybe, one day... But I can feel it now, that certainty. He is gone."

Hugh hooked her hip with his arm and brought her against his side. He put his lips to the wet, fragrant crown of her head. It had been his lasting worry too. But as he took the letter from her hand and read it again, the worry he'd lived with, that had become a part of him, dissipated. He felt lighter than he had in months.

"I don't know whether to feel happy or sad or relieved,"

Audrey said as she leaned against him, resting her head on his shoulder. He folded the letter and brought her closer.

"I think all three are warranted."

She looked up, her eyes a blue so clear and vibrant, they pierced him. "I'm ready."

"Ready?"

"To open my gift, like Philip said."

Hugh kissed her brow. Then, he reached into his waistcoat pocket. "I've been carrying this around, intending to give it to you, but the timing was never quite right."

Audrey sat up straight, her lips falling open before curving into a radiant smile.

Hugh slid from the divan, his knees hitting the carpet as he came to kneel before her. He held up the thin gold band, studded with a brilliant mine-cut sapphire.

"Marry me," he whispered.

She laughed. "I've already said yes."

"I want to hear you say it again. Every day for the rest of our lives would suffice."

He took her hand, and the ring glided smoothly into place on her finger. When Hugh looked up, she wasn't staring at the ring. She was watching him, her eyes brimming.

"Yes. Yes, to every day for the rest of our lives."

When she leaned down to press her lips to his, Hugh did something he never imagined he would ever do: He thanked Philip Sinclair, the late Duke of Fournier.

CHAPTER
TWENTY-ONE

The study inside Violet House was the room Audrey was going to miss the most. It was the one room in the Curzon Street residence where she'd always felt at home. As she stood at her desk, the top cleared, the drawers emptied, she took a deep breath and said goodbye.

It was a strange thing, for a heart to ache with loss and yet at the same time, feel near to bursting with happiness. Over the last week, whenever she thought of Philip, the odd sensation had coursed through her. She'd waited for his promised letter all year, and its arrival, and its contents, had allowed Audrey to finally close a door she'd been holding open.

It had also allowed her to see that she had, in some ways, been standing still all year in anticipation, while everyone around her—Michael, Genie, Cassie, Tobias—had all been moving forward, grieving and healing and *living*.

It was time for Audrey to catch up.

She'd committed the letter to memory, put the paper to her lips for a long moment, and then let it fall into the grate in her bedchamber. She'd wept as the flames quickly consumed it. That someone would one day find it wasn't her primary concern. She'd burned the letter because it was her last link to Philip. And she needed to let go.

On the afternoon following the debacle at Burdick Close, Audrey had been seated at her desk, dipping a quill into her pot of ink to complete a letter to her sister Millie, when the door had flung open. Genie and Cassie had whirled inside.

"Is it true?" Genie had asked just as Cassie demanded, "When did you plan to tell us?"

For the briefest moment, Audrey wondered if they'd learned about Philip's letter. But then, Cassie had stormed to the desk, picked up Audrey's left hand, and stared agog at the sapphire Hugh had presented to her the night before. He'd explained the ring had belonged to his mother, Catherine Marsden. He'd learned the previous year that his birth mother was April Barlow, but Catherine would always be his only mother. Miss Barlow had remained distant, even after their meeting last year. It was something Audrey couldn't fathom. How could anyone not want to know Hugh? How could anyone not want to love him?

"It is true!" Cassie had exclaimed.

The incurable gossipmonger Lady Dutton had just called on Violet House for tea and related that a friend had been taking Gunter's ices in the park the other week when she'd seen Lord Neatham on one knee in what appeared to be a proposal to the dowager duchess.

"I had to pretend that I already knew, and that a formal announcement was to be made soon," Genie said, "all while trying to keep my oolong from spilling into my lap!"

"How could you keep this from us?" Cassie demanded. "Why haven't you said anything?"

It was true that she and Hugh had agreed that they'd wanted to solve Bethany's case and the mystery of the Vauxhall bodies before they married. But that didn't explain why Audrey had not told them at breakfast that morning. Or why she'd kept her hand in her lap to conceal the ring.

"I didn't say anything because I knew the two of you would make a fuss. Hugh and I will marry soon. It doesn't have to be a big affair."

"All right, fine. A small ceremony. But why keep the proposal a *secret*?" Cassie had asked.

It was with those words that Audrey realized the truth. Why she'd been tiptoeing around the subject. Everything involving Hugh had always been a secret. She'd secretly investigated crimes and cases with Hugh; she'd secretly spent time with him; she'd secretly fallen in love with him, and he with her; together, they had kept the secret of Philip's ruse from the rest of the world. When it came to Hugh, she was accustomed to simply being secretive.

But like dawn driving out the night, a revelation had suddenly struck her. Secrets were no longer necessary. Even their largest one, the one involving Philip, had evaporated like morning mist after receiving his letter. There was no threat that someone, somewhere, at some point would cross paths with him and bring news of it back to London. He was no longer an axe hanging over their heads.

The overwhelming freedom Audrey had felt in that moment had been apparent to even Cassie and Genie. At seeing her overcome, they'd apologized, assuring her that they weren't angry and would leave her to do as she wished.

"Don't go," Audrey said as they were backing toward the door. In that moment, she promised herself no more secrets. "Genie, can you send for Madame Gascoigne? We should discuss a wedding gown."

The modiste had come that day, and Audrey had selected a cream silk taffeta and a simple blue embroidered design. She'd finished her letter to Millie and added a postscript, telling her to come to London as soon as possible.

There was going to be a wedding.

"Oh, there you are!"

Audrey turned from her empty desk and found a frazzled but excited Cassie in the doorway.

"It is nearly noon! We need to leave if we're to get there on time and dress you, and—oh! I've forgotten my gloves!" Cassie rushed back into the hall, calling, "I'll meet you in the carriage!"

Audrey laughed as she made her way to the front hall, where Carrigan waited in the open doorway. He was wearing his finest livery.

"Are you ready, Your Grace?" he asked.

Greer had already gone ahead to Berkeley Square to prepare for her arrival. Audrey nodded, then thought of something.

"Carrigan, you may very well be the last person to ever call me that."

"Your Grace?" he asked, sounding confused. She laughed.

"Yes. Exactly."

A PERSISTENT THRUMMING had come alive just under Hugh's skin. He rolled his shoulders, for once at ease with his tall stock and cravat. If there was ever a day to appear starched and formal, it was this day. He hadn't complained once as Basil had meticulously dressed him in the downstairs study at 37 Berkeley Square, where the valet had lain out his suit, complete with tailcoat and boutonniere, the flowers of which Basil had matched to the ones filling the drawing room.

The valet had been curiously silent while dressing Hugh, and while standing close to knot the neckcloth, he'd noticed Basil's eyes glistening.

"Do not tell me you are becoming sentimental," he'd said.

"Don't be ridiculous, I'm merely coming down with a cold."

Hugh had clapped him on the shoulder. "I love you too, Baz."

The valet had admonished him to stand still, but Hugh still caught the slight tug at the corner of his mouth.

The morning after Philip's letter burned in the grate inside Audrey's bedchamber, Hugh told Basil to purchase whatever he thought necessary for a wedding at the new residence. The valet had taken charge of the planning, rapturous with the task, and entirely disapproving when Hugh had rejected his suggestion that the wedding take place in the more fashionable St. George's Cathedral. Audrey had agreed that fashion and convention did not matter. There could be no better way to christen their new home than with their own wedding.

Now, Hugh stood beside Thornton at the front of the

drawing room. As the furniture at 19 Bedford Street had yet to be moved, the new house was still mostly unfurnished, but it wasn't empty. Floral arrangements dressed the corners of the room, and a crowd of about a dozen people milled about. Everyone from Genie and Fournier and Tobias to Audrey's sister and her husband Reggie to Sir Gabriel Poston and his wife, Lady Rebecca, and Hugh's cook, Mrs. Peets. Basil waited patiently at the door to the receiving room, while Sir, who had reluctantly permitted Basil to tie a cravat, looked sharp but bored as he rocked on his heels beside Thornton. A vicar stood on Hugh's other side.

It was a small crowd, and excepting Millie, none of them were blood relations. But everyone here was someone he and Audrey cared for, and who cared for them in return. These were the people who would be in their lives from that day forward.

Hugh wanted to rock onto his heels, as Sir was, but instead, he twitched his nose at the scent of the lily and honeysuckle nosegay pinned to his lapel.

"Patience," Thornton murmured. "It isn't as though she is going to flee. Unless, of course, she comes to her senses."

The bruises on Thornton's face had not had much time to heal, and his arm was still in a sling to keep his broken fingers stationary. But despite his battered appearance, his friend claimed he'd never been so popular. "I can't tell you how many women seem to think I'm a hero for enduring torture just to save your skin," he'd said with a waggle of his brow—which had thankfully pained him.

"The moment this wedding concludes, I'm booting you all out of this house. Beginning with you," Hugh told

Thornton, his voice muted by the murmuring in the drawing room.

Their guests had been mingling while waiting for the bride to arrive, but now, an hour after Audrey had been whisked upstairs to dress, they had taken their seats—the chairs arranged by Basil to create a center aisle for Audrey to come down.

"I know you are eager to be alone with your bride, but I'm afraid no one here cares. I hear Mrs. Peets has made a lovely cake for afterward, and I intend to sit and eat several slices," his friend said.

"These chairs are the only furniture in the house. I kept the rooms bare for a reason. No furniture means no sitting, which means no lingering."

Thornton whispered, "I hope you at least had a bed installed into the bedchamber."

Hugh glared at him. Sir leaned forward to look past Thornton. "Does that mean Baz and I have to go back to the old digs?"

"It does," Hugh replied, his patience wearing thin. Where was she? How long did it take to dress?

"I can't take Baz for a full week all by myself. You won't mind if I go back to Surrey, will you?" Sir asked.

That he'd just returned from there the previous day didn't signify. Sir had been helping his mother and sisters settle into the cottage and small plot of land Hugh had offered them at Cranleigh. Mrs. Givens had accepted it without hesitation, knowing that life would be far better for them there than in London. Spending the last week there had also kept him away from the news in regard to his father's murderer.

The trial against Hammond Abbey had been swift and decisive. Abbey would face the noose. A handful of Sanctuary members had been revealed publicly, including Sir Oliver Pendleton, who, as co-owner of the *Morning Post*, had disclosed the story of the bodies to help along Mr. Gye's crisis at Vauxhall. However, after the fiasco, Mr. Gye decided against selling the lease, and in the last week, Vauxhall had become a crush again.

"Go to Surrey if you like," Hugh said. "So long as no one comes back here for one full week. The duchess and I will get on just fine, all on our own."

Thornton snickered, but Sir leaned forward again to look past him. "You mean the viscountess."

Hugh's chest clamped hard, and all his impatience fizzled. He blinked, his eyes strangely burning. Speaking around a sudden knob in his throat, he said, "The viscountess. Right you are, Sir."

Had he never been named viscount, she would have married him still, of that he was certain. She would have become Mrs. Audrey Marsden just as willingly as she would have the Viscountess Neatham. The only thing that she would care about was simply being his *wife*. He swallowed hard, and Thornton clapped him on the back, as if in understanding.

The doors to the drawing room opened, and Hugh's heart lurched. Basil stepped to the side and cleared his throat. He looked inordinately pleased with the ceremony of it all as he snapped his fingers, and the strains of a violin filled the room. Hugh's butler, Whitlock, had been in an orchestra in his youth and had offered to play.

Everyone turned in their seats to view Audrey's attendant, Cassie, entering first. As she took measured steps down the aisle, Hugh refrained from tapping his foot, though just barely.

"A sloth may have moved faster," Thornton muttered as she came to stand across from them. She shot him a glare, but then faced the doors again.

And then, there she was. Audrey's eyes immediately found him, and Hugh was lost. She was a vision in cream silk. Perfect in every way. He stood tall and waited for his bride to come to him.

Two years ago, Audrey had descended a set of steps, into the dark, dank cellar of the Brown Bear on Bow Street. In that moment, her heart had been in her throat. Her best friend, her husband, had just been arrested for a crime that she knew, in her soul, he never could have committed. When she'd walked into that cellar and met with the arrogant, belittling arresting officer, Audrey never could have imagined that she was, in fact, meeting her next husband. The love of her life.

As she entered the drawing room, clutching the small bouquet of lilies and honeysuckle, the officer she had so detested upon their first meeting blinked to keep his tears at bay. Now, she knew Hugh Marsden was neither arrogant nor belittling. She'd come to know him as the kindest, most honorable, caring, intelligent, and loyal man she had ever met. He could still be infuriating at times, but she'd never felt more loved.

A person's life could take such curious and serendipitous

turns. Though Philip was gone, he would always have a place in her heart. Without him, she would have gone through with the arranged marriage to Lord Bainbury. She would have continued to feel like an outcast, afraid to be who she was.

Most importantly, without Philip, she would have never met Hugh Marsden.

As she walked slowly down the aisle between the chairs filled with their friends and family, a violin playing a soft piece, she felt full of gratitude that they were here, rather than in some church that held no meaning for them. This would be their home. It would be where they would love each other and grow old together and raise children together. There could be no better place to take Hugh as her husband.

Upstairs, after Greer and Cassie had helped her into the gown Madame Gascoigne had turned out in record time, there had been a knock on the bedchamber door. Michael entered, and pulling on his cuffs, announced, "I've come to offer myself up."

Audrey peered at him in the mirror's reflection as Greer pinned a dainty, crystal-studded netting over her upswept hair. The mirror was one of the only pieces of furniture in the room, other than a few trunks and the large tester bed that gave her an electric thrill when she imagined sharing it with Hugh that night.

"How so?" Audrey asked.

"To walk you down the aisle, of course," he answered. "We are still family. Your marrying the viscount won't change that."

Audrey turned from the mirror, the sting of tears biting the corners of her eyes. "Oh, Michael." Greer quickly finished with the netting pins, and Audrey went to him. His alarm at her approach was significant, as if he worried she was going to throw herself into his arms. But she stopped short of that and only took his hands into hers.

"I'm lucky to have you. Both you and Genie. Cassie and Tobias too."

"I should say so," Cassie said, suppressing a grin as she came forward with the pair of tall silk gloves the modiste had sent as well.

Audrey sniffled, knowing she couldn't cry before the wedding. It would make her eyes red and puffy. "Thank you for the offer, Michael, but I want to walk myself down the aisle," she said. "I'm giving *myself* to Hugh."

Michael nodded, a bashful grin forming. "I could not be happier for you."

So, after a long time coming, and a short walk down the aisle, her eyes hinged on her groom with every step, Audrey reached the altar on her own. Though, as Hugh came forward and took her hand into his, she knew she would never be on her own again.

EPILOGUE

One year later

The mantel clock in her study at Cranleigh ticked softly toward the hour. Audrey braced an elbow on her desk, her chin resting in her hand as she checked off columns in the ledger.

Going through the household accounts every week was something she had never done at Violet House or at Fournier Downs. But here at Cranleigh, and at Berkeley Square whenever they were in London, she had taken to it without reservation. Even one year after their wedding, which sometimes felt like a lifetime ago, and other times like a single day, she still marveled at the difference of feeling. She'd never felt much like a duchess. But she did feel every inch the viscountess that she now was. At long last, her life had fallen into place, and the fit was as natural as her next breath of air.

As the clock chimed, Hugh strode into the study. He

shut the door firmly behind him and began to stalk toward the desk, a deeply serious expression fixed on his face. "Rise," he commanded.

She leaped to her feet. "What is wrong?"

"Nothing at all," he replied, the solemn expression vanishing as he sat in her chair and hooked her waist. Hugh brought her down into his lap. "I just realized the little imp is asleep, and I have you all to myself."

She pinched his chest. "That is for making me worry."

Hugh kissed her. "That is for putting up with me."

"I don't know how I do." But when he clasped her to him again in another kiss, she relented. Though only for a few moments. She pulled back. "She won't be asleep for very long."

He kissed the tip of Audrey's nose. "She's too stubborn, like her mother."

Catherine was only a few months old, but from her first breath and wail, she had effectively stolen their hearts. They'd been in London for Audrey's confinement, which had allowed Genie and Cassie to be with her when her time had come. But a few hours into it, and with little progress made, Audrey had only wanted one person at her side. She would not be dissuaded. Against the doctor's wishes, Hugh had entered the birthing chamber, already looking bedraggled in his shirtsleeves after spending the last few hours pacing the halls, hearing her cries. He'd told her afterward that each one had been like a knife to the chest.

Shortly after he joined her, the baby had come, and the disapproving doctor had lain a little bundle in Hugh's arms. Catherine Millicent Marsden Neatham was a little golden-haired angel, and Audrey had never seen Hugh more in love than he was with their daughter.

The heat in his gaze now, however, came close. He rubbed his palm along her thigh, his mouth nuzzling her neck.

"Cassie is due to arrive today," Audrey reminded him.

"Mrs. Simmons can get her settled," he replied, his breath hot on her neck. "We don't need to be standing in the front door to greet her."

Mrs. Simmons was housekeeper at Cranleigh and had been for nearly two decades. Audrey got on well with her, but, perhaps predictably, she had a closer rapport with the housekeeper at their Berkeley Square residence: Mrs. Greer Carrigan.

After Audrey and Hugh's wedding, they'd combined their households, and Audrey had begun interviewing for a housekeeper. But no one, no matter how pleasant and organized and appropriately stern, came up to snuff in comparison to the servant Audrey most admired and trusted. So, after discussing it with Hugh, she'd offered the position to Greer. It was, after all, the next expected step up for a lady's maid. She accepted with one of her rare smiles, and she and Carrigan now resided full time in London.

Audrey's new lady's maid, Dorothy, had been Charlotte Bainbury's maid, and she'd accepted with excitement when Audrey had written to her with the offer. Her relationship with Dorothy wasn't the same as it had been with Greer, but they were beginning to get along well. Audrey didn't have an abundance of time to think too deeply on it anyhow. She was far too busy with Hugh and little Cat and the running of

Cranleigh. Cassie would be staying with them for the summer, too.

She'd written the month before, begging for an invitation. Within weeks, she would reach her majority and while Michael had given up his blustering about her not being able to manage her own income, he had not quite given up on his crusade for her to marry. The Season was ending in London, and Cassie was desperate to get away after his failed attempts to throw potential suitors into her path.

Hugh's palm grazed the old scar from the bullet that had struck her a few summers ago. "How is it that you're even more tempting now than you were before?"

She never felt more loved and cherished than when she was with him. During the last year, he'd shown her so many ways to love, and not just in terms of intimacy. It was in the small things, like the sly wink he'd give when she caught him gazing at her. Or how he'd leave a flower or something else he'd found out on the grounds of their Surrey estate—once, it had been an enormous pinecone nearly the size of her forearm—on her pillow or desk. It was how he'd stand close and keep his hand on her lower back whenever she was meeting someone new and was nervous. Or it was just making a comment about how delicious she smelled after he'd kissed the crown of her head.

"I suppose it is the same mystery that makes me love you more with every passing day," she replied. He growled in appreciation and leaned up for a kiss.

"However," Audrey said, a hand to his chest to keep him back, "It will have to wait. It's nearly two o'clock, and I cannot allow Cassie to arrive without a proper greeting. I haven't seen her in months."

Hugh sighed and sat back, though his hand stayed rooted on her thigh. "Very well, I am content to wait until tonight."

"Your fortitude is heroic, my lord."

He groaned lightly before releasing her leg. Once his arms were back around her waist, he said, "I've heard from Sir Gabriel."

"Oh?" Audrey shifted in his lap, her interest piqued. Albeit, she was a little wary too.

Sir Gabriel had asked for Hugh's assistance on a murder case in December, and the argument that had ensued had been the low point of their first year as husband and wife. At seven months pregnant, Audrey had been close to confinement and Hugh had insisted he work alone. She'd been resentful and, admittedly, not entirely reasonable. Everything had resolved in the end, but she didn't want another incident like that again. In fact, she was rather enjoying the monotony and calm of their life at Cranleigh. Perhaps it wouldn't always be that way, and they may eventually be drawn into another investigation together, but for now, she was content.

"He is thinking of retiring from the magistrate's chair."

Audrey's fingers, which had been combing the ends of Hugh's hair, went still. "And?"

"And he wants to speak to me about taking his place."

Her stomach cinched. "As magistrate?"

Hugh held her eyes. "I've already replied."

Audrey shifted away from him, her fingers withdrawing from his hair. "You didn't think to discuss it with me?"

"There is nothing to discuss. My mind is made up, and the letter is sent."

Her temper beginning to simmer, Audrey braced her

hands on the desk and started to stand. But he pulled her back down and held her tight in his lap again.

"I have said no."

She stared at him as the fire in her chest stamped out. "But...you love Bow Street. You miss it terribly."

"I do," he said softly, nodding. "But my life is here. It's here with you and Cat. I know the job and how often I would be away from you, and I can't. I don't want it more than I want my time with you."

Audrey melted against him, drawing her legs up. This was her favorite place to be, curled up against him, with all the time in the world stretching before them. She kissed him, relieved beyond measure.

The door to the study winged open then, and Sir sauntered in without knocking or announcing himself. Audrey sat up. "He's beginning to take after you," she murmured to Hugh, getting to her feet.

Hugh groaned in disappointment. "Sir, what are you doing? Cat was sleeping."

Now fourteen, Sir was as tall as Audrey. He walked into the study holding Catherine in one arm. She was wrapped in a blanket, the bundling so proficient and tight that Audrey knew at once Sir had done it himself. He was skilled at wrapping up babies, he'd said, while trying to show their first nanny how to imitate his method.

"She was not, she was wailing like a banshee," he replied. "You've got to hire a new nanny, Lady A. I found her sleeping through all Cat's howling, dead to the world, out like a two-penny boxer."

He bounced the baby, who was now burbling happily

with her fingers in her mouth. Audrey grinned as Sir bopped Catherine on the nose and pulled a silly face.

She bit back her smile, knowing Sir would scowl at it, and left the desk. "You are entirely too picky."

Hugh quickly overtook her and snatched the baby from Sir's arms before Audrey could reach them. "What's this nanny's name again?"

"Miss Pierce," Audrey said with a shake of her head. "Honestly, she's been with us for four weeks."

"There she is!" Basil said, as he entered the study. "Sir, did you take that baby again? Miss Pierce is utterly beside herself, sobbing that Catherine has been abducted. Goodness, she's blubbering on and on about nonsensical things like faeries and changelings. Someone, take that baby back to her."

"See?" Sir said, with a pleading look at Audrey. "Changelings! I told you she was no good."

Basil threw up his arms. "I suppose you want to dismiss this nanny too?"

"She's barmy," the boy insisted.

"If his lordship went around dismissing every servant you didn't like, we wouldn't have a staff at all."

"He wouldn't have a valet, that's for certain," Sir muttered.

"I should like to know who else would put up with the lot of you," Basil said, before swiftly bowing to Audrey with a simper. "Not your ladyship, of course. I find you to be the only reasonable one, my lady."

She couldn't suppress her smile this time. "Thank you, Basil. Would you please take Catherine to Miss Pierce for now?" She took her from Hugh, her little fist now glistening with spit, and handed her to the startled and suddenly rigid valet.

He clasped the gurgling baby, holding her far away from him, like week-old laundry. He turned and began toward the exit, muttering under his breath, "I am a valet. Valets do not carry babies..."

"And Sir," Audrey turned to the boy, "will you find Mrs. Simmons and tell her we may need to look for a new nanny after all?"

Sir saluted, bowed, and then darted away with more excitement than she seen in him since they'd relieved the first nanny of her post.

Audrey followed him to the door, then closed it. She turned the lock and glanced over her shoulder. Hugh crossed his arms.

"What are you up to, minx? I thought you wanted to form a welcome party for Cassie."

She sauntered toward him, enjoying the way he watched her. "I have a more important task in mind." Audrey put her arms around his neck, and he dragged her close. "And much more pleasurable."

He lowered his forehead to hers. "You aren't getting away from me this time, my lady."

Audrey raked her fingers into his hair and nipped his bottom lip. "I'll hold you to that, my lord."

Thank you for reading Taken to the Grave and for continuing the Bow Street Duchess Mystery series. Please consider leaving a rating and review on Amazon to help other readers discover the series.

Don't miss The Lady's Last Mistake, a Bow Street Duchess Romance, featuring Cassie and Lord Thornton! Releasing June 15, 2024 and available now for pre-order!

Want to know how Hugh Marsden and Sir met? Subscribe to my monthly newsletter for a free short story, The Officer and the Thief!

THE OFFICER AND THE THIEF

An all-new short story available to newsletter subscribers!

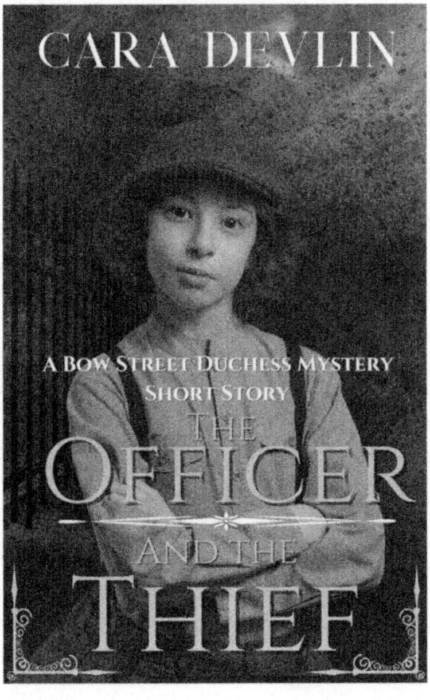

ACKNOWLEDGMENTS

As the Bow Street Duchess Mystery series comes to a conclusion, I want to extend a heartfelt thank you to every reader who has followed this series. To everyone who has eagerly anticipated the next Audrey Sinclair and Hugh Marsden mystery, left a review online, told a friend or family member to check out the series, listened to the audiobooks, or reached out to me to say how much they've enjoyed the series, THANK YOU.

I have loved writing these books for you, and I hope you'll stay with me for my next historical mystery series, releasing in 2025. I can't wait to share more about this new series, set in Victorian London. Stay tuned!

I want to say a special thank you to Tantor Audio and voice actress Allie Rose. I've loved partnering with you to bring the Bow Street Duchess series to life in audiobook form, and I'm so grateful for your support.

Although the Bow Street Duchess mysteries have concluded, there is one more story from that world that needs to be told. Lady Cassandra Sinclair and Lord Grant Thornton will be featured in the upcoming Bow Street Duchess Romance,

The Lady's Last Mistake. This will be a historical romance novel rather than a mystery, and I hope you enjoy it!

ABOUT THE AUTHOR

Cara is the author of the bestselling Bow Street Duchess Mystery series. She loves to read and write across genres, but her heart is reserved for romantic historical fiction and mystery. She lives in rural New England with her husband and their three daughters. Cara is currently at work on her next historical mystery series, releasing in 2025.

ALSO BY CARA DEVLIN

The Bow Street Duchess Mysteries

MURDER AT THE SEVEN DIALS

DEATH AT FOURNIER DOWNS

SILENCE OF DECEIT

PENANCE FOR THE DEAD

FATAL BY DESIGN

NATURE OF THE CRIME

TAKEN TO THE GRAVE

THE LADY'S LAST MISTAKE (A Bow Street Duchess Romance)

The Sage Canyon Series

A HEART WORTH HEALING

A CURE IN THE WILD

A LAND OF FIERCE MERCY

THE TROUBLE WE KEEP

A Second Chance Western Romance

Printed in Great Britain
by Amazon

51208075R00155